CHANCES

PAMELA LEIGH STARR

Genesis Press, Inc.

Indigo Love Stories

An imprint of Genesis Press, Inc.
Publishing Company

Genesis Press, Inc.
P.O. Box 101
Columbus, MS 39703

ISBN-13: 978-1-58571-296-0
ISBN-10: 1-58571-296-5
Manufactured in the United States of America

First Edition 2000
Second Edition 2009

Visit us at www.genesis-press.com or call at 1-888-Indigo-1

INTRODUCTION

In *Fate* you met Vanessa Lewis, a young woman from a strong, black Southern family. She was destined to fall in love with Scott, a man so different from, yet so perfect for her. *Chances* continues this family's story with Vanessa's strong, no-nonsense older sister Monica. After losing the man of her life to a senseless car crash, Monica Jones is determined to live the rest of her life bestowing her love and attention on her three children. She had no idea the annoying, inconsiderate neighbor she had never met would turn out to be her brother-in-law Scott's college buddy, her dad's good luck charm and a brand new honorary member of the family. Everybody loved Devin. She was even beginning to feel something for him herself. How could she possibly give love to someone else when her late husband was still in her heart? Could she give Devin a chance?

CHAPTER 1

Hot! More like sweltering, Monica Jones thought.

Spring was here, but summer wasn't far away and it was coming with a vengeance. She sat in her truck, windows down, hoping to catch a spring breeze.

Monica had volunteered to pick the guys up after their camp-out. She'd been doing this for three years. Somehow it didn't seem that long since her brother Warren convinced Tony to join the Scouts. Monica sighed, then shook her head. Something as simple as remembering when Tony became a scout had triggered those memories again.

Keith was gone. Killed in an senseless car crash. If he were alive today, it wouldn't be necessary for Warren to fill in. Keith himself would have been right there with his son, guiding him through Scouts. And right now, Monica would be anxiously waiting for both her son and her husband.

She took a deep breath and let it out slowly. The memories were good but bittersweet, simply because there would be no more. The what ifs got to her once in a while, but for the most part she'd gotten on with her life. A new life without Keith. At times, the impact of losing him had been too much—it hurt just to think about him, but still, she did.

Keith was her first love. She thought back to when they met. Her best friend D'Juan had invited Monica to a high school football game. She remembered how she'd resisted going. Monica was familiar with the rival schools but hadn't known any of the players on either team.

D'Juan's uncle was the football coach of the more popular team, and she had promised that, before the night was over, Monica would be introduced to all the football players on that team, and maybe half of them on the other.

It all seemed like a lifetime ago. Monica smiled to herself, remembering how nervous she'd been as they entered the bus behind the players. If her parents had known her mode of transportation , she wouldn't have set one foot out the door. But she'd gotten on that bus with D'Juan dragging her down the aisle crowded with muscular male teenage bodies outfitted in football gear. Monica quietly, shyly, nodded her head at each boy she passed, holding onto D'Juan arm with a death grip. Monica was glad the intros were quick. She couldn't wait to glance away from one boy so she could say hi to the next, anxious to finish the embarrassing introductions.

D'Juan had called as she passed, "That's Mike and here's Joe! There's Ryan, and hidin' back there's Keith."

And that's where it all had started. Their eyes locked. Keith stood out from all the others, his uniform the only proof that he was part of the team. He sat alone, at the back of the bus, staring at her with serious eyes.

D'Juan's uncle called out to them as he stood next to the driver, "D'Juan, you girls had better come up here, right now, or you'll be walking to the game!"

Monica was quickly dragged back up the aisle with D'Juan whispering in her ear, "Hurry up! He means business!"

Monica remembered looking back to find Keith smiling at her behind his helmet. That was how it all started. She was in love from that day until the day he died.

He wasn't perfect by any means, sometimes too quiet and determined. And they had their problems, but despite them, Keith was her rock and she nearly crumbled when she lost him.

Monica shook herself. Remembering always made her feel so sad and alone. She'd gotten over asking why and gone on to deal with her life and raise their kids, whom she loved to death. But she always regretted holding Keith back from fulfilling his dream. He'd just gotten to the point where his business was making a good profit, with a few young men wanting to learn the trade of carpentry, when a drunk driver ended his life. If Keith hadn't been so adamant about her finishing college, he would have had a real chance to run his business the way he wanted to.

"Stop it, girl!" she told herself. It was a good thing he had insisted on it or she wouldn't be able to provide for their kids. Her job as a speech therapist in Orleans Parish Schools, money from the insurance policy Keith had taken out, and monthly payments from her tenant living on the other side of her double house left her secure. All in all, she was doing well financially. Keith had even taken care of them in death.

The steamy heat forced her to come out of the truck. It was Keith's, a four-door crew cab. He had bought it used, and it wasn't too pretty to look at with the dents and peeling paint, but Monica couldn't part with it. Monica closed the door, patting it affectionately. She wiped her finger across her forehead, feeling the moisture there. The open windows had offered no relief from the heat, and the moisture in the air was causing her hair to frizz, irritating the back of her neck. Monica gathered her thick, shoulder-length black hair into a ponytail.

Ridding herself of that minor irritation was easy. She wished she could erase the ache in her heart as quickly. The only way to do that was to have her husband back, alive and sharing their life together. Of course that was impossible.

Deciding to deal with a problem that she could actually do something about, Monica walked to the corner grocery to buy herself a drink. C & C Food Store, she read as she entered the small building. It was comprised of two narrow aisles. She squeezed her way to the back, passing a deli, which of course offered po-boys as well as a variety of other New Orleans-style dishes. She went right past it, wanting but not needing anything more to eat. It was tough resisting as she sniffed the mixture of smells filling the small store. But she'd already eaten an early lunch with her sister-in-law Jackie and didn't need another meal.

Taking a long sip of her diet iced tea, Monica stepped out of the store. Today, April felt more like June, she thought as she crossed the street. She stood outside the school, not wanting to get back into the truck. This school in the middle of the Quarter was the troop's meeting place. She walked around the building, wondering at its location, directly between Bourbon and Royal Streets.

Monica finished her drink and threw the plastic bottle into a nearby trash can. Her interest in the building increased as she walked up to the large, wooden double doors in the front of the red stucco building. They were locked of course, but to the right of the door was a huge plaque attached to the outside wall.

"Ah-ha, it was more than just a school once!" she whispered to herself. According to the plaque, this was once the site of the first New Orleans opera house. A moment after her discovery, a mule-drawn buggy stopped in the middle of the narrow street, right in front of the school. It was full of sightseers on a French Quarter tour. Monica watched the curious faces of the tourists as the guide stopped. She listened.

"Right here, in this very yard, Elvis Presley performed a scene from one of his many movies..." The guide continued in a loud 'N'awlins' drawl.

You learn something new every day, Monica thought. Not that that particular fact interested her much. She wasn't an Elvis fan. But that plaque was something interesting. Her sister Vanessa would be more than interested in that little bit of history. She'd have to remember to tell her about it.

Checking her watch, Monica began to get a little worried. Jackie had told her they'd be back by twelve-thirty. It was almost one now. She absently rubbed the empty ring finger on her left hand. She'd lost her wedding and engagement rings about a year ago. Monica couldn't find them anywhere, and had finally gotten used to the idea that she probably never would.

Sitting on the edge of the curb, she was relieved to see her old friend D'Juan drive up in her car. Her husband was the den leader and extremely precise. Warren obviously had gotten the time wrong.

"Monica, well, look at you! Where's the rest of you! But don't you look good!" D'Juan said all in one breath.

Monica hadn't seen D'Juan in a long time. She cocked her head to the side and looked up at her friend, grinning with pride. "I just got rid of all that extra baggage. The fat is gone!"

She hadn't really been fat before. But during the past three years she'd slowly let the inches and pounds creep on without realizing it. Keith had always helped her keep fit with volleyball, baseball, tennis, any kind of activity. He loved it all! And he'd pulled Monica and the kids right along. But then Keith wasn't there to keep her busy and those frequent stops at those fast food places hadn't helped much either. Consequently she acquired an image she couldn't stand to look at in the mirror.

During the Christmas holidays she'd gotten a part-time job at The Family Sports Spa as a tutor for kids at vacation camp. She stayed on with after-school activities in return for a free membership. Newly built in eastern New Orleans, it wasn't far from home. Three months later, with regular exercise and a low fat, low sugar diet, she was her old self again.

Talking to D'Juan, Monica found out that she was here an hour earlier than she should have been. Just wait 'til she got her hands on Warren.

"So," D'Juan began, "I like that outfit you squeezed yourself into. White shorts that can't get any shorter, and a tank top you're almost falling out of. Girl, you are too much!"

"I don't know what you're talking about. It's hot out here and these shorts are not that short and this top is not that full. Besides, I've got a blouse over it!" Monica exclaimed.

"I think you're just showing off that new body. Got anyone in mind?" D'Juan asked.

"You know better than that, D'Juan. I don't have time for some no-good man out for one thing. I've got three children to raise! And I didn't get this body in shape for anyone but myself!"

"Just what I thought. But you never know. One day you might fall in love again."

"After Keith?" Monica gave a short laugh. "Nobody can ever take his place."

"Calm down, Monica, I didn't say anybody had to take his place. Maybe someone can find another place somewhere…" She trailed off. Monica watched as D'Juan's eyes surveyed her. She looked up and down and finally agreed. "Oh, it's hopeless!" She leaned back and crossed her feet at the ankles. Turning serious, D'Juan told her, "It's been years, Monica, and you're only twenty-eight years old. You can't honestly tell me you're not interested at all!"

"No, not at all. I have three beautiful kids and lots of memories. I'm happy!"

"You do look happy, but it's been a long time since you've hung around with the gang."

"It's been awhile."

"Since Keith died," D'Juan clarified. "Monica, I'm worried about you. I feel as if you closed yourself off after he died."

"I wouldn't say that!" she protested. "I'm busy. I'm a single parent. I have to do it all. I don't have time for anything else."

"I understand that, girl! I wasn't criticizing. I don't know anybody who can juggle work and kids the way you do. I'm just worried about you. You need some time for yourself once in a while. Everything you do revolves around your kids."

"And I like it that way."

"Okay, I understand. Butt out!" D'Juan laughed. "But hey, losing that weight, that was for you, right?"

"You better believe it!"

They both laughed. Then naturally lapsed into a quiet moment.

"Pssst," D'Juan suddenly whispered from the corner of her mouth. "Take a look at what's coming down the street."

"What? Where!" Monica asked, loudly wondering what D'Juan was up to now. She was hoping that her brother Warren and D'Juan's husband Ray were finally here.

"Hush up, sit back, and watch that fine hunk of a man coming down the street!"

"'Hunk of a man!' What are you talking about, D'Juan? I've already told you, I'm not interested, and you're married, you can't look!"

"I can look all right, I just can't touch," she informed Monica in her usual sassy way. "Watch! He's almost here, look at the way he struts down the street. If I weren't married…" D'Juan shook her head side to side.

"You forgot the happily part," Monica reminded her.

"That's right, if I weren't happily m-a-r-r-i-e-d," D'Juan dragged out.

Monica did watch, and she had to admit, she wasn't unmoved. He was fine, but he was too fine! He walked down the sidewalk as if he owned it and the whole world. That thought became more evident as he came closer. His stance, that long-legged stride. It all seemed to ooze confidence. Finally taking her eyes off his body, Monica glanced up at his face as he came closer. He wore a patch on his left eye. It gave him a dangerous air. He was dark-skinned, darker than she, a deep, deep brown. He wore his soft wavy hair cut close to his scalp, and had the beginnings of a receding hairline. But instead of making him look old it only added to his good looks.

The man was more than good looking and somehow vaguely familiar. His long strides took him past them in no time. But it was long enough for Monica to notice the way those jeans molded to his body, and the steady swing of those muscular arms. Boy, was he in shape! Not that she cared. Monica was just more aware of a firm body in excellent shape from all the time spent at the Sports Spa, she assured herself. She confirmed that thought by looking until he turned the next corner.

"Monica!" D'Juan called. "Monica? Still not interested? For someone not interested, you sure got an eyeful."

"Hey, I can look, I just don't want to touch!" Monica informed her friend in a cool voice, trying hard not to let her see just how interested she had been in the fine hunk of a man. Today was chock-full of new discoveries. This one had taken her by surprise.

Luckily, D'Juan was stopped from commenting by the arrival of the two vans used to transport the Cub Scouts.

She was relieved. She didn't know what had gotten into her. That was the first time she'd even looked that closely at a man since Keith died.

Tony spotted her and was about to run over to her, but suddenly remembered to act cool. Too bad eight-year-olds had to stop running into their mama's arms, in public at least. Tony was a very affectionate child, but preferred to keep it a secret. So she had to make do with a "Hi Mom" after his two-day absence.

Warren, Ray and the other fathers were unloading the vans that had transported them to Camp Salmen, the Boy Scout camp a little over sixty miles from New Orleans. Every Cub Scout had to have a father or relative for the trip, Scout guidelines. Thank goodness she had Warren, or Tony would have missed out. Of course she could have filled in, but there was something different about having a guy to do guy stuff with.

Monica was blessed with an abundance of male role models for her kids. Warren, and every male in her family, took great pains to make sure not only Tony, but her younger son Mark, now four, had regular male guidance in their lives, and Jasmine, her little girl sandwiched between the boys, was being spoiled rotten by all the men in her life. Yes, her kids had an abundance of male influence, which strengthened her decision to remain single.

Monica smiled to herself as she helped to unload the camping equipment. She thrust a tent into D'Juan's hands. She grunted and pretended to fall to her knees under its weight.

Monica laughed out loud as she watched her friend pretend to struggle until her husband came to her rescue.

At the sound of that deep laugh, which was unique to Monica, Warren peered over his shoulder and into the face belonging to the hands he'd been passing the equipment to and flushed guiltily.

"Oh, hey, Monica. I thought Jackie was coming to pick us up."

"Hm-m-m." Monica stared at her older brother. "And is that why I got tricked into coming at twelve-thirty. I've been waiting for over an hour!"

"Sorry, Monica. If I'd known…"

"I know," Monica admitted, "I should have known better. I'd completely forgotten about Jackie's little problem. If I'd remembered, I could have saved myself a wait. Next time, Warren, tell me the real time!"

"Sure thing, sis. Grab that last sleeping bag for me, will ya?"

Warren was only three years older than she was, and the most even-tempered person she knew. Everyone knew about Jackie's habit of never being anywhere on time. No one ever gave her the right time to be anywhere. Besides, waiting hadn't been that much of an inconvenience. She'd learned some interesting things during the wait—and got to see one fine hunk of a man. Now where'd that thought come from?

After loading up and gathering Tony and Chris, her nephew, into the truck, they were on their way.

"So, what delicious campfire dessert did you guys make?" Monica wanted to know.

The boys broke out laughing hysterically.

"Uh-oh, what happened, Warren?"

Warren was a connoisseur of sweets and could create a masterpiece of desserts, even at a campfire site. He let out a big chuckle.

"It was a disaster from start to finish," Warren stated.

Tony and Chris helped to tell the tale. As a requirement, the boys were supposed to cook a full meal on a campfire. Dinner went without a problem, but dessert...They were making apple crumb pie. Everyone had a job. Two boys, Gordon and Brice wanted to trade jobs. So they switched.

"Gordon wanted to spray the pans, and Brice wanted to handle the sugar," Warren explained.

"So I let them switch."

"Yeah, but Dad didn't know they switched back again," Chris added.

"And Gordon decided he didn't want to spray the pans. So they never got sprayed and both Gordon and Brice added sugar!" roared Tony.

"I didn't notice with so much going on. I was just happy to get the ingredients together and baking on the campfire. A half hour later I had two pans of burnt globs that stuck to the pans."

"Yeah, we hung them upside down and banged them around, but nothing happened," Tony guffawed.

"So Dad threw them away in the garbage can next to all the food supplies. And in the morning ants were all over the can, in the food and on our tents! They were everywhere!" Chris roared, nearly falling out of his seatbelt.

"Oh no!" Monica laughed.

"Oh yeah!" Warren warned, "Don't say a word, I'll hear enough from Jackie."

Monica quietly chuckled and asked, "This didn't by any chance happen on your first night?"

"You bet."

"Don't worry, Aunt Monica. We're Cub Scouts, we survived!" Chris assured her.

"On grasshoppers and worms?" she asked.

"No way, Mom. We ate at McDonald's every day!" Tony answered.

"Poor, poor Warren. Your pockets must be empty by now."

"Mine and every dad's on the trip. I'm glad it was only two days! I don't want to go on another camp-out for a long, long time."

"Good thing that was the last one this year, huh, Dad?" Chris said, trying to console his father.

CHAPTER 2

Monica pulled into the driveway of a modest single-story brick duplex in Gentilly Woods. She smiled with pride. Monica loved her house. This house was an investment Keith had insisted on. When they first bought it, the inside was a complete mess. There were holes in the walls and the ceiling and one room had no floor at all. It looked like the day after. Whether it was the day after a hurricane, tornado, or wild party, Monica could never decide. Maybe it was all three. Whatever had happened was a blessing for them because that was the only reason they were able to afford the house.

With Keith's know-how and help from family and friends, they were able to repair it one room at a time. Working and buying supplies when money was available, they completed the repairs on the entire house a year later. This house was at least one dream Keith was able to fulfill and enjoy for a while.

As Monica made it to her front door, her neighbor and tenant opened his own. He stood behind his iron security door, as always. "How are you and the kids doing today, girl?"

"Just fine, Mr. Reaux," she answered. He was a nice old man and an excellent tenant. He thought it was his responsibility to watch over them, but only did so from behind the security door.

"Kids, come say hello to Mr. Reaux."

The children came over to say hello, giving him a low five through the bars of the iron door.

"I'll be going inside to start cooking dinner. Do you want me to bring you a plate, Mr. Reaux?" Monica asked, knowing the answer. He never accepted, but loved to be asked.

"No, thank you, girl. You know I only eat my own cooking."

"Let me know if you change your mind."

"I won't," he told her with a smile in his voice. "You just call me if you need any help," he said.

"I will," Monica promised as he closed his front door again.

Before she could close her own door, Jasmine, Monica's six-year-old daughter, poked her head out once more. "Mommie, look! Someone's movin' in next door!"

Without needing to turn, Monica knew exactly what house Jazz was talking about. It was a two-story

brick house right next door to her own. The biggest
house on the block, it was empty. Well, from the looks
of things, it had been empty. A moving van was parked
in the driveway, but no one was around. The van was
enough evidence for Jasmine.

"At last! Do you think a little girl might be moving
in? Maybe she'll be six years old like me!"

"Sweetie, I don't know. We have to wait and see."

"New neighbors! All right!" Tony hooted.

"All right!" Mark echoed, forever imitating big
brother.

The house that held their interest had been empty
for the last six months. Monica felt better knowing it
wasn't going to be vacant anymore. There was something about an empty house that made her nervous.
While her neighborhood was quiet, with many families, unfortunately for her kids, the children were
mostly teenagers. It was especially so for Jasmine
because there was not a female among them. Jasmine
was hoping to tip the odds a little. Even if their new
neighbors happened to include a teenager, Monica
didn't think Jasmine would mind as long as that
teenager was a girl. For now it was comforting to know
that someone would be living in the house.

As it turned out, four days passed without anyone laying eyes on their new neighbor. Jasmine kept an eye out the front window for hours after dinner but the new neighbor was never seen. Which was just as well, Monica thought. If she herself caught up with him he'd get an earful about what she'd heard. Music—loud music—early in the morning and late at night pouring right into her bedroom. Was *he* deaf? Monica didn't know why she was referring to the neighbor as 'he.' For all she knew, it was a 'she' but somehow, for some reason, 'he' felt right!

He seemed to leave his house very early in the morning and come back long after everyone was in bed. It was in those in-between hours that Monica had to deal with the disturbance—from eleven at night to two A.M., and then again from five in the morning until six A.M. when she had to get the kids up and ready for school. She couldn't deny that he played some good music, but enough was enough! Monica figured that both she and her unknown neighbor were getting only three hours sleep a night. If this kept up, she'd be marching over there one night soon to put a stop to it. Better yet, she would call her brother Randy, a police officer, when he was on duty and ask him to cite her inconsiderate neighbor for disturbing the peace. Something had to be done.

Monica could not survive on three hours of sleep a night and function the next day, especially with all the reports and records she had to complete before the end of the school year. She'd already caught herself falling asleep at her desk more than once this past week.

The next morning, not long after the second round of music began, Monica woke up to find Tony in her room with his official pirate spyglass, practicing the art of being a Peeping Tom.

"I see you, Tony, and you have five seconds to move away from that window."

Tony jumped, almost dropping his spyglass. "Aw-w, Ma, I was close to getting a good look at him!"

Monica looked over at her son, his face so much like Keith's she wanted to go easy on him, but instead sternly informed him, "That's against the law!"

"I just wanted to know what he looks like," Tony reasoned, hopping on her bed. "He plays some good music; too bad we can't hear it from our room," he added, trying to change the subject.

"We're not talking about music. How would you like it if that man you were spying on was standing in the window with a spyglass looking at me?" Monica Asked, pointing to the window at the side of her bed.

"That wouldn't be a good idea. I'd just have to call Uncle Randy."

Call Uncle Randy, Monica thought. They were of the same mind with thoughts on how to deal with this neighbor. Randy was Monica's oldest brother, a police officer and all-around clown, but serious when matters concerned the safety of his family.

"So that means you'll never spy on anyone again, or that," she pointed to the spyglass, "will be confiscated."

"Yes, Mom," he agreed politely, knowing when she used that tone of voice, she meant business.

Tony crawled to the head of the bed where she lay. He hugged her and landed a loud kiss on her cheek. "Good morning! It's time to get up!" Then he hopped off the bed and ran out of the room.

So much energy, Monica thought with disgust as she turned off the alarm that had just begun to buzz in her ear. But then, he wasn't kept awake half the night listening to loud music.

Just then, the music changed to a soft tempo that, without much effort, lulled her back under the covers, for just a minute, she told herself.

Sunday morning, she thought, listening to the Commodores sing. I don't have to wake up yet, it's Sunday morning.

"Mom! It's seven o'clock!" Jasmine shrieked, jumping on her bed in her frilly pink nightgown. "We're gonna be late! We're gonna be late!" she sang as she bounced up and down.

"It's not Sunday morning!" Monica yelled. She sprang from the bed and ran into the kitchen.

"Tony, why didn't you—" Stopping mid-sentence, Monica could see why Tony hadn't warned her about the time. He was normally a stickler for time, but this morning, a bowl of cereal and the cartoons held him spellbound. Tony and Mark sat on the stools in the kitchen with their faces glued to the TV, oblivious to anything else. It was a good thing they were eating cereal because that's all they'd have time for this morning.

Turning off the TV, Monica announced, "It's after seven, and you have fifteen minutes to be brushed, washed, dressed and completely ready. That includes socks and shoes!"

"After seven! Why didn't you tell me, Mom!" Tony wailed. "C'mon Mark!" They made a bee line for their bathroom. Monica brought Jasmine into her room. With no time for anything fancy she combed Jasmine's thick, wavy hair into a single pigtail, deftly plaiting it and absently noticing just how long it was growing. It seemed to take forever to finish that one little plait. She secured the end with one of Jasmine's barrettes and went to check on the boys.

Entering their room, she discovered them completely dressed, but Mark was, of course, shoeless. Recovering the shoes from under the bed and brushing Mark's hair left her with five minutes to finish getting ready. She'd done it before and proved it was possible to do it again. With hardly any time for her own hair, Monica grabbed a barrette, brushed it until she got all the tangles out, and put it up in her old reliable pony-tail. She quickly hopped into the only outfit that didn't need to be ironed, a two-piece, lightweight pant set. There were very teacher-like ABC's and 123's on the shirt. Although she wasn't actually a classroom teacher, she still thought of herself as a teacher. A speech thera-pist taught the basics of language sounds so children would have confidence in themselves and be able to speak without being self-conscious.

Monica grabbed a piece of fruit, her breakfast, as she directed everyone out the front door and into the truck. She backed out of her driveway but almost immediately slammed on her brakes when she heard a loud crash. Monica put the truck in park and got out, muttering to herself the whole time. She said words in her head she wouldn't dare repeat in front of her kids. Even if she said them, they probably wouldn't come out right. Monica had been told by many a relative and friend that she couldn't curse. While she didn't approve of foul language, a good damn it, said out loud, would probably make her feel better right about now.

Behind her truck were her new neighbor's garbage cans. This was the second time this week they were thrown directly behind her truck. Last time, at least, she'd spotted the cans before rolling over them. Feeling more irritated than ever with her absent neighbor, Monica continued to mutter to herself as she removed the cans. She flung them as far as she could onto his yard, taking pleasure in the loud crashing sound the metal trash cans made as they landed.

Monica knew it wasn't entirely his fault that the cans landed in her driveway. The garbage men were mostly to blame. But her inconsiderate neighbor could have moved them this morning. If he had enough energy to wake up at five o'clock in the morning, then he had enough to move two trash cans out of her driveway! This was another strike against him, and she hadn't even met him yet. And it had to be a him; no woman would be so inconsiderate.

When she got back into the truck, she was pleased to see the helter skelter way the trash cans had landed and a huge dent she'd spotted on one. "Serves him right!" she muttered as she drove to her sister Vanessa's house. "Who buys metal trash cans nowadays anyway?" Vanessa's husband Scott drove the kids to school every morning since Vanessa's stepdaughters Vicki and Megan went to the same school. Vanessa had assured Monica that it wasn't a problem. This arrangement helped Monica because her day began a half hour before her children's.

Monica was six years older and married by the time Vanessa was twelve, but they were always very close. Monica could always rely on Vanessa to babysit, paint a room, run an errand or just hang around with her.

As Monica pulled into the driveway of the two-story house, she spotted two little blond heads peering through the large front window as usual. Today, their faces were full of worry.

"What happened?" asked Vicki.

"You're late, late, late!" Megan paused and began again. "I mean, you're late."

Monica smiled. Megan was trying so hard to break out of saying everything three times. She'd had the habit for as long as she'd known her, and according to her dad, ever since she started talking. Monica was impressed by her persistence in correcting herself because it was strictly Megan's decision to change.

She'd declared, "I'm fours years old, I'm a big girl, and big girls say things one time!"

Monica couldn't help teasing her a little. "Yes, I'm late, late, late! And I have to go, go, go!"

"You're silly, Aunt Monica!" Megan laughed, her blue eyes dancing.

"I know, know, know! Where's your mom?"

"Mom!" Vicki called. "MaNessa!" she called again when Vanessa didn't immediately respond.

MaNessa was Vicki and Megan's special name for their stepmom.

"It's okay, Vicki, I'll get her," Monica told them, walking toward the stairs.

"Monica, is that you? It's not that late already!" Vanessa called from upstairs.

Monica moved up a few stairs leading to the bedrooms. "Yes, it's us!" she answered, surprised at her sister's disheveled appearance. Vanessa was usually dressed and ready to greet her at the front door. Today it seemed as if she'd dressed, undressed and dressed again, and in a hurry. Her hair was sticking up, and her denim dress was misbuttoned, revealing her slightly rounded stomach.

"Daddy grabbed MaNessa and brought her upstairs," Megan informed her.

"Oh, I see," Monica answered with a knowing look as her sister blushed.

"Monica, you're late! You'd better get out of here!" Vanessa urged, glancing at the clock on the wall.

"I know, I'm surprised you haven't noticed before."

"My fault," Scott answered, peering around their bedroom door, his hands casually rubbing Vanessa's stomach.

Monica smiled at the sight of her sister and brother-in-law. To some people they'd be an odd couple. Scott was young, handsome, and white, and Vanessa a beautiful pecan brown, black woman. Odd or not, different or not, they were meant for each other. Monica felt good inside whenever she saw the two of them together. It was such a perfect picture of what true love was. No racial barriers, no restrictions, just love.

"I just wanted to know," Monica asked, "if you need me to pick up the girls today?"

"No, my doctor's appointment's early, and Scott's coming. Today's my first ultrasound. We'll be finished in time to get them."

"All right, gotta go!" Monica called, pausing long enough to give each child a kiss on the forehead.

Monica drove off, recalling that Vanessa wouldn't give the time of day to any guy, until she met Scott. And he was definitely getting more than the time of day.

Racing up the stairs, she made it to the school office just as the bell rang. She signed in for the day before the secretary could take the staff book away to mark tardies. Her principal frowned on tardiness, and had a way of making a grown person feel like a kid who'd played around on the way to school. Fortunately Monica prided herself on being on time.

"Made it just in time!" Monica told the secretary, a tall, thin, dark-skinned woman who was always cool as a cucumber, a necessary skill for a school secretary. She had to handle everything: needy teachers, misbehaving students, uncertain parents, and a demanding principal, sometimes all at once.

Waving her red pen at Monica, Evelyn Brown said, "You missed being circled by the skin of your teeth. Next time I think I'll ring the bell a little early, just to shake you teachers up a bit."

"Then you'd have a mutiny on your hands," Monica told her. "Every teacher, aide and staff worker would be in this office to protest."

"I can handle that. I'll ignore all requests, questions, and desperate cries for copy paper until they come to their senses."

"That'll work, but remember Secretary's Day! It comes but once a year!"

Evelyn laughed as Monica left. If she got to her room unseen by her principal, she could immediately start on the mound of paperwork she had on each and every one of her students. For some reason Mr. Boute thought she had time to squeeze in a number of extra hours each day. But she was swamped. Monica had sessions with her autistic students in primary and pre-school to the various levels of regular ed students in kindergarten to sixth. Each student required a separate IEP, Individualized Education Program. Near the end of the school year Monica had to revise and make adjustments according to a student's progress. School-wide she had sixty-six students, enough to keep her based in one school. She couldn't really complain because being an itinerant speech therapist would be even more hectic.

She got down to business and was able to put a small dent in her workload by the time her first session with her autistic students began. The day went by smoothly, with no interruptions. As soon as the last group, the third graders, left her office, Monica's head fell flat on her desk. She didn't have the strength to use the last half-hour for the designated record keeping, or the inclination to move. The next sound she heard was the ringing of the bell, then the voice of her principal

through the PA System. "Mrs. Jones, I've been meaning
to see you all day. Could you stop by my office, please?"

"I can spare ten minutes," she answered. Monica
really couldn't spare a second but she didn't want to give
him a straight no. He was her boss, after all. She sighed;
something more to do.

Monica made it on time to pick up the kids after
school. Their school day started a half-hour later, but
also let out a half-hour later, which allowed her to pick
them up every day, then head straight to the Sports Spa
for her second job.

She felt more relaxed. Not just because she'd gotten
a nap in, but also because her principal was only
informing her about an end of the year workshop for
speech therapists, and because today was Friday. No
rushing home to fix dinner, do homework, and put
children to bed. And who knows, maybe, just maybe,
she'd finally get a decent night's sleep.

Monica found all three of her kids, along with Vicki
and Megan, waiting in the school yard. Jasmine stood
facing a little girl almost twice her size. She was
screaming at the top of her lungs. "They're my cousins,
I don't care what you say! They're my cousins forever!"

"Not your real cousins," Monica could hear the
little girl tell Jasmine. "They're white!"

"No, I'm not, not, not!" Megan shouted forgetting to say the last word only once.

Monica continued to walk toward the yard, she moved slowly, wanting to see how the children would respond. They'd never had to defend their right to be cousins before.

This whole scene was unusual. Everyone who attended St. Ann's Parish School knew Scott and Vanessa, how they met, and that the Jones children, her crew, were related to the Halloways, Scott and Vanessa's girls.

"You're just new here and don't know anything!" Tony told the girl in front of his sister.

"Yeah, you don't know anything!" Mark repeated.

"I know those two are white," the girl answered pointing to Vicki and Megan. "And you three are black, so you can't really be cousins."

"We are not just white," Vicki answered, adding her own brand of logic. "My mommie is black so I can be black, too."

Being equally logical the little girl insisted, "You don't look black."

It was time for Monica to intervene. She walked up just as Vicki finished talking to the intruder. "But I am black. On the inside, I could be white, black, brown, red, even yellow."

"That's right, Vicki," Monica said, grabbing her hand. Her little face, as well as Jasmine's, was flushed red. Megan had tears in her eyes. Tony's aggressive stance was copied by Mark. They were ready and waiting to defend against any outside force their right to be cousins.

"Tell her, Mommie," Jasmine pleaded, grabbing Monica's other hand and leaning against her for a hug of reassurance. "Tell her Vicki and Megan are our cousins!"

"Yes, they are. Why are you telling them otherwise?" Monica asked the little girl who seemed to be a bit embarrassed.

"I don't know, they just don't look like cousins, and she told me she's black. She's not! That's silly! Nobody can be white, black, brown, red and yellow all at the same time!" The little girl might have been embarrassed, but she was persistent. She shook her head, obviously not believing a word Monica had said.

"Tell her, Aunt Monica," Megan insisted.

"Are you a person?" Monica asked the little girl. "Yes," she answered.

"Do you have two eyes that see, a nose that smells, a mouth that you eat with?"

"Yes," she answered again, a perplexed look on her face.

"How about a heart that beats, a stomach that gets full when you eat pizza and hamburgers, and lungs that breathe air?"

"Of course I do!"

"That's right, you do, just like everybody else in the world. You could be black, white, brown, yellow, or even red. It doesn't matter what we look like on the outside. Inside we're all the same. Do you understand?"

"I think so."

"You're new here, aren't you?" Monica asked, hoping to show the kids that sometimes you have to teach others by example.

The little girl, a subdued look on her face, nodded her head up and down in answer to Monica's question.

"Then I'll tell you something. They are cousins and have been cousins for a long time. It's not nice for you to continue to tell them that they aren't. I don't want you to do that anymore, okay."

"Okay," she answered, relaxing enough to smile.

"I'm Miss Monica, Jasmine, Mark, and Tony's mother. I'm also Vicki and Megan's aunt. Can you tell me your name?"

"My name's Laura," she whispered, "I'm in Tony's class."

"Well, Laura, welcome to St. Ann's."

"Thank you, I'm sorry," she said before running to a car that had just pulled up on the curb.

Monica could hear the little girl shouting, "Guess what, Mom? I'm black, brown, white, red, and yellow!"

Monica sighed in relief. That went okay. She turned to the sound of clapping. Scott and Vanessa had been right behind her the whole time.

That was very good, Monica," Scott complimented. "I just tore a page from your book. It made sense to me."

"It seemed to work on that little girl. I don't think she meant any harm. It wasn't logical to her."

"Well, a lot of things aren't logical," Vanessa added.

"Take, for instance, the fact that I'm carrying twins. Looking at my belly you couldn't tell I have two babies in there. The doctor was as shocked as we were today."

"Twins! That's great, Ness!" Monica yelled, grabbing her sister for a hug.

The little girl and the incident we forgotten as the kids jumped up and down, excited with the prospect of having not one, but two additions to the family.

CHAPTER 3

Monica waved at Mark as she finished lap twenty-five of her exercise workout. When she first came to the spa Monica had tried every form of exercise. She'd gone from the body toning and muscle strengthening machines in the weight room to the Stair Master and the Life Cycle. Then to the one form of exercise she'd never try again, aerobics. There was too much moving, bouncing, and jumping involved.

The track was her place. She could move at her own pace and not look ridiculous as she exercised. Besides, she got to watch the action below her. The track was on the second floor directly above the gym. She enjoyed being a spectator. A variety of different teams practiced every day. At any time T-ball, volleyball, kickball or basketball players could be seen running across the gym floor.

Monica had only just realized how much she enjoyed watching the men run across the court. But as she'd told D'Juan, Monica liked to look; she just wasn't interested in touching.

Fortunately for her, a group of men were, at this moment, prepared to play a game of basketball. Pumping her arms and adjusting her walkman, Monica picked up her pace to something between a walk and a jog, her adrenaline increasing as she anticipated the scene below. By the end of the workout, her heart would be pumping and her body sweating, exactly like those men down there.

"Lap twenty-six, Mom!" Mark called out to her.

Monica made a goofy face at Mark as she passed by. He raised his stack of index cards high above his head to show the number twenty-six. More than halfway there, Monica thought.

Mark helped her keep track of the number of laps she'd done with numbered and laminated index cards Monica had put together on a metal ring. It benefited Mark as well as her because he learned his numbers, and the duty gave him a feeling of importance. He wasn't old enough to take karate lessons with his brother and sister, but he could trace, wipe, and reuse the cards over and over again. He had become both coach and cheerleader without suspecting that he was learning.

"Lap thirty! That's a three and a zero together!" he yelled loud enough for Monica to hear over the music coming from the walkman.

"That's right, baby, keep writing!" Monica told him as she passed, keeping pace with the fast beat of the music in her ears. The music was what kept her going. She didn't think she could get past ten laps without it. After passing Mark, she looked down again and couldn't help noticing one particular player on the court. He'd been moving as fast as lightning between and around the other players. He'd be a challenge for her younger brothers, the twins, who slaughtered anyone they played against. She noticed him because his play made him stand out, at least that's what she told herself. It had nothing to do with the firm muscles she could see as he dribbled the ball across the court to make a perfect shot.

Monica used a towel to wipe the perspiration from her forehead. She couldn't have sweat dripping into her eyes and spoiling her view. Was she lucky or what? Monica thought, thanking whoever or whatever was responsible for putting him on the shirtless team.

"Lap forty, Mom! Slow down!" Mark reminded her.

Monica automatically went into her cool-down. She really should be ashamed of herself, gawking at the man like that. Not at all, she corrected, she was only appreciating a well-toned, well-shaped body. And what's wrong with that? Not a thing, she assured herself as she stopped gawking long enough to concentrate on her cool down. Besides, the game was breaking up anyway. She marched around the track in a slow walk until she'd completed fifty laps. That was over three miles altogether.

The next song on her walkman brought to mind her mysterious neighbor. If she ever caught up with him…Monica let out a frustrated breath. She'd handle it when the time came.

"Number forty-five," Mark called.

Monica nodded and sang a little of the song to her son.

As she turned Monica came face to face with the man she'd been gawking at a few minutes ago. She covered her gasp with a cough and pretended to adjust the volume on her walkman. He was wearing an eyepatch. How could she have missed it? He was the same man she and D'Juan had seen walking through the French Quarter. The one that had looked somewhat familiar. She'd been staring at the man's muscles so hard she hadn't even noticed his face. How could she have missed the eyepatch? She had sunk to such a low level, and so fast!

He smiled at her and commented in a friendly tone. "That's one of my favorite songs. I listen to the Commodores every chance I get. I think I'll do a few laps myself."

Monica shrugged her shoulders. She didn't own the track. He could do whatever he wanted. He walked half the track with her, keeping pace and making idle conversation. Why? She hadn't even looked at the man since the first glance. All right, the first two glances. Since then she had kept her eyes straight ahead and offered no encouragement.

"This is a well-equipped facility. I'm considering becoming a member." When she didn't respond, he continued as if she had. "Yes, I definitely will. if for no other reason than to see you again."

Monica's head turned in his direction, her gasp sounding like a gasp this time.

"I look forward to seeing you here often. I can tell that you feel the same," he added before stopping at the side of the track where most people stretched before and after workouts.

It took her a minute to realize what he'd actually said. He was joining the spa! He hoped to see her often, and he could tell she wanted to see him again. God forbid! He was just too much, oozing with confidence, too fine and good looking for his own good. Monica's eyes strayed back to the corner where he continued to stretch. Just too fine. She had a clear view for at least half the track. Why didn't he put a shirt on? Those muscles were too much to handle up close.

He stood and began to jog, making his first lap around the track. When he passed he almost, but not quite, brushed against her. Monica felt a chill, a warm chill, move through her body.

"That's fifty, Mom!" Mark yelled.

Thank God, she was finished!

"Mom!" Mark called. "Mom, you forgot!"

"What did I forget?" Monica asked.

"Remember, when you're done? You move your hands up and down like this." Mark demonstrated, pumping his little arms up and down.

"Oh yeah, like Rocky." How could she forget? It was all because of Muscles. He was nothing but trouble. He was distracting her and she wouldn't allow it. Monica hoped she wouldn't see him too often. Never would be better, she thought, bopping and humming the theme of Rocky with Mark.

Instead of thinking of Muscles, Monica finished her cool-down with a few stretches while she waited for Jasmine and Tony at the back of the karate room. Her thoughts returned to the possible luxury of sleeping all night or getting revenge on her neighbor if he interfered with her plans.

Devin eased into a slow jog, increasing his pace until his tenth and last lap. That he ended with a slow walk around the track. He hadn't really been in the mood for a run after such an intense game. The guys downstairs had given him exactly what he was looking for, a competitive game of basketball. He had a complete gym in the house he'd just bought, with every exercise machine imaginable, but there was nothing like the high he got from the challenge of pitting his skills against worthwhile adversaries. So why had he come up to the Track? Not to jog, that was for sure. He simply couldn't resist the call of those brown eyes. He'd known she was watching him. He hadn't caught her once, but he knew her eyes had been focused on him. Not that he was conceited. Devin was just used to women eyeing him and could always feel the vibes. Tonight, he'd felt plenty of them, from more than one pair of eyes. But the vibes coming from upstairs were the only ones that had interested him.

Devin had watched as she did her 'power walk' around the track over and over again. He didn't know what she called it, but power came to mind as he watched her. The determined swing of her arms, her long, long legs moving faster and faster with each step, the sway of those round hips and the deep concentration on her face. That was power, Devin laughed to himself.

She probably wouldn't appreciate his interpretation of her exercise. And she most definitely wouldn't appreciate him even thinking about her, not after the cold treatment she'd given him. But he sensed that she could be warm, just by the way her eyes lit up when she sang to the cute little boy sitting on the side of the track. And those goofy faces and the smiles directed at the little tyke. Those weren't the actions of a cold person. Devin had hoped to receive one of those smiles himself. Instead, he was blasted with frost. Getting to know Brown Eyes, he could see, would be a challenge, and he loved a challenge.

That's why he'd moved to New Orleans to begin again. He needed to meet new people, more specifically the average American. He'd gotten tired of catering to the rich, extravagant clients whose desire for the unusual had helped him to make his fortune. Becoming one of the most sought-after architects in the country, however, had its drawbacks. Satisfying the needs of his clients, he had gotten away from creating and designing from the heart. He was restless inside and his desire to build again, to create a structure from paper to reality, was too strong to ignore anymore. What better place to start again than New Orleans, with its unique style in architecture.

He had always yearned to visit, and come to know the city.

He'd taken his first step away from the life he'd tired of by fulfilling his final commitment, designing a string of first-class condominiums along the Gulf Coast, the last one in Mississippi.

With relaxed hands-on participation, he had been happier then he'd been in a long time. Until the bigoted lunatic had shown up. Devin deliberately cleared his mind. Thinking of T. J. and the disaster he'd almost caused would waste the benefits of a good workout.

He forced himself to relax as he bent into a stretch. First to the right, then the left, straight down, and what do we have here? Brown Eyes dribbling a basketball? And that cute little tyke was trying to take it from her. So were two other kids. Devin stopped to watch. They sure looked like they were having a good time. The kids tackled Brown Eyes, knocking her to the floor as the ball bounced to the other side of the court. Tackle basketball, that's what it looked like to him. Brown Eyes got away and retrieved the ball, only to be attacked from all sides again.

"Come on, Mom! It's our turn!" Devin heard the older boy say.

Mom! It hadn't occurred to him that the two older children could possible belong to Brown Eyes. The little one, yes. He hadn't seen a ring and she looked way too young to have children that old.

"I'll give you two kisses if you let me shoot," the older boy was saying. He was using his brains to get what he wanted, Devin thought. My kind of guy.

"In public!" Brown Eyes asked in a shocked tone.

"Since it's in public, only one," he answered.

"Deal!" she told him, moving close to collect her payment.

Devin watched the exchange of a kiss for the basketball. Soon the other kids were covering her with kisses too.

Mom? Maybe she was so cold to him because she was married. Somehow he didn't think so. If she were married, she'd have a ring on her finger. She looked like the kind of woman who'd not only wear, but cherish a wedding ring.

Did he want to get involved with a woman with three kids? Not really. It had nothing to do with his liking or disliking children. Kids just seemed to complicate matters. Looking down again at Brown Eyes running across the court in her skintight exercise jumper, he thought again. Maybe complicate was the wrong word. Challenge, yes, that was the word. It would be another challenge. One he was ready for, he thought as he went to sign up for a membership he didn't need. It would be a sure way to catch up with Brown Eyes again.

CHAPTER 4

Monica rolled over and stretched. A smile spread across her face as she buried herself deeper into the covers. She felt rested, refreshed. Monica didn't know what happened to her annoying neighbor, but she hadn't missed him one bit!

The silence was such a relief. An uninterrupted night's sleep was so blissful. It's funny how you don't really appreciate something until it's gone or impossible to get. She'd always taken a good night's sleep for granted. Maybe there was a slim chance that she'd get along with this new neighbor after all. She could afford to be gracious after such a satisfying night. Monica turned over to look at her digital clock. Eight o'clock, a decent time to get up on a Saturday.

She went into the den to see what her little monsters were up to. Strangely, no faces were glued to the TV screen for Saturday morning cartoons. They were all staring out the back window into the annoying neighbor's backyard.

"He's big," Mark said, obviously referring to whoever was on the other side of the window.

"He looks dangerous," Tony commented.

"I think he's ugly!" Jasmine said, matter-of-factly scrunching up her nose.

"That's not a very nice thing to say," Monica told her, thinking that they'd finally caught a glimpse of the mysterious neighbor.

"But he is, Mommie, take a look!" Jasmine insisted.

Monica braced herself, figuring that she'd probably encounter the face of a severely deformed man who played music all night to take his mind off his troubles. That would explain a few things. That is, if Jasmine's description was right. She wasn't normally a child to speak negatively about anyone. The children moved aside so that she could have a look for herself.

Monica stared into the scariest face she'd ever seen. She jumped back, dropping the curtain that automatically swung into place.

"See, I told you," Jasmine smiled smugly.

"Yes, you did. That is one big, ugly, dangerous-looking Rottweiler."

"And he's loud, too," Mark added.

"Yeah, he's disturbing us. We can't even watch cartoons in peace," Tony told his mother.

"He's quiet now. That's because we're at the window. Whenever we leave he barks and barks, and makes all kinds of noise. What's wrong with him?" Jasmine asked.

"I don't know, but you kids better stay away from him. That means no one can go into the yard."

"Don't worry, Mom, we're gonna stay far away from him," Tony assured her.

Monica couldn't believe it! She'd finally gotten a decent night's sleep, but in exchange for what? A killer dog living right next door. If so, her kids couldn't play in their own backyard anymore.

Monica threw on a pair of stretch pants and an oversized t-shirt she usually used to exercise in and stormed over to the house next door. She quickly lost her steam when she saw the empty driveway. Not that she'd ever noticed a car during the day. But those nights when she couldn't sleep, she'd peer out her window and stare daggers at the house and the sports utility vehicle in the drive.

The lack of a vehicle in the driveway didn't stop her. Monica kept going. She suddenly froze when the dog came bounding toward the gate, growling deep in its throat. That growl sounded like an animal war cry. He was on the attack and Monica was his prey. The gate, closed and latched, looked strong enough to keep him where he belonged. Just in case she looked around for someplace she could run to quickly, some place high, knowing she probably wouldn't have enough time to make it back into her house. In a matter of seconds he'd nearly reached the gate but stopped short just as Monica began to climb the oak tree in front of her neighbor's house. The Rottweiler whined in pain as he was suddenly jerked backwards. He was attached to a long chain.

Monica came down from the tree, slowly releasing the breath she'd been holding. She stared down at the crescent marks her fingernails had made on the inside of her palms. The dog had almost frightened her to death. This was grounds for neighbor eviction. If it were up to her she'd kick him out of the neighborhood this minute! Loud music, trash cans, killer dogs, what next?

She stood in front of the tree waiting for her heart rate to go down. At that moment Mr. Reaux opened his front door. "Everything all right there, girl?"

"I'm fine, Mr. Reaux."

"What's all that barking out there? Y'all got a new dog or somethin'?" he asked.

"No, but our neighbor does."

"The new boy."

"You've seen him?" Monica asked, surprised that Mr. Reaux had caught sight of him before she had.

"Yeah, nice fella, he is. I think you gonna like 'im. His dog, too, I bet. Now you just call if you need me."

"I will," she promised, not believing he liked the dog. Because he thought 'the boy' was a nice fella, the dog had to be nice. Mr. Reaux didn't know anything about their new neighbor and even less about the dog.

Knowing that he probably wouldn't be home, Monica banged on his front door, releasing her anger on the heavy wood. She leaned on the doorbell. No answer; she knew it! As she passed the gate again, the dog went into a frenzy trying to reach her by gnawing through his chain. Considering the size of his teeth Monica thought he might do it if he tried hard enough.

For the safety of her kids and the entire neighborhood, Monica knew what she had to do.

"Mom, who are you calling?" Jasmine asked.

"The SPCA. We need someone to come take care of that dog before he hurts himself or someone else. That's why I want you kids to stay away from him."

Monica reported the crazed dog and gave the address for the house next door. She didn't want to be anywhere around when they came for the dog. For all she knew, he could break away and attack other people. With that in mind, she got the kids ready and they left to do Saturday errands. They'd do their weekend cleaning when they got back.

After getting back home Monica took a few cautious steps toward the gate.

"He's gone?" asked Mark.

"Looks like it," she answered, pleased to see no sign of the dog.

The SPCA must have come and gone. The kids helped her unpack the groceries and started doing the jobs they were responsible for every Saturday. Monica mopped the kitchen floor and vacuumed the living room carpet. By the time she finished, the kids were cleaning their rooms.

As Monica rewound the cord onto the back of the vacuum, she could hear a soft whimpering. It was coming from outside. She went to the back window and pulled the curtain back. The dog was still there, and in a precarious predicament. The chain that had kept it from bounding through that gate this morning was twisted around his body and neck. The same animal who'd looked so dangerous and wild a few hours ago looked downright pitiful now. The poor animal stood on its hind legs trapped against the fence. It was a wonder that it hadn't strangled to death. What was keeping the SPCA? She went to the phone and dialed the number she'd written on a pad earlier.

She hung up a few minutes later. The SPCA had gone to the wrong house. They'd gone to Piety Street instead of Piety Drive. The woman on the phone assured her that someone would be there shortly. Monica peeked out of the window again. Pity replaced the fear she felt this morning. What would Keith have done? Try to ease the animal's pain, Monica knew. But she didn't like dogs, was afraid of them. At that precise moment the Rottweiler moaned again, a hollow pitiful sound that went right through her. She had to do something.

An idea forming at the back of her head, Monica went into the kitchen to get the broom. She had to free the dog enough so that it could at least breathe normally.

"What's going on, Mom?" Tony asked as he came into the room. "What are you doing with the broom?"

"That dog's still out there, Tony. It's gotten itself all tangled up. I'm going to help him."

"No, Ma, that dog's dangerous! Call the SPCA!" he shouted, grabbing her hand.

He had a mighty grip for an eight-year-old. "Tony, take a look at him. He looks hurt; I have to do something. I already called the SPCA. They're coming, but I don't know how long they'll take to get here. Look at him, Tony."

Tony looked between the curtains. "Oh, Mom, he's gonna die. He's gonna choke to death."

"That's what I thought."

"You can help him, but be careful. He could still be dangerous," he cautioned.

"I will, Tony, I will," she repeated, trying to assure herself. "You stay right here."

"I'll keep watch," he promised.

"Good idea," Monica answered, stepping out into her backyard. She had no intention of getting any closer to the dog than necessary. She could hear Tony inside talking to Jasmine and Mark.

She was sure all three faces were pressed against the window.

She looked into the dog's glazed eyes, trying to let him know that she wasn't going to hurt him. The dog growled, twisted, then yelped, causing itself more pain.

She thought talking to it might help. Monica had seen enough animal shows on TV to know that a soothing voice helped to calm a scared animal; maybe it would help to calm her nerves. If he was scared, she was terrified.

"Now Mr. Rottweiler, I'm just going to help you out a little. You wouldn't be in this predicament if it weren't for the irresponsible, insensitive jerk who owns you." Monica addressed the poor scared creature in the same tone she would use if one of her kids were frightened. It seemed to calm the dog—until Monica lifted the broom handle in its direction. Then it went wild. She jumped back.

In a frantic voice Tony yelled through the window, "Be careful!"

"I know, I will," she told him as confidently as possible. She couldn't help picturing scenes from a TV news program about a pair of Rottweilers that attacked a jogger for no apparent reason.

Monica knew this Rottweiler felt threatened. She did too. After a minute the dog had worn itself out and stood still on its hind legs. Monica slowly approached, humming "This Little Light of Mine."

"Mmmm-mmm-mmm-mm-mm." *Help me Jesus,* she thought. She continued to hum as the dog watched her warily. The soft sounds coming from her mouth were having a quieting effect on him. Monica stretched the handle again, standing a good four feet away. She hummed nonstop, adding a little prayer now and then. Monica inched the broom forward, then under the link of chain that lay on top of the fence spoke and lifted. As soon as the chain was free, Monica dropped the broom and quickly went back into the house. She stood at the window with the kids, waiting to see if her efforts had helped the dog. That one loop was enough to allow the dog to get down on all fours and promptly collapse.

"Mommie, is he dead?" Jasmine asked.

The dog lay on the concrete ground, the rest of the chain still wrapped around its body.

"I don't know, sweetheart," Monica answered.

"No, look," Tony shouted, "he's breathing."

"Yeah, he's breathing," Mark repeated.

"Yes, he is. Let's all go sit on the front porch to wait for the SPCA."

They waited. Fifteen minutes later the SPCA finally arrived, a half an hour after she'd called. The dog probably would not have survived. When the young man and woman asked about the owner, Monica had absolutely no information to give besides an address, which was enough for now, they assured her. Monica hoped her neighbor would be slapped with a huge fine for all the trouble he was causing her. Whatever the case, the dog was gone.

CHAPTER 5

Two hours later, still a little shaky from her experience, Monica walked into Ness's kitchen complaining. "If ever I lay eyes on this new neighbor of mine, I won't be able to resist wrapping my hands around…"

"…him for a big hug," Ness answered, effectively stopping her big sister from voicing her negative thoughts in front of the kids. "Why don't you kids go outside to see how many fish Papa Cal's caught." The men in the family had chartered a boat for a day's fishing in the Gulf and had just returned.

"Can we count them?" Tony asked.

"Sure," Ness answered.

"I'll just watch," Vicki decided as they all ran out.

"From what Dad says, they caught a lot of fish—" Ness paused, and they both added,

"—for a change!" before exploding with laughter.

"Well, Dad said it was all because of their good luck charm," Ness told her.

Monica could hear the men outside talking to the kids. "Good luck charm?" she asked.

"Yeah, Scott's old college buddy just moved to New Orleans. They majored in the same field, shared a dorm, hung around together. He seems like a nice guy."

"In that case he has nothing in common with my new neighbor. The most insensitive, inconsiderate excuse for a human being has moved next door to me."

"So?" Vanessa asked nervously. "Is one of your neighbors are giving you trouble? I thought you got along pretty well with everyone."

"I do, but this one's new. This one I've never laid eyes on. But I tell you, Ness, I can't stand the man already!"

"You've never met him? So, how do you know it's a him?"

"I just know. Or I should say I just knew. Mr. Reaux confirmed it this morning," Monica answered. "I haven't laid eyes on him, but Mr. Reaux, who rarely steps out of his house, has seen and talked to the insensitive jerk."

"Exactly where does this self-centered man live?" Vanessa asked.

"Right next door in that big split-level house that's been empty since the beginning of the year? Why?"

"Well."

"What do you know about this, Ness?"

"I hope that what I'm suspecting isn't true. I mean Bug seems like such a nice guy."

"Bug? Who's Bug?" Monica questioned, knowing she wasn't going to like the answer.

"Scott's college buddy from Pennsylvania."

"The good luck charm?" It was obvious Ness had some information she needed to know, and it looked like she'd have to drag it out of her. "And?"

"And— I think your new neighbor is Bug, and you're about to meet him because he's outside right now with all the guys," she got out in a rush.

The memory of many sleepless nights, the trash can fiasco, and her recent fright with the dog sparked her anger. It grew. Soon she wasn't angry, she was mad!

Bug is a fitting name she thought. Before she went storming out to confront him Monica had to make sure this man was her mysterious neighbor. "Ness, how do you know it's him?"

"Scott and I told him about the house," she admitted.

"And he bought it. He said he wanted to stay in a nice, quiet, normal neighborhood."

"And you never mentioned this to me?"

"I planned to—today," Ness answered.

The steam rose in Monica's eyes. "And he had the nerve to want to move into a quiet, normal neighborhood?" Monica asked, her voice rising with each syllable.

"Those were his words," Vanessa answered carefully. "Exactly what has Bug done to make you so mad?"

Monica paced up and down the kitchen her arms moving in agitation.

"It can't be that bad, Monica. Wait until you actually meet Bug and talk to him face to face. He is good-looking and I was hoping that…"

Monica heard Ness's voice but was too mad to listen to what her sister was saying. She was too busy dwelling on the noise and inconvenience she had put up with this past week. "Ness, I'll tell you what he's done. This Bug has been anything but quiet or normal so far. He plays music all night, he keeps strange hours. He's left trash cans in my driveway, a potential hazard for both me and my truck. And he has the most dangerous, vicious animal I've ever seen for a pet! This takes the cake. This abnormal man wants to live in a normal neighborhood. Unbelievable!"

Monica watched Vanessa's eyes grow wide as she finished her tirade. It was rare for Monica to get so upset. "Vanessa, you have to admit, it's unbelievable!" Monica repeated, prompting a response. "Vanessa, are you even listening to me!" Monica asked, waving a hand in front of her sister's face. She was really worked up.

"Yes, Monica, you might as well tell me what you want," Ness answered, resignation in her voice.

"Could you please tell that obnoxious, annoying, abnormal bug of a man to come here. I would go outside, but I don't want my children to witness what I might do or say."

"Monica, maybe you should wait."

"Why? Now is the perfect time."

"What I mean," Ness clarified, "is maybe you should stop and think, give yourself some time to cool off."

"I'm cool, Vanessa, I'm so cool I'm hot," she answered.

"But…"

"It's okay, Vanessa. The obnoxious, annoying,— abnormal, was it?" he questioned before going on, "bug of a man is right here."

They both turned at the sound of the deep, smooth, confident voice behind them. Vanessa smiled up at him. Monica scowled.

"Well, hi there, Bug," she casually answered. Then with a touch of wariness in her tone, "Monica, this is Bug."

"You!" Monica shouted, instantly recognizing him even without the eyepatch. "You're my new neighbor?"

"The obnoxious, abnormal bug, yes," he answered evenly, a smile spread across his handsome face.

Devin couldn't help smiling at Brown Eyes. He couldn't believe his luck. He'd already decided that attempting a relationship with her would be a challenge because of the kids. He could see from the molten copper of her gaze that there was even more of a challenge than he'd anticipated. One he would win. Devin never backed down. She would have caught him at a disadvantage if the kids hadn't come outside when they had. Instead, he caught her off balance.

He'd recognized Brown Eyes' children, especially the littlest one. It was an interesting coincidence, one he was going to take advantage of. Brown Eyes was Scott's sister-in-law. It was the children's uncensored, full description of this morning's happenings that gave him the upper hand, as well as the little extra news about the loud music that had been disturbing her every night. The kids hadn't used those exact words, but their comments were enough for him to put two and two together. And they added up to him appearing to be an inconsiderate jerk. It had been a long time since he'd lived so close to his neighbors. The house in the mountains he'd designed and normally stayed in to work was secluded. So secluded he hadn't realized that his odd hours and need for music had disturbed her. He felt bad about that. But being fore-warned would help him to redeem himself.

"Dad called this arrogant—" Monica paused, concentrating on finding a word that would insult the man smiling at her as well as make her feelings about him clear. Her mind drew a blank. She spat the only thing she could think to call him "—this arrogant so-and-so can't be Dad's good luck charm!"

Bug watched as Vanessa looked from him to Brown Eyes and then announced, "I think I'll go outside to join the kids and the guys. Since you two have obvi-ously met before, I'll leave you to talk this over. As adults," she emphasized, walking out the back door.

Ness was right, Monica thought as she watched her sister leave. Name-calling was pretty childish, and she wasn't all that great at it anyway. She would deal with this like an adult. If she hadn't been so angry she wouldn't have resorted to name-calling to begin with. She'd cooled off enough to talk. Taking a more civil tone, Monica requested, "As your unfortunate neighbor I would appreciate it if from now on you refrain from playing your music so loudly in the early morning hours when normal people are asleep." She didn't quite know what to expect from this handsome, arrogant man, but the smile that had remained plastered on his face was unexpected.

"I understand. I certainly will. I had no idea that your bedroom window was directly across from the room I use as a home office. I promise that you won't be disturbed again by loud music coming from my house." His tone was serious, but his eyes danced as he talked. They were dark, as dark as his deep brown skin.

His music wouldn't disturb her any more, but now she had to deal his presence here. Stunned at his easy compliance, she nodded in acceptance of his apology. "I'd appreciate it." His acquiescence didn't fit with what she'd learned about him so far. But wait, she hadn't tackled him with the dog issue yet. She'd let him know what she thought about a man who could be so cruel to his pet.

"I also want to apologize for the trouble you had today," he said before Monica could sink her teeth into him.

"Trouble?" she asked.

"The kids mentioned a dog you rescued in my backyard."

"Yes, that trouble. I almost got mauled trying to save your dog." She would have gone on in great detail if Bug hadn't interrupted.

"That wasn't my dog."

"What?" Monica asked, dumbfounded.

"I don't own any pets, never have. But I did find a strange note in my mailbox informing me that a Toby was coming Saturday. I had no idea who Toby was and assumed the note was for somebody who used to live in my house. I never thought twice about it. I'm guessing the dog was Toby."

"I guess it was," she slowly agreed. His explanation was incredible, but it sounded like the truth. What was left of her anger and resentment completely melted away.

"I'm sorry you had to deal with that," he went on to say. "Your son, the older boy..."

"Tony," she said, supplying his name.

"Yes, Tony, he's a very nice little boy. He told me you were afraid of dogs."

"Thank you." Monica found herself warming up to Bug. Anyone who complimented her kids couldn't be all that bad. Through unusual circumstances she had misjudged him. "And for the record," Monica continued, a hint of a smile in her voice, "I wasn't scared, I was terrified. But I had to do something; that dog was in bad shape."

"You look as if you came away unscathed," he commented. Encouraged by the warmth in her voice, he inched closer.

Now that the anger had melted away, Monica became aware of a new feeling that had been trying to break through earlier. She could feel herself inch a little closer to him. After all he was one fine hunk of a man. There was that thought again. Monica sighed. It was inevitable, the fine hunk of a man was standing in front of her. How could she help thinking it? His lips started to move, he was talking. Monica tried to focus on what he was saying.

"Now that we've gotten all of that out of the way, why don't we concentrate on what's really on our minds." He whispered this as one of his long brown fingers made a trail up her arm.

"Discuss what?" Monica asked taking first one, two, and just to be safe, three steps back. She knew she wasn't going to be warming up to him like that. If that's what he was thinking, Bug had better bug off. Monica watched as he put his hands in the back pocket of his jeans, satisfied that he seemed to get the message. He was making her nervous, but she refused to show it.

"Us," Devin answered, as if it made perfect sense.

"Us?" Monica asked, as if it make no sense at all.

"I thought there might be a possibility for an us."

"You? Me? What gave you that idea!" Monica shouted.

"What gave me that idea? You gave me that idea."

"I never did!" she answered with force. "I just met you today!"

"The basketball court," he continued, his voice even but firm. "You stared holes in my back."

"Muscles," she softly groaned.

He moved closer and quietly asked, "What did you say?"

"There's no way I—"

Devin stopped her by placing a finger on her lips. "You did, I know it, and you know it. You gave me the cold shoulder afterwards, but I was hoping to melt it down a bit. I don't like to see ice in your eyes. I prefer the warmth I see in them now." Devin slowly leaned closer.

When Vanessa left Bug and Monica, she stood at the back door. Scott spotted her. He wiped his hands on a damp cloth and went over to his wife. "What's going on in there, Nessa?" he asked. "It's been years since I've seen Bug, but I don't remember him being able to move that fast."

"And I don't remember ever seeing Monica so mad before."

"From what the kids say, Bug hasn't endeared himself to Monica as a good neighbor."

"That's the understatement of the year! He seemed like such a nice guy. And I'd hoped…"

"That Monica would be interested in Bug," Scott finished for her.

"Yes," she admitted.

"You can't force your sister into a relationship, Nessa."

"I know, I just wanted to provide the opportunity."

"It's sounds like you provided an opportunity all right, for verbal warfare."

They both stopped to listen to the exchange behind them in the kitchen. Monica's voice loud and forceful, Bug's as calm as a cucumber.

"It doesn't sound good," Vanessa said.

"Don't worry, Nessa, this might be a good thing," he whispered in her ear, hugging her close.

This little show of comfort had two effects. The first one was instant arousal, something Scott knew would happen the minute he went anywhere near her sensitive ears. The second was stronger and even more powerful. Her stomach reacted to the suffocating odor of fish as Scott held her close.

"Oh no!" she moaned. Unable to hold the nausea back, Vanessa ran back into the house with Scott not far behind her.

Monica didn't take offense at the pressure of his finger on her lips. The contact was light, warm, and electrifying. She suddenly wanted Bug to kiss her. But the sound of running feet was enough of a distraction for Monica to realize what a ridiculous reaction she was having from the touch of a finger meant to shut her up. Monica turned, her head first moving away from his touch and then his presence. She trailed behind Scott.

Scott was at the bathroom door looking worried. "She told me to go away. Nessa closed the door on me. Monica, help! What should I do?" he asked, worried about his pregnant wife. "She's supposed to be past this stage!"

"I know, Scott. Calm down, and tell me what happened." This crisis was more manageable than the one Scott and Ness had unintentionally interrupted in the kitchen.

"I was hugging her one minute and the next thing I know she was running, and now she won't let me near her. She's throwing up in there."

"I realize that," Monica said, trying to suppress her laughter. "And I'm not surprised. You smell like rotten fish. It must have turned her stomach. Do yourself and Ness a favor, go take a shower and come out smelling like roses."

Scott raced off to do as Monica suggested.

"Wait!"

"What?" Scott turned back.

"Don't come back smelling like roses. That might set her off again. Fresh and clean will do it."

"Right. Thanks, Monica." Scott raced off and almost collided with Devin. "Oh, Bug, sorry."

Devin eyed his old friend, unable to miss the worry in his face. "Vanessa okay?"

"Yeah, she's going to be fine, just morning sickness. Ha! More like all-day sickness, even fish-smelling sickness. Man, I don't know. I don't remember going through all this with Kathy."

"You probably weren't around enough at the time to notice." Devin remembered the long hours both of them worked as they tried to make a name for themselves at the beginning of their careers.

"You're probably right," Scott admitted, the feeling of guilt surrounding him as always when he thought about his first wife, who'd died when his daughters were still babies.

Depressing Scott not being his intention, Devin added, "But hey, man, you're here now, for Vanessa."

"Yes, I am," Scott answered, immediately feeling better about himself. "Monica said the fish smell had set off Nessa's stomach. I'm going to take a quick shower. You don't mind if I leave you guys to clean the rest of the fish?"

"Your father-in-law guts those fish so fast he's probably finished and made every man outside feel like a two-year-old with a butter knife to boot. Go on- bathe!"

"Will do. Thanks, Dev."

Devin grunted. He wished all he had to do was shower to attract Monica. But, he reflected, she hadn't wanted to run a second before Vanessa and Scott raced through the kitchen. Monica had wanted to kiss him. Devin could tell by the heat burning in her eyes. They weren't just warm, they were hot.

CHAPTER 6

The brown eyes staring at Devin from across the yard were now as cold as the frozen tundra that covered the Arctic. He shivered inside. Those expressive eyes accused him of sins he was sure he'd never committed. He had apologized, but he guessed that hadn't been enough. Monica had probably not only doubled his sins but multiplied them by ten while he ran home to shower.

Devin had hurried back to find all of Scott's in-laws, as well as his sister and her family, outside feasting on the catfish, redfish, and trout they'd caught. A large picnic table laden with the crispy fried fish, potato salad, a huge pan of bread pudding and pecan pies. New Orleanians really knew how to feed you, he thought, taking in all the food.

Devin took a long, slow survey of the yard. When he'd gotten in touch with Scott, Devin never expected to be welcomed into his extended family in such a way. During the fishing trip all of Scott's male in-laws had welcomed him as if he were part of the family simply because he was a friend of Scott's, not because he was the famous D.J. Prescott. It felt good.

Family had been lacking in his life. As busy as he was, only technology kept him connected to them. He telephoned and e-mailed often, but made it home only once or twice a year. Today, in the midst of this big family, Devin was flooded with memories. There were only his brother Joe and his mother in his family, but their feelings were the same as those of this large family. Devin wondered if Scott's relatives realized what a special thing they had: three generations in this backyard—grandparents, parents, children. Devin looked around for the family member he was deter- mined to get better acquainted with. He spotted her sitting between her parents. He'd met them both only today. Monica's coloring was the perfect mix of both her parents. Her mother was very fair, her father very dark. A few shades darker than Joyce's, yet a few shades lighter than Cal's, her toasty complexion reminded him of a pair of warm, fuzzy moccasins he'd had as a child. Devin laughed to himself at the comparison. So far, she was nowhere near as warm and soft as those slippers.

His laughter floated to Monica and caused her to scowl. He came toward her anyway to speak to her parents, brushing against her arm as he reached past her to shake Cal's hand. He moved on to mingle with the rest of the family as they settled around two sets of patio tables or in lawn chairs to eat. The kids filled up two wooden picnic benches.

When he paused at the kids' table, he found them to be a good source of information. He discovered when Tony and Jasmine took karate; how often they went to the sports spa; that he really should pick up his trash cans before their mom dented them. The kids were open and friendly and viewed him as family friend. After all, he was their new neighbor.

Tony had been doing all the talking and providing him with tons of information when Jasmine interrupted. "I thought a little girl might move in next door, but it's only you."

"Hey, I'm not so bad," Devin told her, a mock hurt look appearing on his face.

After studying him a few seconds, Jasmine agreed. "No, you're not."

He tapped her nose with the tip of his finger to show that he was glad she thought so too. It was unfortunate that her mom wasn't as easy to convince.

Devin looked around the spacious yard and caught sight of Monica at the food table adding more freshly fried fish to an empty platter. It looked like a good time for him to get something to eat.

Joyce had obviously been thinking the same thing. Before he could so much as stand, a large plate piled high with catfish, potato salad and french bread was placed in front of him. "We can't have you going hungry, Devin. After all you're the good luck charm."

"You bet he is!" Calvin bellowed from across the yard.

Devin sighed, his plans ruined. Monica had now vanished into the kitchen. But the evening wasn't over yet, he thought. He turned to Monica's mother. "Thank you, ma'am, that was really nice of you to fix a plate for me." He was touched by the gesture.

"He's not only a good luck charm, he's polite too. You've got a nice friend there, Scott," Joyce called out to her son-in-law.

"Bug's one of a kind," Scott answered.

"Bug," Calvin said, now standing beside him. "I've been meaning to ask you. How'd you get that nickname? There has to be story behind a name like Bug. And I know my son-in-law must have something to do with it. When he uses it, I can swear I hear some kind of hidden meaning."

"You're very perceptive, Mr. Cal. Scott was a witness, no, I should say a participant in one of the strangest things that ever happened to me."

At that moment Monica walked out the back door into the yard again. "Monica," Joyce called, "come listen to the story about how Devin got his nickname."

Monica took in the expectant faces of her family members. They'd all surrounded Devin, waiting for the next words to come out of his mouth. How had he, in one day, entranced her family this way? How had he entranced her a few hours ago? She wasn't going to allow him the opportunity again. Pointedly speaking to her mom, Monica said, "I'll listen, as long as it doesn't revolve around music, trash cans, dogs, or mu—" Monica stopped herself. She was about to say muscles. Her eyes darted across the yard straight to Devin's. She wondered if he noticed. He wore that broad confident grin as if he knew what she was going to say.

"Stay, Monica," he encouraged. "This particular story has no music, trash cans, or dogs, but it's bound to be enjoyable. After all it's about me." He grinned.

Monica had planned on staying to listen to his story. She was interested, despite herself. But he'd rubbed her the wrong way, again.

You big-headed, arrogant…, she thought, just stopping herself from spitting it out. Instead, acting as a mature adult, she answered, "No thank you, I have something to do in the kitchen."

As she made her way to the back door she heard Scott suggest, "Bug, you better let me tell the story. I'll be able to relay it from the view of an innocent bystander."

"Innocent," he calmly repeated, eyebrows raised. "I'll let you tell it, but I reserve the right to a rebuttal afterwards."

"Agreed," Scott answered.

"In that case," Monica did an about face and sat down in an empty lawn chair, "I'll stay to listen."

Devin noted the satisfied look that came across Brown Eyes' face when she openly revealed her supposed dislike of him. He vowed that before the evening ended the warmth, no, the fire, would return to her eyes. And she would remember the kiss she would willingly participate in each time she saw him. Which was going to be often.

Devin relaxed and listened to Scott, knowing there was much he'd need to refute.

"Well, it was the middle of summer. Bug and I had decided to attend the rural studio course for the summer session at Auburn. We hung out together, studied, and as part of the requirements helped to build a community center for the locals. When we had time on our hands, we did the regular crazy things college students tend to do when they're bored."

"Would chasing and harassing girls have been one of them?" Monica asked looking toward Devin.

Scott answered for them, gazing at his wife as he traced her ear with a finger tip. "We refuse to answer that on the grounds that it might incriminate us."

"I think you've already incriminated yourself." Vanessa shuddered as she answered her husband.

"Scott, the story," Devin prompted. Watching Scott with his wife just now stirred a feeling inside him he'd never felt before. Not even when they were roomies and their landlady openly showed favoritism to Scott and virtually ignored him because he was too dark. Plain and simple, it was jealousy. Scott had a wonderful wife, two beautiful kids, two more on the way, and some great in-laws. Top that with success in his career and he could say that Scott had it all.

Devin himself had a successful career and tons of money. And he made a new beginning based on what was important to him. But it wasn't enough. He wanted what Scott had. Glancing at Monica again, Devin wondered if he'd find it with her. She'd already sparked his interest like no other woman had before. Time would tell.

Devin returned his attention to Scott. "We'd been having an awful season with mosquitoes. That summer, if you ventured outside at night, you'd better be prepared to get eaten alive by those little blood suckers."

"Those female blood suckers," Devin added.

"Hey!" Every female objected at once.

Devin held both hands up in self-defense. "I didn't mean anything by it. It's a fact of nature. Only female mosquitoes are blood suckers."

"Bug, you should know better than that," Warren told him, years of experience with his mother, sisters and wife behind his warning. "You almost dug yourself into a hole you could never hope to crawl out of alive."

"But I'm sure these sweet, understanding women realize that I had no intention of insulting them," Devin humbly responded, an apology in his voice.

Except for one, all of the females in the group were appeased. Monica was disgusted. Scott went on with the story.

"Anyway, if you had any sense you didn't go out without using insect repellent. Something we did regularly, right, Bug?" Scott asked.

"Some of us thought we were using insect repellent," he answered.

"Okay, all right, you're getting ahead of the story. Let me finish. Late one night Dev and I were starving. There was no way we were going to survive until breakfast the next morning. So we decided to raid the kitchens in the community hall. In order to do that, we had to brave the mosquitoes. I had no problem walking across a wide field to get to the kitchen. Bug, on the other hand, kept slapping himself and asking me, 'You're not gettin' bit?' "

"Scott," Devin interrupted, "was having no problems whatsoever. The mosquitoes that night just seemed to like my blood. But then, I started to get a little suspicious. Every time I'd slapped one of the annoying pests, Scott would laugh."

Scott laughed now in remembrance, "Yeah, but before I could let him in on the joke, we seemed to step right in the middle of mosquito hell. They were all over the place! In seconds he was covered with them. He started to look like one big bug. Dev had so many mosquitoes covering his arms and neck, it was hilarious. That is, until they started biting me!"

"You weren't much of a good luck charm that night," Cal told him.

"I had luck that night, but it was all bad. It was bad luck that we chose that summer to work in the country, and worst luck that my roomie was out to get me and planned to watch me slowly die from mosquito bites."

"Hey, I didn't let you die, I was the one who saved you," Scott reminded his friend.

"You did, I'll give you that much," Devin confirmed, attempting to rein in his laughter just like everybody around him.

"Well, how'd you finally get the mosquitoes off?" Monica was the only person around not falling all over herself. She obviously didn't find much humor in the story. Devin finished it for the sake of the other listeners. "Running didn't help. I'd run the rest of the way across that field to the community hall, but they were still all over me. The only part of my body that had any protection were my legs. Mr. Cal, I felt lucky to be wearing jeans instead of shorts that night."

"What happened, then!" Monica asked again.

"I'm getting there," Devin told her. "I knew if I went into the building for cover they'd come in right along with me. I was thinking about throwing myself on the ground and rolling around in the grass like a dog when Scott blasted me with a garden hose. I had never been so happy to be drenched with water."

"Did you ever figure out why they attacked you and not Scott?" Vanessa asked.

"Oh yes. Your husband failed to mention that he'd given me some special insect repellent. He'd dumped the real stuff and replaced it with lotion and baby oil!"

Bug and Scott looked over at each other and cracked up laughing again.

"You did this kind of thing to each other often?" Monica asked.

"Yep," they agreed simultaneously.

"That was just payback for the time I put itching powder in his underwear," Devin told her.

"Hey, we were young and bored, and not many girls were interested in architecture that summer. We missed having them around to drool and stare at our muscles while we played basketball."

"Bug!" Scott cautioned.

"Yeah, Scott?"

"Dev, you're about to get me in big trouble."

"Naw, Vanessa knows that I'm only kidding," Bug insisted.

"What I know is that Scott's mine now. It doesn't matter what happened before we met," Vanessa declared.

"You better believe I'm all yours, Nessa," he laughingly answered. Then he whispered something into her ear.

"Scott!" Vanessa yelled, playfully hitting him on the shoulder.

Devin noticed that everyone was smiling indulgently at the happy couple. Jealously hit him again full force. As he turned and tried to suppress the feeling, his eyes collided with Monica's. At first content and happy, her eyes quickly turned as cold as ice. Ahh— more sins on his plate. Maybe he'd gone too far with the basketball and muscles crack.

"Ness, I think we're going to be leaving soon," Monica told her sister. "I'll help with the clean-up before we go."

"I'll give you a hand," Devin suggested. "It'll make the job easier."

"No, you're a guest, sit down and relax, Bug." She pronounced his nickname as if it were a dirty word.

"I insist. I got the use of a boat and fishing tackle, enjoyed good company, and I was fed. I need to return the favor."

"Guests don't have to return favors," Monica muttered with clinched teeth.

"It'll make me feel so much better, as if I contributed in some way."

Before Monica could open her mouth to refuse, again Calvin Lewis put in his two cents. "Let the man help, Monica! He's the good luck charm. He's bound to make the job easier. Hey, Bug, while you're at it, why don't you tell her about some more of those pranks. She could use a few more laughs."

"That's exactly what I intend to do, Mr. Cal." Devin got up and was through the back door in a flash.

Monica turned to her father and asked, "Dad, why did you do that?" Not waiting for an answer, Monica followed Devin into the kitchen.

"Joyce, what's wrong with that girl?"

She just smiled and told her husband, "Time will tell."

CHAPTER 7

Monica stepped into the kitchen to find Bug already hard at work loading the dishwasher. She'd decided to tolerate his presence, nothing more. That meant she didn't have to talk to him. She'd been embarrassed by what she'd let slip out and angry that he'd caught her so easily.

He looked as if he knew what he was doing. At least she didn't have to help him help her.

"Oh, there you go, I'm about done here. I only need to sort the silverware. You want to handle that greasy mess over there? I never know what to do with used oil."

"Ness normally keeps some old gallon jugs around that she uses so she can dump it into the garbage without making a mess." Too late, Monica realized, she'd opened her mouth. His attitude was so friendly and open he'd taken her unawares. He was confusing her. He went from being too forward to graciously asking her forgiveness to revealing his arrogance. Her head was spinning from all the different facets of his personality. He'd shown concern for Ness, spent time with the kids, went back to being arrogant again, and now he'd turned into Mr. Friendly. Monica wasn't used to this. Keith had always been straightforward and easy to read. He was loving, but was serious. Serious about his job, serious about her education. He was even serious about the sports he played.

Devin, on the other hand, had proved that he could laugh at himself, a trait she'd found endearing until he added that comment about muscles and basketballs.

Monica froze in the middle of searching for a funnel to help pour the oil into the jug. She couldn't have compared Devin to Keith just now. There was no comparison. There was no room, no way.

"Finished."

Startled, Monica jumped and turned toward the deep voice. "What?"

"Looking for something?" Devin asked.

"Huh-um. A funnel," she finally remembered.

"One like this?" Devin asked as he reached around her to pick up the small blue funnel two inches from her hand.

"Yes, that's it." Monica breathed in deeply, determined to get some oxygen into her lungs in the hope it would make it to her brain. His aroma was so masculine, so intense, she felt brain dead. She'd breathed in too much of him, and nowhere near enough oxygen. Monica was annoyed that Devin was standing so close to her, but it was just like him to think she wanted him there, right behind her, so close she could feel his warm breath on her neck. She pushed the drawer with her hip and turned to empty the huge cast iron skillet they'd use to fry the fish, disgusted with herself because she realized that she'd been thinking of him as Devin instead of the bug he really was.

"While you do that, I'll just put the good oil away." He grabbed two gallon containers of oil, one full, the other half empty.

Monica pointed him in the right direction. Two seconds later he called, "Monica!"

"Yeah," she answered absently.

"I can't find the light switch. Where do I put these?"

"It's right inside the doorway."

"I can't find it, and my hands are full. Can you help me out?"

Now this Monica was able to deal with, a helpless male. She found him at the pantry door, hands full, just as he said, but he could have easily put the jugs down to find the light. "Men," she muttered as she flipped the switch. "Muscles, but sometimes no brains."

She turned to find her way blocked by a fine hunk of a man full of muscles, empty-handed, and standing directly in front of the closed pantry door. He reached over and flipped the switch back down, instantly covering them in darkness.

"Bug, what are you doing?"

"You can call me Devin."

"Bug-g-g," she emphasized, dragging his name out, "let me pass."

"Not until we finish the discussion we were having earlier today."

"It was finished. It is over and done with." He was making her nervous—afraid, standing here in the dark with him. Funny, she didn't feel threatened, as if he would harm her. She was scared, but for a whole other reason. When he was around he made her forget Keith. She couldn't tolerate that, not for a second. It wasn't right. Keith was the love of her life; she couldn't simply forget him.

"No, Brown Eyes, it isn't over and done with. We were interrupted."

"Fortunately, it was at just the right moment," Monica quickly answered.

"More like unfortunately," he whispered, slowly moving toward her, causing the atmosphere to change. "I would like to finish the discussion, now," he requested in a more reasonable tone.

"Well, you know, I remember where it was headed, and there's no way I care to continue that line of discussion, thank you," she answered in a surprisingly calm voice considering the gentle but direct shift in the air between them. The need to protest was melting away, being replaced with acceptance of the inevitable.

"Do you know that you become very polite when you argue?"

"I am not arguing. I was only stating a fact. I will not continue the discussion, and you will not lay another finger on me," Monica declared in a last-ditch attempt to gain some control of the situation.

"Okay."

Okay. There he goes again from arrogant to agreeable. He was nuts. And she was disappointed. Monica shook her head in exasperation and moved to pass him. He gently wrapped his arms around her from behind, holding her close. His hold was light; she could easily break away and leave anytime she chose. She sighed and leaned back against him. She was his—for the moment anyway.

Monica stared at his hands. They were big, strong, working hands. "Devin, I told you not to lay a finger on me. You didn't listen, and being such an arrogant man, you went overboard. You couldn't use just one, you've got all ten of them on me."

"No, I don't."

"No? Really?" she chuckled. "I can count."

"So can I," he whispered. 'Eight fingers." He moved all eight, sending tiny shocks of electricity along the soft skin of her arms. "And two thumbs," he added, moving them up to caress her cheeks and gently turn her around to face him. His eyes peered deeply into her own.

Obviously finding what he sought, Devin smiled at her.

"If I promise to keep my fingers and thumbs off you, will you kiss me?"

"I suppose we should end this discussion," Monica answered, drawn to him by the darkness, his voice and some kind of magnetic electrical pull surrounding him. "But I still don't think you should lay a finger on me." Monica had an overpowering need to feel his hands on her. To feel him holding her close. "That won't be enough," she told him in a soft whisper. "I'm going to need eight fingers and two thumbs."

Devin's smile widened as he pulled her closer, lowering his mouth to her lips. He softly tasted them. That was sweet, she thought. He nibbled on her lower lip. Oh, so sweet. He stopped. She opened her eyes to stare at him in question. He came back for more. She savored and enjoyed the feel of his lips, his tongue meeting hers with the same thought, the same rhythm, the same intensity. She was astounded. He held her, his chin resting on the top of her head.

"Brown Eyes," Devin whispered as he lifted her chin to look into her eyes.

"Dev?" she sighed, making it a question.

He answered by kissing her again. They both jumped at the loud metallic banging noise on the other side of the pantry door.

"Cut it out, John. Mama asked us to help clean up, not to come in here to bang on pots and pans."

John dropped the two metal spoons and stopped the copper pots from swaying above him. "Ness would probably kill me if I knocked down all her fancy pots and pans. And don't get all grumpy with me, man. It might ruin your mood for that hot date you've got tonight," Josh answered, trying to get a rise out of his brother because he'd interrupted his drum solo.

"Don't worry about my date. Just get busy so we can both get out of here."

Monica didn't want to leave the warmth and the electrifying feel of Devin's arms around her. But the sounds of her younger brothers in the kitchen forced her to focus on something besides his arms, his lips and the things he could do with his tongue. She looked up at him, but not for long. There was such an intense look of longing and seduction in his eyes she couldn't face it.

After a few minutes of silence in the kitchen Monica could hear John's voice. "I thought Mama said that Monica and that guy Bug were in here cleaning up."

"Well, it looks like they got started. There's not much left to do," Josh answered with his usual impatience.

Monica stood in the dark pantry next to Devin, wondering how they were going to get out without anyone noticing that they'd been closeted inside longer than it took to put away a couple jugs of oil. Devin squeezed her hand in reassurance. Strange, that he could sense how she was feeling. They stood together quietly, both wondering how they could get out of this situation.

"You know, man, I had a real good time fishing today. We haven't gotten together like that in a long time," John commented.

"I know what you mean. But it felt funny, I mean it wasn't the same, without Keith," Josh clarified. "After all these years I still miss having him around."

"It did feel weird without him," John agreed. "But I like that guy Bug, Scott's friend."

"Yeah, but he's not Keith. I guess we'll always miss him," John said ending the discussion.

He's not Keith! Monica stared down at their entwined hands and dropped Devin's like a hot potato. She began to slowly back away. He watched her, a look of confusion on his face. He's not Keith! Then why was she kissing him? Kissing him and enjoying it. She continued to back away until she was at the other end of the pantry. She held both hands straight out signaling for him to stay where he was. She was as far away as possible. She had to get herself under control again.

Despite being at the far end the pantry Monica could hear Vicki's voice loud and clear as she came into the kitchen.

"Uncle John! It's time for dessert!" she yelled excitedly. "Maw-maw Joyce said to bring the ice cream outside when you're done."

"Okay, Miss Victoria."

"I love you, Uncle John, and I'm going to marry you one day!" she announced.

"You bet," John answered as usual. There seemed to be a special bond between the two despite there being no blood ties.

"I love you too, Uncle Josh. But I'm not going to marry you," she told her other uncle so he wouldn't feel left out.

"I understand, Vicki. As long as I get to dance at your wedding."

As Monica nervously waited for them to finish this little ritual, Devin edged closer. She waved her hands wildly to keep him back. He halted.

Monica heard Vicki's feet run across the kitchen floor and the slamming of the back door.

A minute later she heard Jasmine asking, "Where's my mama?"

Guilt washed over her. Her baby girl was looking for her, and where was she? Hiding in a pantry after being locked in a lustful kiss with a virtual stranger.

"Ah, we'll find her, Jazz," she could hear Josh tell her. "I've got the ice cream, you get to hold the scoop."

They all made a loud exit, letting the back door slam again. Monica motioned for him to leave. Devin quickly slipped out the door, but Monica froze when she heard John's voice loud and clear. "Oh. Hey, Bug. We were just looking for you."

"I've been around," Devin answered.

"Have you seen Monica?"

"Yeah, just a second ago. We started cleaning the kitchen together. I guess she finished without me."

"No, me and Josh finished it up."

"Oh, thanks."

"No problem. It was an order. You know mothers. Once you hit twenty you think you're grown and independent, then wham! One look, a couple of words and you're doing exactly what she wants."

Hoping to draw him out of the kitchen so Monica could come out of the pantry without embarrassment, Devin walked toward the back door. Laying a hand across John's shoulder he casually explained, "It's the same way with all women. You might as well get used to it."

"If that's the way it goes, I think I'll stick to my music."

They were at the door, almost home free, when John suddenly stopped. "Cones! That's why I came back inside. Josh forgot the ice cream cones. We've got kids out there screamin' for ice cream."

Cones; they were in the pantry. Monica had seen them when she'd flipped the switch earlier. She grabbed them and slipped out the door just before her brother turned around. "Cones? Here they are!" she announced.

"Monica, we were looking for you, too." John eyed her suspiciously. "Something going on here that I need to know about?" he asked. "Two missing people showing up at about the same time in almost the same place."

"Not a thing to worry about, okay?" Monica pleaded with her eyes.

John eyed her before agreeing. "Okay, I'll let it slide. But I'll be watching you young people," he said in a mock stern voice.

"Take the cones, John. There's nothing for you to worry about. I'm more concerned about the kids mobbing you because you're holding up the ice cream."

"You're right ," he said, hurrying to make it out before the kids did decide to jump him.

Monica watched as he ran outside waving the box of cones high in the air pretending to save the day. It only excited the kids, causing them to jump all over John anyway, ice cream cone hero or not. As she took in the scene, a familiar feeling of contentment over-rode those new feelings Devin had brought to life.

"Monica," he began from behind her.

She turned toward him. A deafening silence stretched between them.

"Brown Eyes," he tried again.

"Please don't call me that. Don't call me anything. This is it! All right? There is no us, Bug," she stated clearly, finally turning to look up at him.

"What happened to Devin?"

"That was a mistake, and it won't happen again. You made me forget everything, and it won't happen again. Do you understand?" Devin shivered inside as he looked into her eyes. They'd turned cold again. He knew he'd found what he wanted, what he'd been looking for all his adult life. A woman he could love. But he couldn't have her until the ice melted perma-nently. She had been his for a short time, until her brothers started talking about the fishing trip. It couldn't have been talk about the fish that turned her cold. She was frying and eating the stuff all afternoon.

He was trying to remember, what was that name? Kevin…Casey…Keith! That was it! Keith. He was probably her ex-husband. There was a story behind this. He needed to find out about this guy. Scott, he thought, should be a wealth of information.

CHAPTER 8

Monica pulled into her driveway. Devin drove into his at almost the exact same moment. She glared at him as he got out of a dark green Durango Dodge 4x4. It had never been parked in the driveway when she came and went during normal hours of the day. The Durango was a perfect match for his personality. It was a strong, sturdy, no-nonsense sports utility vehicle that matched his smooth, dark looks and bold, confident manner.

"Mom, can I unlock the door?" Tony asked, peering through the open window of the truck and interrupting her thoughts. She was getting ridiculous, now she was comparing the man to a car. At least it was better than comparing him to Keith. She handed Tony the keys and went back to glaring at Devin as she got out of the truck. Monica wanted him to understand the message she was sending across the width of their adjacent driveways. While she glared he stared with an appreciative spark in his eyes. She didn't want or need the compliment.

It was obvious that her glare wasn't doing its job. Before she could dwell on it Mr. Reaux opened his front door and called out, "How are you and the kids doing today, girl?"

"Just fine, Mr. Reaux," she answered.

"I was wondering, it's not like you to take so long getting out of the truck."

"I was just thinking," she told him, unable to come up with a better explanation.

"Maybe you oughta think about thinking inside. I can't stand at this door all day waitin' for you to decide to get into the house," he told her from the safety of his iron door.

"Good evening, Mr. Reaux," Devin called as he passed Monica. He headed straight to the old man's front door with what looked like a grocery bag full of newspaper.

"Well, how ya doing, boy?" he called.

"Good as ever. I brought you some of the redfish we caught today. It's all wrapped up tight. We even cleaned it for you so it's all ready to cook."

"Why, thank you, boy. You didn't chop the heads off, did you?"

"No. They're right where you told me to leave them, still attached," Devin answered.

"Such a nice boy. I think I'll go right in and start making myself some coo-blee-ya." He pronounced it the Creole way. Mr. Reaux turned to go back into his house, excitement in his movements. Just before he closed the door he told Monica, "You call me if you need any help?" Then he slammed and locked the door.

Mr. Reaux had been her tenant for the last two years and he'd never taken anything she'd offered him. And just now, right before her eyes, he had looked at Devin as if he'd offered him gold. An irrational anger was working its way under her skin. This went way beyond what she'd felt before. That was a mild irritation.

Now she was angry because he was so fine that she couldn't help noticing him. She was angry because it had been so easy for her to accept his apology, even after all the trouble he'd caused this past week. She was angry because her whole family and Mr. Reaux were all under his spell. She'd fallen under it too, and that's what got to her the most. What was it about Devin that made people like him?

Monica spun around to glare at him again. He was still in front of Mr. Reaux's door, too close to her own, and he showed no reaction to her efforts to show how much he annoyed her.

"What's a coo-blee-ah?" he asked, a puzzled look on his face.

"It's a stew. Fish heads in a red gravy," Monica answered, not bothering to elaborate. It was really delicious. The heads were added to the stew, more or less as a garnish.

"Okay," he answered with a look of disgust. "At least that's better than thinking he wanted the fish heads for some kind of voodoo spell."

"Ump," she answered, still glaring. He finally got the message and started toward his own front door. Monica stood where she was, her eyes following and glaring until he made it to his own house.

The short wail of a police siren brought her attention to the curb. A police car had pulled up behind Devin's driveway. Monica recognized her brother, a sergeant in the NOPD, in the patrol car. Her neighborhood happened to be in the same district he supervised. Randy had to work a double shift and missed the fun.

Devin stood and waited, a friendly smile on his face as Randy and his partner Frank got out of the patrol car. They headed straight to his house. Monica had assumed that they were stopping by her house for some reason when she remembered the people from the SPCA informing her that they were required to make a report to the police for cruelty to animals. From the confident expression on his face Monica could tell that Devin simply knew he was going to be able to talk his way out of the criminal charges that could be brought against him. Monica had no doubt that the arrogant man could. After all, the dog wasn't his to begin with. But he deserved to be taken down a notch or two. She'd see to it that he was.

Before Frank or Randy could utter a word, Monica hurried down the walk way. "Officers, you have to arrest this man! I've never seen such a horrible case of cruelty to animals. He starved that poor animal through neglect and made it suffer by wrapping him in chains. The poor thing couldn't move. You have to put this man behind bars." Monica tried to wink at Randy and his partner. She needed them to go along with the gag. Winking had always been a problem for her. She usually ended up blinking both eyes crazily, having no control over her eye muscles whatsoever. Randy seemed to catch on though and responded just as she wanted him to.

"Yes, ma'am, that's exactly why we're here."

"Hey, something wrong with your eyes Mon—" Frank grunted when Randy's elbow connected with his ribs, effectively stopping him from blurting out her name.

"Frank, why don't you take a look at the crime scene. I'll question the suspect."

Monica could tell Frank found the request strange, but he pretended to be interested in the crime scene. "Ma'am, if you could just show me the scene of the crime..."

"Yes I can, officer," she said, ready to lead the way.

Devin's smile had disappeared the moment Monica spoke up. He'd stood rooted in place listening in stunned silence as they discussed a crime he had nothing to do with.

"Crime scene?" Devin looked from the gleeful, determined expression on Monica's face to the serious look the officers conveyed. "Now officer," he addressed Randy. "If you could wait a minute I can explain to you why there's no need for any of this. There's no reason why criminal charges should be filed against me."

"Oh, is that right?" Randy said, narrowing his eyes. "You're special or something? You don't have to obey the laws?" he demanded. "You think you can break them and get off scot-free?"

"No, of course not—"

"I'm glad to hear you say that, sir," Randy answered cutting him off. "Now, ma'am, the crime scene."

"This way, officers." She happily led the way, glancing back at Devin as she spoke. "And I have to tell you, the moans of pain I've heard coming from this backyard were heartbreaking."

Looking more than a little bit disconcerted, Devin followed behind them. "Wait officers! You can't do this!"

"You bet we can, and a whole lot more. Try six months in jail or a thousand dollar fine," Randy sneered at him.

Monica was impressed. Randy was doing a really good job of scaring Devin. Mr. Cool, Arrogant, Macho Man appeared to be a bit nervous. But he was still holding up pretty well.

"Hey Randy, we could recommend both," Frank suggested. "One thousand and six months."

"This is absolutely uncalled for, officers. If you would stop to listen I can explain." As if it suddenly occurred to him, Devin added, "And wait just one minute, do you have a search warrant?"

Frank and Randy both stopped in their tracks, glanced at each other, then Devin. "No!" they answered and continued to make their way to his backyard with Monica leading the way.

Taking two long strides, Devin caught up with them and demanded, "All right, take me in if that's the only way you're going to listen to me. But you're going to have to hear me out because this woman is lying!"

The police officers spun around to stare at him. Devin stood firm, keeping eye contract, and not backing down from either officer.

Randy relaxed and quietly released a long, slow breath. "Hell man, I know that. Monica's my sister and she was just pulling your leg. The name's Randy, nice to meet ya."

It took a minute for Devin to adjust. "This was all a joke?" he asked quietly.

"Yeah, and a pretty good one from the look on your face," Randy told him.

"Did you plan this?" he asked Monica.

"No, it was just a spur of the moment idea, but it worked. Thanks, guys." Monica hugged each officer, her pleasure in making Devin sweat obvious.

Devin stared at them with a look of disbelief. A minute later the kids came out yelling, "Hey Uncle Randy and Mr. Frank!"

Monica enjoyed the change of expression on Devin's face as the two officers who'd just intimidated him hugged and spun children around on the front lawn.

He didn't stay stunned for long. "Stop! Wait a minute!" he demanded with force. Everyone stopped at the tone of authority in his voice.

"I need to get a few things straight," he continued, now that he had everyone's attention. "You played a Low-down, dirty trick on me, and although unplanned, you all enjoyed it at my expense."

"Yeah, that sounds about right," Randy nodded.

"You summed it up real good, man," Frank agreed. "I can't remember when I had such a good time. And you should have seen the look on your face."

"The opportunity was too good to pass up," Monica told him. "I knew you'd appreciate a good joke, especially after hearing that story you told today," Monica threw out as dare for him to utter one complaint. If he really wanted to, Devin could file a grievance against both officers and it would be all her fault for starting the charade to begin with. His features softened, transforming him into the same man who'd cast a spell on her whole family with his easygoing, open attitude.

"Okay. You got me," he admitted. "I can take a joke. But am I to understand that you actually came here about the problem with the dog?"

"Yes, we did," Randy answered switching to his professional mode. "We do need a statement from you," he told Devin as he flipped open a small notepad. "The owner of the dog has been tracked down and we've determined that he left the dog at the wrong address. Apparently someone had planned on breeding Rottweilers. He should have delivered the dog to a house on Piety Street, not Piety Drive."

"Correct."

"And I suppose you have an alibi," he stated, a little of his humor breaking through his serious demeanor.

"Your whole family," Devin answered, admiring Randy Lewis's change from joker to professional. He wouldn't have a problem getting along with this member of Monica's family. Monica, on the other hand, was a different story.

"There won't be any charges filed against you," Randy assured him. "The owner of the dog—he might have some trouble on his hands."

"Thank you, officers. I think," Devin responded.

Devin absently waved as he told everyone good-night, his thoughts preoccupied with Monica. The mere thought of her lying about him had thrown him off balance, unable to react to this little crisis with his usual flair and confidence. Now, having relaxed from the fear of jail, lawyers, injustice, fines and crazed police officers, Devin stopped at his door and turned to stare at Monica. Shining in her face was happiness, pure and simple. Her eyes had been dancing with it, and probably still were. And what had made her so happy? Seeing him sweat, that's what. Devin was sure she hadn't meant to, but she'd accidentally revealed something. He concluded that the only reason she was so happy to get even with him was that Brown Eyes didn't like the fact that she enjoyed kissing him.

Well, tomorrow was another day, another opportunity. Devin figured the more he kissed her, the better she'd respond, and the more she'd enjoy it.

Devin hadn't slept a wink. The idea that had been buzzing at the back of his head had exploded. His brain was filling with details and specifics for his new project. It had been simmering in his head since his walk through the French Quarter the first day he'd come to New Orleans. The project he had in mind would involve the Spanish style architecture in the French Quarter. Despite the Vieux Carre's French name, many of its customs, traditions, food, and architecture were mostly Spanish, he learned. Control of Louisiana had passed back and forth between France and Spain during its early history. The Spanish influence in architecture came about in the rebuilding after two enormous fires, one in 1788 and another in 1794.

Devin found all aspects of the city's history rich and interesting, from the settlers of France and Spain, to the many free people of color who settled there to the slaves, who seemed to have more freedom than other slaves in the South and were more likely to learn a trade. He'd spent many a night pouring over books he'd bought at a bookstore or borrowed from the public library. Not to mention the hours he spent surfing the Internet. Those were the many nights he'd disturbed Monica's sleep. Sitting in his workroom now, he was tempted to play some music. Not just to play it, but to blast it, just to get her attention. But no, he'd let her be for now, let her think about him, think about the kiss they'd shared. She seemed like an intelligent person. Hopefully she'd realize that what was happening between them was a good thing. Maybe if he gave her some space, was a little less arrogant, she'd be more receptive. Devin chuckled. Being a little less arrogant was like being a little less Devin. He'd settle for giving her some space.

He spent the next hour moving his stereo, speakers, and computer to another room. His drafting desk and other tools of the trade, he moved last. He was going to make this room, the one closest to

Monica's bedroom, his own. It would be something else to tease her about the next time he saw her. He'd do or say anything to get her attention.

Programming five different discs to play consecutively, Devin got to work at his drafting desk. The ideas were bursting forth, and his fingers and his brain were set at two different speeds. He forced his thoughts to slow down. The hours flew by.

With his plans outlined and the general details in place, his thoughts slowed. A song ended on one of the CDs. Devin hit the power button. He walked across the hall to his room, straight to the window facing Monica's house. He looked down. He couldn't see them, but Devin could hear the children's voices as they carried down the alley between their houses. Then he heard Monica's. He couldn't understand a word. He lifted the window and peered out, catching a glimpse as they loaded into the truck. They were all dressed in their Sunday best. Even from this angle, he could see that Monica looked gorgeous with her hair hanging down to her shoulders.

Devin let the curtain fall back into place and fell onto the bed completely exhausted. He was tired. Church, that's where they were going. Mr. Cal had invited him to mass and dinner today. He looked over at the clock, nine forty-five. There was no way he'd make it. He hadn't slept in over twenty-eight hours. He'd exceeded his limit. It would be a missed opportunity to see Monica again, but it was all for the better. He'd already decided to give her some space. Unable to stay awake a minute longer, Devin rolled over and lost himself to sleep.

CHAPTER 9

Monica was free. This Friday was movie night at Scott and Ness's house. Ness had begun the monthly tradition of having the kids sleep over three years ago. It was Vanessa's way of helping Monica cope with Keith's death, and it had helped, especially at the beginning. It had given her some time alone to deal with her grief, time alone to collect herself. Now it was just a nice treat.

Scott had gotten involved, adding more fun activities to movie night. So the kids always looked forward to going. They even gave up karate this Friday to be there early, so Monica was even free from having to pick the kids up from school. Ness volunteered to get them.

Monica had no idea what Scott had planned for them. But she knew it involved wood, hammers, and nails. She hoped he knew what he was getting himself into.

Monica drove straight home after work. She glared at the empty driveway next door. No sign of Devin.

He seemed to be keeping the same strange hours, but it wasn't as noticeable. True to his word, there was no loud music to disturb her sleep. Another added plus was the absence of metal garbage cans blocking her driveway.

She sighed, wondering what he was up to. Not that she cared. She was certainly happy that his interest had faded so quickly. It saved her from the problem of rejecting his advances over and over again. She was glad that he hadn't come over to her house making a nuisance of himself. Or hung around the spa bugging her.

Stop. Now wait a minute, she told herself. Monica had to admit that she felt slighted. Why would he give up so easily? Men! That's exactly why she wasn't interested.

She was also relieved that he hadn't shown up at her parents' house last Sunday. Her father had invited Devin to their weekly get-together after church. Her dad was doing it again, throwing Devin her way.

Every Sunday her family ate dinner together as families used to. Monica enjoyed the time they spent together and was proud that they kept this particular tradition alive. It kept them close. She didn't want Bug to have anything to do with it. He wasn't family. Keith was family. His memory should stay strong and clear to everyone, just as Josh and John had said. Devin, with his arrogant ways, would somehow cloud Keith's memory. Monica just knew it.

Monica turned the key inside the lock as Mr. Reaux called out of his open door. "Tonight's your night off, right, girl?"

"Yes it is, Mr. Reaux."

"Well then, you go have yourself some fun. Maybe ask that nice boy next door to go with you. Better yet, I could send over a pot of my con-blee-ya. You two could sit down and enjoy some good Creole cooking."

"No thank you, Mr. Reaux, I already have plans," she told him. The last thing Monica wanted to do was sit down anywhere and do anything with Devin.

"You're not scared to ask him out, are you? Times have changed, girl. I wish some foxy girl like you had had the nerve to ask me out when I was your age."

"That's about enough of that, Mr. Reaux. I prefer my own company."

"Too bad, that's one fine young boy over there."

That he was, but Monica only said, "If you say so."

"All right then. Call me if you need me."

"Thanks, Mr. Reaux."

Monica went into her house and came out with her exercise clothes in hand. She had to be at the Sports Spa by three-thirty when her students arrived.

Three hours later Monica headed up to the track for her workout. She spent the first few minutes warming up, adjusted her walkman and got started. By the fifth lap she was really moving, her thoughts cleared of Devin. She concentrated on the rhythm in her ears and the movement of her feet.

"Excuse me!"

Monica looked up to find the owner of that voice. There he was, jogging just ahead of her. His elbow had grazed her as he passed. She could feel the fast beat of her heart. Must be the fast pace she was keeping. Attempting to ignore her reactions and him, Monica kept moving.

"Excuse me!"

How had he made it around the track so fast? she wondered. This time he brushed her shoulder with his own. He was doing it on purpose! She scooted closer to the rail, hoping to avoid any more contact. No luck. He was deliberately moving as close to her as he could. And again, he didn't have the decency to have a shirt on. He was solid muscle. He needed to cover up. She needed him to cover up. This was not helping her need to forget the things Devin made her feel in the short time that she'd known him.

Monica would just grin and bear it. If she didn't acknowledge him, then he'd understand that there was nothing between them. Giving him the cold shoulder should make him see that she meant what she said.

So Monica endured the "Excuse mes", "Pardon mes", and even a "Watch out, Brown Eyes!"

At the end of her workout, it was a relief to move to the corner for her cool down. As she stretched, Monica seethed with annoyance because Devin slowed to a walk around the track.

Why was he deliberately making her aware of him? Try as she might, Monica couldn't control the erotic flood of electricity whenever he was near. But she didn't want Devin to know.

Monica kept that in mind when he began his cool-down stretches beside her, leaning as close as he could with each stretch. He started up a conversation.

"So, no kids today?"

"No," she answered, executing the cold shoulder without being rude. One syllable answers were more than he deserved.

"I guess they missed karate."

"Yes."

"Looks like you had a good workout today."

"If you say so." Oops—that was more than one syllable. He bugged her so much she couldn't think straight. Disgusted with herself, Monica stood after one final stretch and left him to talk to himself. Devin watched her walk away. It was exactly what he deserved from waiting almost a week to talk to her. She'd built up that frozen wall of hers. What a time for his brain to be working overtime. He couldn't control the need to record what had been developing in his head. Well, all was not lost. He could still detect a hint of nervousness. And those vibes were still there surrounding them both. He could feel them each time he passed.

He'd given her enough space. He needed to concentrate on melting the ice. Tonight had possibilities. First, he had to pump Scott for some information. He'd asked Devin to come over and help with a special project. Maybe Monica would be there too.

CHAPTER 10

Stepping out of the shower, Monica decided that a movie would be a good idea. No sense in sitting around the house with nothing to do but think about that big, muscular Bug. Even when Devin was no where around, he was more irritating than the mosquitoes that gave him his nickname.

Monica called Ness just to let her know where she'd be in case of an emergency. From the sound of children laughing and hammers pounding in the background, Monica realized they'd already started on their special project.

Avoiding traffic that was extremely congested on Friday evenings she decided to grab a light dinner while she waited for it to die down. The nine o'clock showing at the Galleria theater, inside an office complex off the interstate, right outside New Orleans in Metairie, was her choice. She liked this particular theater, especially at night. Instead of just a lot, there was a well it parking garage. It made her feel safer somehow.

Monica couldn't go to the movies without indulging in a big bucket of buttery popcorn, which was why she only had a salad for dinner. She settled down in one of the seats midway to the screen. When the kids were with her they'd always insist on sitting in the first row. Oh, the freedom of being alone!

Monica got comfortable in her seat at the far end of the row, ate her popcorn and watched the bits of trivia flash across the screen as she waited for the movie to begin. She savored each kernel, enjoying her treat because it was a rare indulgence.

The lights dimmed. At the moment the previews started, Monica wished she was anywhere but in this movie. She heard a familiar voice repeating a recently irritating phrase.

"Excuse me! Excuse me!"

Devin was making his way down to the last empty seat in her row. Probably the last empty seat in the theater. It was packed.

"Hello, Brown Eyes. Is this seat taken?"

Monica looked up. He towered over her. Sitting made her feel at a disadvantage and what was even worse, her heart was pounding a mile a minute. She wasn't working out, what was her excuse now? Monica didn't have a good one, because she knew she was staring up at the cause of her accelerated heartbeat.

"Yes, it's taken," she said, setting the popcorn bucket into the folded seat, nearly spilling the entire contents.

Devin continued to stare down at her, his expression showing that he didn't believe her for a minute. He didn't move an inch.

"Hey mister, are you gonna sit down?" a voice from behind them called out. "Some of us like to watch the previews!"

Devin smiled, waved a calming hand, and waited. The teenagers in their row found the previews not nearly as interesting as the battle of wills a few feet from them.

Monica had no choice. She wasn't used to all this attention and wasn't fond of riots or being the cause of one either. Besides, these people paid full price to see a movie. If they wanted to see the previews, she wasn't going to be the cause of them missing a second more.

She ungraciously removed the popcorn bucket, not bothering to brush away the kernels that fell into the seat.

She hoped he would sit on them and get a nice little butter stain on his jeans. Monica shook herself. She was becoming mean and spiteful. This wasn't like her at all. It was just that he made her remember what it felt like to be a woman. A woman in lust, that is, not a woman in love. She loved Keith. Devin—she lusted after him. The problem was she didn't want to lust after him. She was the mother of three small children and had no time for extracurricular activities involving a man.

There, now that that was straight in her mind, maybe she could enjoy the movie.

But that was not to be. To prove to herself that she could be nice, Monica shared her popcorn. Despite the vastness of the supertub, Devin's hand seemed to constantly encounter hers as she reached inside. Monica kept peering into the tub, expecting the few unpopped kernels to shoot up from the heat of his touch.

But that wasn't the worst part. The movie she'd chosen was a romantic comedy. There was a particular bedroom scene that was sizzling hot. If she were alone, the scene wouldn't have affected her in the least. With Devin beside her constantly touching her hand, quietly arousing her with his presence, she was one big fountain of need, want, and lust.

She couldn't ever remember feeling so aroused before, even with Keith. They'd had not only a satisfying love life but an explosive one. But this, this felt like the Big Bang happening all over again inside her body. Monica peered up at him. He seemed to be completely unaffected by the scene. She reached for some more popcorn. Maybe the chewing motion would help to calm her down. Just as before, his hand brushed against hers. Monica dropped the popcorn and instead savored his touch. The tip of his finger caressed each one of her own. He slowly turned her hand over, cradling it in his palm. Devin traced every line on the soft, pink center of her hand. Completing his exploration, Devin stared straight into her eyes as he slowly lifted her palm to his lips. Monica had no explanation for what she did next.

She couldn't remember deciding to do anything. It was a reflex action. She turned his hand over, cradling it just as he did hers. Monica lifted his strong brown hand to return the kiss and held onto it for the rest of the movie. Devin was anything but unaffected. Monica, of her own free will, had looked at him with those melting brown eyes, taken his hand and kissed it. That simple gesture did to him what no woman had ever been able to do before. His heart expanded as well as other parts of his body. His mind reeled from the certain knowledge that he was falling in love. The movie was over but he had no idea what it was about. The feature presentation for him was Monica

Lewis Jones. And he was so glad he hadn't missed the show.

He had found out where Monica was heading from Vanessa, and had gleaned a bit more information from Scott as he helped to build a tree house with the kids earlier in the evening.

Devin had gone home to shower and returned to pump more information from Scott. He'd convinced his friend to give him a ride to the Galleria so they could talk without so many little ears around.

"Okay, Bug, out with it," Scott said as he backed out of the driveway.

"Out with what?"

"Out with the reason you begged for a ride to someplace you could have easily driven to yourself if you asked for directions. Out with the reason for all the questions about Monica, and why you're following her."

"You want a lot of information here, Scott."

"I'm entitled. I'm family. And she's been hurting for a long time."

It wasn't as easy as he'd thought it would be. Devin had to deal with Scott's protectiveness toward his sister-in-law. He had to swear that his motives were for a serious relationship, and that he wouldn't intentionally hurt Monica in any way before Scott would take him to the Galleria. They had driven around for an hour before Scott was satisfied.

Devin had learned about Keith, his death, and Monica's reaction to it. It explained a lot. His goal would be to help her realize that what was happening between them wasn't a bad thing.

One factor was in his favor. Keith was only a ghost, but Devin was alive, a living, breathing man. And he would make sure he was always around, beginning with tonight.

He had gotten to the movie theater right before the lights were dimmed, and was able to spot Monica. And now here they sat, holding hands as the last of the credits signaled the end of the movie. The room was empty except for the two of them sitting together holding hands like teenagers on their first date. Monica broke the silence by asking, "Devin, can I have my hand back?"

"No," he answered. "It was given to me freely, so I plan on keeping it for a while."

She smiled, "Okay."

This was some night, Devin thought. She'd given him the smile. The one she reserved for her family. Devin couldn't help himself. With his other hand he caressed her cheek and gently kissed her lips.

"Thanks," he whispered.

"For what? My hand? I do expect to get it back one day."

"No, the smile. You have a beautiful smile, Brown Eyes."

At that moment when she looked as if she would die if he didn't kiss her again, an usher came into the theater. "Sir? Ma'am? You have to exit the theater for the next show."

"We were just leaving," Devin informed him, still holding tightly to Monica's hand.

She laughed as they left.

"Where are you off to?" Devin asked.

"I'm going home."

"Me too."

The laughter suddenly disappeared from her eyes and a serious look crossed her face. She dropped his hand. "I mean, I'm going home. To sleep—in my bed— alone."

"Still sounds like a good idea to me," he casually answered, his hand feeling lost as he finally put it into his jean pocket. "Can I get a ride home?"

"What happened to your Durango?"

"I left it. I got a ride here. I thought I'd catch a cab back, but since I ran into my neighbor I was hoping you'd do the neighborly thing and give me a lift."

"I've got a feeling that you somehow planned this."

"How could I know you were coming here?"

"That's a good question, but I won't ask you to answer it. I'll be neighborly," she agreed.

The wait to get on the elevator was long because of the crowd. Then they were stuck in the parking garage. It seemed as if hundreds of cars were waiting to exit into the traffic that was moving at a snail's pace.

Monica stared at the line of cars. She turned the air conditioner on full blast to combat the heat and the smell of exhaust fumes. "What do we do now?"

Wanting to see that smile on her face again, Devin thought talking was a good idea. He didn't want her to feel threatened by his presence. He much preferred the warm look in her eyes right now. Maybe before the night was over it would go up a few degrees. "Since I have your undivided attention, I can entertain you with some more stories about myself."

"Okay, I'm game." Monica leaned over to whisper, "I hate to admit this, but I liked the other one."

"You did? From the looks you threw my way, I could have sworn you thought my story was tasteless, crude, and immature."

"It was. But I enjoyed it anyway."

"Because I was bitten unmercifully?"

"That was reason enough, but mainly because you tell a good story. And you certainly kept the children entertained that day. I wondered what it was you were talking to them about."

Devin began to tell Monica about his mother and brother in Pennsylvania. She laughed so much Devin found it easy to forget the frowns and suspicious looks she'd cast his way more often than not.

"You have to be exaggerating," she told him between deep breaths. "Your brother couldn't have been so gullible to believe every lie you ever told him. Especially that last one."

"That cats come from catalogs? That wasn't one of my original pranks. I got that one from a book. Ever heard of *Stories Julian Tells?*"

"Yes, I have. Tony's read the whole series. The books were written by Ann Cameron. Julian was a very mischievous little boy."

"And I always wanted to be just like him. Reading his books stirred my imagination."

"And telling all those lies caused you to get into more trouble than Julian ever did, I bet."

"Not really, I was just having fun, I didn't hurt anyone. And for the record, they were not lies. They were jokes."

"M-m-m, I understand. They were innocent little episodes just for fun."

"Exactly!" he answered, enjoying her laughter. It was full-bodied and unique, and it seemed to come from deep inside of her, bursting forth like a geyser.

"Good, then you can laugh at the little joke we played on you last week."

"I don't know about that. That was a dirty, under-handed trick. That was not a joke. It was a boldfaced lie."

"So the rules are changing now! You're going back to being Mr. Arrogant, positive that you're always right. I've been enjoying Mr. Suave."

"I'm always arrogant, even when I'm suave. It's one of my many positive traits."

"I understand," she laughed again.

Devin stopped to stare. Her eyes were closed, her head thrown back. He captured that laugh with his lips, pulling her close to him. So, so sweet, he thought, resting his head against hers.

"Monica," he breathed, gently placing his hands on her cheeks. "I want you, you do know that?"

"Yes," she answered.

"Good, I thought you should know." He moved back, to his side of the truck. "I think we'll be able to leave now."

Monica leaned back and drank in the sight of this handsome man. He was arrogant, suave, and mysterious. Devin was also pushy and persuasive, yet understanding. It was too much to handle.

Monica started the engine but paused before putting the truck in reverse. "Devin, there's one thing I'm curious about."

"Yes."

"The eye patch, was there a reason for it or was it one of your little jokes?"

"You'd like to know, wouldn't you?"

"It was a simple question, Devin," she told him.

"I'll save it for another entertaining evening."

"What makes you think there'll be other entertaining evenings?"

"Brown Eyes, I don't think it, I know it." Before she had a comeback for that too-sure-of-himself comment he asked, "Why do you want to know about the eyepatch?"

"I liked it."

"You did?"

She nodded her head up and down. "It made you look sinister, dangerous and sexy all at once."

"Thank you," he answered, moving toward her again. "And how do I look without it."

"Exactly the same," she whispered, surprised and regretting every word that she'd uttered in the last sixty seconds. She decided to concentrate on getting home before she revealed how much she wanted him, too.

CHAPTER 11

Devin's hours of work were finally becoming more normal. The first couple of weeks in New Orleans he worked at developing a connection with the design and history of the area. He studied the architecture of the French Quarter, leaving every morning before dawn to view the Vieux Carre in the early morning hours just as the city began to rouse. Devin roamed the main avenues and side streets that made up the Quarter, noticing the subtle differences in the newer buildings built alongside older versions of similar style, how they blended with the original artistry.

He loved the style and beauty of the Pontalba Buildings gracing each side of Jackson Square. Devin's research revealed that they were meant to be apartments for rich patrons. Now they housed shops and restaurants that tourists visited by the thousands.

He blended into the crowd and soaked up the essence of the city, discovering that he loved it here. He spent an entire day sketching Jackson Square and the surrounding buildings from an elevated view in

Washington Auxiliary Park. He had only to turn in the other direction to enjoy the setting sun over the muddy Mississippi when he was done.

He did a close study of St. Louis Cathedral, as well as the Presbytere and the Cabildo, which flanked each side of the catholic church. His fascination with the intricacies of the wrought iron balconies and grillwork had nearly gotten him arrested for trespassing. But he'd easily talked his way out of that trouble. Brown Eyes would probably say he deserved to be put behind bars because it was his arrogance that had gotten him into the trouble to begin with, thinking his fascination was reason enough to invade people's privacy. He studied the Seignouret and the Dujuarreau Rouquette Houses on Royal Street. He also visited Gallier Hall with its high ceilings and beautiful courtyard. He was intrigued with the Merierilt House, the only one to escape the fire at the end of the eighteenth century. Devin was dying to get into some of the other houses in the Vieux Carre, but he settled for what he could see from the outside. Or the houses he could sneak into. He found it more adventurous and, most times, more effective.

Devin's powers of persuasion and his knowledge of carpentry gave him admittance into Cucullu Row, a three-story row of red brick houses built in 1828.

Some workers were doing repairs on an outside wall as Devin studied the building. He started up a conversation with the men and soon they were talking and laughing like old friends as he helped with the repairs. It turned out to be one of his most productive days.

Devin had enough contacts and money to have the famous homes opened for him. But he preferred researching his own way. He could have rented one of the houses or apartments in the Quarter or even stayed in one of the hotels. The Andrew Jackson was located in the Quarter. It had the distinction of being the site of the first U.S. District Court in New Orleans. But he hadn't, and was glad he hadn't. Wanting to be in a quiet environment had, almost literally, led him to Monica's door.

The majority of his time now would be dedicated to concentrating on his new dream, the one he'd always had in the back of his mind, the one that wasn't relevant until he met the right woman. In Monica he had found a woman he could love as well start a family with. Devin wasn't giving her any more space. That would only give her more time to make up all kinds of crazy reasons to keep them apart. The biggest reason, the largest obstacle, was Keith, a man who was dead and buried but still alive in her heart.

Devin hoped she'd find room in her heart for him. That's why, the morning after their night at the movies, he showed up bright and early at Scott's house under the guise of working on the tree house. He arrived before Monica and just in time to make pancakes. Devin considered himself a pro at pancake flips.

"Mind if I take over?" he asked.

"Be my guest," Vanessa told him, relinquishing the spatula.

Devin entertained the kids as he piled two plates high with pancakes. He demonstrated the straight flip, backwards flip, and his all-time famous spin flip as the kids watched wide-eyed. The kitchen was soon full of noise and fun. Devin was having a good time. He couldn't deny that he enjoyed being the center of attention. After he ended with one final spin flip, the kids and adults attacked the huge stacks of pancakes.

In between bites Tony told him, "Mr. Devin, that was incredible!"

"Yeah, incredible!" Mark echoed.

"Why, thank you, Tony—Mark."

"I liked the spin flip the best. Can you show me how to do that one?"

"Me, too?" Mark asked, his mouth full.

"What are neighbors for?" Devin promised to teach them after they got permission from their mother.

"All right!" Tony shouted. "She'll say yes. Mom thinks it's important for us to learn to cook and bake and clean and do all kinds of stuff. That way we'll be round people when we grow up."

"That's right, round people," Mark agreed, nodding his head up and down.

Devin smiled and nodded, though he was a little confused. Round people? Realizing what they meant, he held in a chuckle as he attempted to correct the boys. But Jasmine beat him to it.

"That's well-rounded people, Tony."

"Oops, I made a mistake. My mom wants us to be well-rounded people."

"I want to be well-rounded, too," Megan informed him.

"Jasmine and me, too," Vicki added.

Devin looked to Scott and Vanessa for help. Scott shrugged his shoulders and Vanessa stood to answer the phone. He wasn't going to get any from either of them. "Then I guess I'll have to give you all lessons."

"Good idea, Bug," Scott told his friend when the cheering children went back to their breakfast. Scott brought his empty plate to the sink and peered into the almost empty mixing bowl. "Dev," he called, "there's some batter left."

"You want more pancakes?" Devin asked, watching the familiar look of mischief appear on his friend's face. He hadn't seen it in years, but there was no mistaking it. Scott was up to something.

"I was thinking, since the kids were so excited about the pancake flips, why don't you show them the triple spin."

"Triple spin?" Tony asked.

"The triple spin!" Devin's eyes widened. "I haven't done that in ages, I'm a bit rusty."

"You can do it!" Scott coached.

Vanessa, finishing her phone call, grinned and asked, "Is it dangerous?"

Devin turned to look at them, a serious expression on his face causing Vanessa's grin to disappear and the children to fall silent. "It's very dangerous—for the pancake!"

They all laughed.

Scott turned on the burner. "Come on, Dev. Do the triple."

"You might as well," Vanessa told him. "Monica's on her way, and she'll be upset if she missed out on her favorite breakfast."

Monica was on her way over? Good! "Well, we can't upset Monica."

"Then get that grin off your face and get started," Scott told him, banging the griddle onto the burner.

Scott began to chant and encouraged the kids to join in, "Triple, triple, triple."

Soon the kitchen was booming with the chant.

"The triple," Devin said. "For this, I'll need to make a big one."

Devin went to work. He stirred up the batter, sprayed the griddle, and when it was hot enough, dramatically poured the batter in the circular motion until almost every inch of the square pan was filled.

"Wait, wait!" Mark called. "Mom likes pecans!"

"Well then, get the pecans!" Devin insisted.

Vanessa handed him a small bag of chopped pecans from a cabinet as everyone continued to chant.

With a flourish Devin sprinkled pecans onto the batter as it began to bubble and dry along the edges. It was time for the triple. As dramatic as a magician performing a death-defying trick he turned to his audience, placed a finger on his lips and sliced his hand through the air in a bid for silence. All was quiet. Every eye was on him.

Devin turned, flipped the pancake high into the air in one quick motion, spun around on the balls of his feet three times, grabbed the griddle and caught the pancake just before it hit the floor. There was a long silence. Five kids regarded Devin with awe.

"That was close, but it was good, Bug," Scott told him.

The kids started talking all at once. Monica walked into the kitchen in the midst of the noise.

"What's all the excitement?" she asked.

Devin glanced her way, flipped the griddle again, and neatly caught the pancake with a plate.

"Breakfast is served." Devin put the plate in her hands, sprinkled a few more pecans on top, drowned it in syrup, pulled back a chair, and handed her a fork, all done with style and grace.

"Milk or juice?" Devin asked.

"Oh, he's got it bad," Scott whispered to Vanessa.

"What does he have?" Vicki asked, her rabbit ears always honed in on what was being said.

"Mr. Devin has to fix Aunt Monica a glass of milk to go with her breakfast," Vanessa told her.

"And we have to put in another hour on the tree house before your cousins have to leave," Scott added.

The kids turned to run out the back door, anxious to get to work. Tony, Jasmine and Mark remembered to stop and give their mom a kiss.

"Mr. Devin did a triple. You should have seen him, Mom!" Tony informed her.

"It was great!" Mark told her.

"He says he'll teach us how to do it so we can be well-rounded people, okay Mom?" Jasmine added.

"I'd better get out there before they decide to saw or hammer something," Scott announced.

"I'll come and help." Vanessa quickly moved out of the chair.

"Your only job will be supervisor, mother-to-be," Scott told her.

"But Scott I…" She sighed. "Okay, I'll supervise."

Devin watched Vanessa give up before finishing her protest. If Monica were carrying his child he'd probably be just as protective, maybe even more so.

"Bug, don't rush out," Scott suggested, "Finish your breakfast and keep Monica company. We're only painting their names on one of the inside walls."

"No problem," Devin readily agreed, setting two glasses of milk on the table.

Monica sat staring at the milk in front of her. "What happened? I could have sworn that I just walked through the door two minutes ago."

"Dig in, it's going to get cold."

"What is?"

"The pancake. You're not going to let my efforts go to waste, are you? Mark said you liked pecan pancakes."

"Yes, I do."

"Then you have to taste this one," he said, taking her fork and cutting a small triangular piece.

He lifted it to her lips. Monica opened her mouth . "M-m-m," she said. 'Just the way I like it, full of pecans."

Devin watched the expression on her face as she ate. It reminded him of the satisfied look she wore after he kissed her. Surprised, but pleased that she allowed him to, Devin fed her piece by piece until the entire cake was gone.

Taking a sip of her milk, Monica leaned back. "I shouldn't have let you do that."

"Make you breakfast?"

"No. If that's a sample I'd let you do that anytime," she smiled. "What I mean is that I'm perfectly capable of feeding myself."

"I realize that. I can tell that you're a very capable woman. You're a single mother taking care of three kids on your own. But tell me if I'm wrong, it looked as if you enjoyed it."

"I did, but Kei— well nobody's ever fed me before, not since I was a baby."

"I don't see the harm—if we both enjoyed it."

Monica's eyebrows drew together. "Is that comment supposed to have a double meaning? That's just the kind of thinking that I'm steering clear of."

"Now you see, Brown Eyes, I wasn't talking about anything other than the enjoyment I got from watching you eat something that I cooked. You really need to keep your mind out of the gutter," he told, her making a tsking sound as he shook his head. Davin picked up his glass of milk and drained it in one gulp. He grinned to himself as he walked out the door.

CHAPTER 12

Monica peered at her bedside clock. She had ten minutes before her alarm went off. She stretched and tried to relax, her mind easily drifting to Devin. It was inevitable. Devin was everywhere. No matter where she went, he was there. He seemed to be following a normal routine that strangely coincided with hers.

Every morning Devin just happened to step out of his house as they were leaving. At first he would walk over to say good morning. Soon those good mornings began to stretch into lengthy conversations about everything and nothing.

To make matters worse, Tony had invented a special handshake in honor of the triple spin. So every morning her children did the triple shake with Mr. Devin. Tony, Jasmine and Mark thought that he was the ninth wonder of the world since that morning at Scott and Ness's house.

He'd come to church and her parents' house the last four Sundays in a row. His presence still bothered her in too many ways to count, but she was finding it easier to deal with each passing week. What began as a barely controlled tolerance grew into acceptance. Devin wasn't family, but he was her father's guest and Scott's friend. It would be mighty cheeky of her to tell her dad who he could invite to his own house.

One thing she couldn't figure out was why such a fine, young, handsome man would want to spend so much time with her family. Maybe he missed his own, or it could be that he'd never had a real family. Devin had talked about his brother and his mother, but nobody else.

Whatever his reasons, Devin was too visible, too accessible. Even when she was in her yard enjoying a warm spring day, he was either cutting grass, pouring over a stack of books, or sketching. Sometimes he sprawled out in a hammock, shirtless, relaxing. Something she couldn't do when he lay there, eyes closed, yet silently daring her to look just because he was there.

Another place she couldn't get away from him was at the Sports Spa. Monica would find Devin on the court in the middle of a basketball game long before she made her way to the track, so she couldn't accuse him of following her. He no longer brushed past her with fake apologies, but instead slowed his pace so that they could talk.

Devin did most of the talking. He told her about
the many places he'd traveled and the different things
he'd done as they exercised together. With Devin
beside her she had no need for music. His voice had a
timber and rhythm all its own. Monica was ready to
admit that she enjoyed his company.

On Fridays when Jasmine and Tony's karate class
ended, he would let them practice a few karate moves
on him, showing Mark a thing or two because he was
so anxious to learn. Then they would all go down to
the basketball court. Sometimes they'd challenge
Devin to a game of four on one. They even beat him
once.

As promised, he came over one Sunday morning
to teach the kids how to do pancake flips, without the
spin. Monica wasn't prepared for dodging IFO's—
Identified Flying Objects—pancakes.

He hadn't told her he wanted her again, and hadn't
even attempted to kiss her, or maneuver to get her
alone. But he was always touching her—to show her
the right way to shoot a basketball, to brush her hand
as he gave her a handful of lilies he'd save from being
chopped with the high grass in his yard. And whenever Devin talked to her, there seemed to be some
reason for him to touch her—a friendly pat, a speck
of lint he'd remove from her clothes. There was always

something. She wasn't complaining. She'd grown used to it. Monica figured he was one of those touchy, feely kinds of people. And because she felt comfortable in their relationship—platonic, friendly, non-threatening—she didn't mind.

Monica had come to consider Devin her good friend, and she liked it that way. At least that was what her brain constantly reminded her. Her body, on the other hand, was experiencing cravings she didn't want to examine too closely. Unfortunately, when she slept, her subconscious kicked into high gear and her mind explored physical longings.

Every morning Monica worked hard at suppressing those feelings before she saw Devin again. It was working so far. She would wake up with the desire to feel his lips on hers, to have the freedom to hold him close and feel his muscled arms around her. And then she would glance at the side of her bed and see the picture of a smiling Keith staring at her as she lusted after another man.

So, she would greet Devin with a friendly, and what she hoped was a platonic, smile and talk to him coherently, without revealing where her mind had wandered yet again. Devin would greet her the same way. Unreasonably, Monica was a little hurt that he could turn from potential lover to friend so easily. Oh well, she couldn't have it all, she thought, as she shut off her alarm.

Devin shivered under the cold spray as he reached for the soap. A cold shower every morning helped him face Monica as a friend. Man, did he hate that word! Monica used it often when referring to him.

"Devin, you're such a good friend" or "Joann, I'd like you to meet my friend." And the one that killed him every time, "I'm so glad we were able to become friends."

Every chance she got Monica threw that word up at him. Devin understood her reasons for doing it. What she meant was, "Stop. This is as far as it goes."

But every morning when he looked into her eyes he saw a different message. When she would say "Good morning, Devin," her eyes would say, "Where's my good morning kiss?" When she'd say, "You're such a good friend," her eyes would scream, "I want to be more than your friend." Monica had no idea what she revealed with those eyes.

"Friend," Devin growled to himself as he shut the water off. Stubborn, stubborn, stubborn woman. She'd rather hold on to the love of a dead man instead of reaching out to one who was alive and loved her so much it hurt.

Devin released his frustrations on the towel and his aching body as he dried himself. He got dressed and sat on the edge of the bed. Feeling a bit calmer Devin admitted that he enjoyed and valued their friendship more than any he'd ever had. But he wanted it to develop into something more. If he let Monica set the pace, it would never happen. Devin had to do something. He couldn't take much more of seeing her every day and never being able to kiss her or hold her.

The phone rang, interrupting his thoughts.

"Hello," he answered briskly.

"Good morning, Devin."

"Mom?" His mother rarely called because Devin phoned her on a regular basis to check up on her, and they chatted on the Internet from time to time. It was her favorite form of communication. Besides her house, her computer was one of the best gifts he'd ever given her. "Why are you calling? Is something wrong? Do you need me there?"

"Don't get yourself all worked up. I'm calling to see about you."

"Me?"

"Yes, you."

"There's nothing wrong with me."

"I see."

Devin cringed. He hated those two words. There was always censorship in the way she let them hang in the air. When he was growing up, those two little words had always prompted a confession. As a grown man they didn't have quite the same effect—still, he hated to hear his mother utter those particular words.

"What about me, Mom? What's going on?"

"That's what I called to find out. I haven't gotten my regular calls since you moved to that dangerous city with all those good-time drunken people. I thought you might be dead or lying in a gutter on Bourbon Street."

"I'm fine. Not everyone in New Orleans drinks all the time, and the city is not as dangerous as it used to be. It's no worse than some of the other places I've been."

"I see."

"Okay, I'm sorry I forgot to call," he told her calmly. "I got so wrapped up in this new project I've been working on I hadn't realized how long it had been since I talked to you."

"Is that all? A project's never made you forget your family before. Your own brother Joseph hasn't heard from you in over a month. You're not letting one of those New Orleans ladies mess with your mind, are you?"

"Mom, aren't you forgetting that I'm a man of the world?"

"Yeah, but if those women know you've got money they'll do anything to sink their teeth into you. You know what they say in that song about those New Orleans ladies."

"Nothing to worry about. But if it makes you feel better, I've got my eye on one. Unfortunately she only wants to be my friend."

"Good girl! She must have a lot of sense."

"Ma, I think you've just insulted me."

"Devin, you're my son. I know that you're a player. Why else would you still be single at the age of thirty-four?"

Devin chuckled. "It could be because I never wanted to get married." There had been women in his life but nowhere near the number his mother was implying.

"I see."

"Ma, stop." He paused, trying to gather a respectful tone. "Tell me exactly what it is that you do see?"

"I see that you're in love."

Again, amused at the direction their discussion had taken he asked, "And how do you know that?"

"I know my sons. You've fallen. It's over. When are you going to marry her?"

"It depends."

"On what?"

"On her."

"I see-e-e-e-e," she answered, dragging out the last word.

Devin clenched his teeth to hold back his frustration. He had the utmost respect for his mother. She had been both a mother and a father and from the ghettos of Philadelphia had raised his brother and himself to be productive citizens. She was his hero, his role model.

"Is she a good Baptist church-going woman?"

"No, she's Catholic."

"That's fine."

Devin laughed, "I'm glad you approve."

"As if you need my approval. I know you're just humoring me, son…"

"Look Ma, I'd love to talk, but I've gotta run." Devin could hear Monica and the kids getting into the truck. "Look out for your Mother's Day present, and check your e-mail."

"Dev—" He'd hung up on her. Lisa Preston stared at the receiver. She'd taught her sons to be respectful and well-mannered. This was the first time her elder son had ever hung up on her. It must have something to do with the 'New Orleans lady' he was in love with. She smiled and whispered, "I see."

CHAPTER 13

It shouldn't have bothered her, but it did. Her whole day was thrown out of whack because of it. When she got to work, Monica discovered that she had been assigned the privilege of being a workshop attendee. She wouldn't have minded going if the workshop hadn't been so boring. It was not worth the time away from her students and the mountain of paperwork she had left on her desk.

Lunch was provided, but for some reason they were five plates short. The problem was quickly solved with the arrival of Popeye's chicken and biscuits—a delicious, but fattening meal she didn't eat. A few too many indulgences of pecan pancakes forced her to stick firm to her diet of weekdays on and weekends off.

So here she sat through the boring presentation with an agenda that had nothing to do with speech therapy and even less to do with education, while her stomach growled and her eyelids hung heavy.

It was all Devin's fault. If he'd come outside as he usually did to wish her good morning and have their talk, she wouldn't have lingered. And if she hadn't lingered she would have missed being caught by the principal as he got off the phone with a sick co-worker, who was supposed to go to this god-awful workshop. But she was convenient and she was there, so she was drafted. It was all Devin's fault.

Monica knew that wasn't true, but felt better blaming him. She'd rather do that than admit that she'd missed him this morning. She missed their talk. Monica hadn't realized how much seeing him every morning brightened her day. She had not expected to feel so much disappointment.

What she could do, she thought, as the presenter turned to yet another irrelevant chart, was to ask Dev to go to the movies with her. Not to go out on a date, but to see a movie with a friend. Yeah, that was a good idea. The kids would be at Scott and Ness's again for movie night after they had their karate lesson. She'd definitely see him at the Sports Spa and ask him then. Monica perked up a little and actually appeared to be interested as the speaker droned on and turned to another chart.

Much later that same day Mark held up the number twenty-five. Monica nodded her head and kept moving, using her headphones again for the first time in almost a month. She was halfway through her workout and Devin was nowhere to be seen. Monica continued with her laps, trying to pretend that it didn't bother her. Just because he had been with her every time she hit the track for the last month didn't mean she couldn't do her workout without him. She'd never had a problem working out alone before Devin, so she didn't have a problem with it now.

Even after assuring herself of that, Monica had to push herself to make it through her workout. She was relieved when Mark held up the number forty and slowed her pace into a cool down with a slow march around the track.

"Excuse me, Brown Eyes."

Monica's head jerked up, her stomach did a somersault. She felt as if the day was starting all over again. She watched, a smile on her face, as he continued around the track slowing to a walk when he caught up with her.

Devin was nearly thrown backwards by the enthusiastic welcome spread across her face. This was the look he'd been dying for. And how did he get it? By not being where she expected him, when she expected him. That was purely accidental, of course, but fortunate for him, it seemed. The phone call from his mother had caused him to miss her this morning, and a run in with the lunatic at Scott's office was why he was late getting to the Spa.

But it was worth it. Now, he realized, was the time to change tactics.

Monica had come to depend on his friendship and expected him to be around, and he had been. But it was getting him nothing but safe smiles. If he wanted more from her, he would have to make himself unavailable.

"So, you missed me," he told Monica, soaking in her smile.

"I won't answer that. That head of yours is too big already."

"You think so? That sounded exactly like something my mother would have said."

"You have a mother?" she joked.

"That's normally how it works. I was on the phone with her this morning. That's why you didn't have the pleasure of my company." He stopped to bow to her in the middle of the track, blocking traffic. "I'm so sorry to have deprived you. I know how much you look forward to seeing me every day."

"I do?"

"At last! You've finally admitted it," he said, smiling apologetically at the two women who had to squeeze past them. He tapped her arm and started moving again.

"That was a question, not a statement of fact, Devin."

He loved the way she said his name. She'd start with a touch of annoyance and end with a lingering caress. He was sure she didn't realize how possessive it sounded.

"I see that one morning without me putting you in your place has allowed that arrogance of yours to come pouring out again."

"Not me. I was only telling you a little bit about my mother."

"Yes, your mother. I think it's sweet that you take time to keep in touch with your mom."

She stared at him as if he'd done the most wonderful thing in the world. He knew it was because she valued family so much.

"We try to stay in touch."

They walked for a while, stopping to encourage Mark with his numbers and exchange the necessary triple shake. Monica and Devin enjoyed each other's company, the conversation and the occasional silence between them.

"Dev?" she asked after one of those silences. "Are you busy tonight?"

"Why?" he asked, bracing himself and promising to hold firm to his resolve to be distant, even though he knew he could have her all to himself tonight.

"I was wondering if you'd want to see a movie tonight?"

"All five of us?"

"No, the kids are spending the night at Scott and Ness's for movie night."

"Oh."

"Well, do you want to go? We could see what's playing, talk, maybe get stuck in the garage again—who knows?" Her eyes were warm and full of antici-pation. "I enjoyed myself last time. I can admit that I didn't want to, but I did."

"Ah ha, this is a night for truths! Tell me some more."

"The truth was that I didn't want to be bothered with you, but I'm glad I did because that's the night we became friends."

Devin had been softening. The temptation was great. Alone, in a dark movie theater with Monica. But that one word stopped him—friends.

Having heard it one time too many prompted him to take a slight detour from his plan. "Are you asking me out on a date?"

"A date? No, we'll be two friends going out together. You know, to have some fun."

"I don't know, it sounds like a date to me."

"It's not a date. I don't go on dates."

"That could be what you believe, but maybe you're only telling me it's not a date. Deep down in your subconscious mind you might really believe that it is a date."

"Devin, don't be ridiculous. I don't consider friends going out together a date. If it'll make you feel better, you can call it anything you want. I, the adult, will know better."

"Okay, then, I choose to call it a date. Sorry, I can't make it, I'll have to take a rain check. I've got other plans."

"Why didn't you say that?"

"I did, just now."

"You know what I meant. Why did you let me go through all that?"

"I don't know. It was fun. A joke between friends?"

Monica laughed. "So you made me a little crazy. I'll forgive you. What have you got planned? Maybe we could do something a little later. I have all night."

That sounded so good. But Devin swallowed his disappointment and put on his cocky act as he stopped on the side of the track to stretch. "Sorry, I can't, I've got a date."

Devin could feel her eyes on him. "A date? With a woman?"

"Yes." From the corner of his eye he could see her blink, and he thought he heard her mutter, "Damn it." Devin wanted to laugh. Had Brown Eyes cursed? The words didn't sound right coming from her lips. He pretended he hadn't heard. Devin watched as she went through her stretching routine in complete silence.

"You okay?" Davin asked as she stood to leave. "How about a game of basketball?"

"Not today. I need to drop the kids off so they can have a couple hours of daylight to work on the tree house."

"Oh yeah, I heard it was almost finished." He glanced at his watch. If he didn't hurry with his workout he'd be late for his date with Scott, the tree house and the kids. She shook her head absently. "The kids are excited about it."

"You'd better go then. I'll see you around, friend."

Monica walked down the stairs with Mark gripping her hand. Friend? Somehow she didn't like that word anymore. Brown Eyes had sounded a whole lot better.

CHAPTER 14

Devin didn't get to Scott's house until after six-thirty, giving Monica more than enough time to have dropped off the kids and be gone. He went straight into the yard to join Scott and the tree house gang. The kids took turns holding the rungs for the ladder as Devin and Scott attached them to two thick pieces of rope. Before the rope ladder was finished, a sudden shower sent the kids racing into the house. Devin grabbed the toolbox and Scott the tools. They followed the kids to the back door and stood under the overhang out of the rain. Devin opened the toolbox so that Scott could return the hammer, pliers, and whatever else they'd used. He turned to go inside, but he stopped in surprise at the back door.

Scott caught the look on his friend's face and the direction of his gaze and whispered, "You can say something, but don't dwell on it. And don't stare at her like that."

"But her stomach. It looks like it's doubled in size."

"We're having twins, remember," Scott told him. Devin detected irritation as well as a touch of fear in his tone.

"Sorry, Scott. I didn't mean to be insensitive."

"She's healthy, the babies are fine. I'm just…"

"…worried." Devin finished. Staring at Vanessa's stomach again, he slowly moved his gaze up to her face but imagined Monica's instead. If he were Scott, Devin knew he'd be worried too.

"If you two stand out there all night playing with tools, the kids are going to eat all the pizza," Vanessa called out to them.

Scott answered, "Can't let that happen. We'll be right in, Nessa." Then he whispered to his friend, "Remember, Bug, you have to say something. If you don't make a comment she'll think I told you not to say anything, and I don't want Nessa to start crying again."

"Tough to deal with?"

"It's not so bad. Nessa's first trimester was smooth sailing if you looked beyond the nausea, cracker crumbs in bed, and watching your wife come face to face with the toilet on a daily basis. It's all part of the pregnancy, but lately, she's been so sensitive. Nothing I say is right."

Devin listened with quiet interest, absorbing Scott's first-hand knowledge on the subject and storing all away for later reference. He would need this information when he and Monica made babies of their own, adding of course to the family they'd become as soon as he could get her to marry him. Devin had spent so much time with Monica's kids they felt like his own. He hoped he didn't have too long to wait.

"Speaking of sensitive, I guess that you haven't told Vanessa what happened at work today."

"Not yet, but she'll agree with me one hundred percent."

"Are you talking about the pre- or currently-pregnant Vanessa?"

Scott paused a second. "Either way, she has no love for T.J. and will agree with the decision I had to make today."

Devin walked into the kitchen ahead of Scott. Another glance at Vanessa confirmed not only her tremendous growth, but an added beauty. He said the first thing that popped into his head. "Those babies are sure making room for themselves, Ness."

Vanessa turned to him, a thoughtful expression on her face. She gave him a hug and a kiss on the cheek.

"You have to tell me what that was for. If I can do it again, maybe I can get Monica to kiss me."

"It's because you're right. That's exactly what the babies are doing, making room for themselves. You have to be one of the smartest people in the world."

Scott turned to Devin, then Nessa, a stunned expression on his face. "What about me?"

"You are the smartest person in the world. That's one of the reasons I married you. What Devin said made sense. There's nothing wrong. I'm not too big. The babies are only making room for themselves," she answered and gave Scott a kiss.

"While she's in this logical frame of mind," Devin whispered to his friend, "you might want to tell her about quitting your job and investing a very large sum of money into a brand new partnership."

Scott shook his head in response. Devin was having some trouble connecting this nervous-looking man with the completely enraged person he'd seen earlier today. Would he ever be this nervous with Brown Eyes? Not ever having dealt with an emotional, pregnant woman, Devin wasn't so sure. Just as he was about to leave, thinking to give Scott and Ness some time alone, Vicki came into the kitchen.

"MaNessa, where are the fish cards?"

"On the bottom shelf in the den. Did everyone wash their hands?"

"I think so. Tony and Mark are still in the bathroom."

Devin stood. "I'll go check on them for you."

"No, it's okay. Tony will have Mark out of there as soon as he rinses all the bubbles away. You need to stay anyway, Bug. Whatever it is Scott has to tell me involves you too, I'm sure."

"You think so?" Devin asked. He wondered if pregnancy made women more perceptive as well as overly sensitive.

"I've known since about four o'clock today. That's when I got an interesting phone call."

"Who was it?" Scott asked.

"T.J."

"That no good son of a b—"

"Scott, his parents are very nice people. They can't help what T.J.'s become."

"What did he say?" Devin asked as he watched Scott sit and fume, red-faced. His friend looked as if he was going to explode all over again.

Before answering, Nessa leaned over to whisper something in Scott's ear. It had instantaneous results. Scott's face relaxed, the tension slowly easing the lines in his face. In a few seconds he calmed down enough to listen.

Amazed, Devin turned back to Vanessa as she began to explain.

"T.J. sounded so wild and crazy that I didn't recognize his voice at first. He was ranting and raving about firing Scott because he associated with scum like Preston. Knowing Devin was meeting you at work today and T.J.'s opinion about any black person, I could only assume he meant you, Bug."

"That's right, my last name's Preston."

"He mentioned your name over and over again, spitting it out like a dirty word. I was about to hang up on him when he claimed that you framed him. I listened because I wanted to know what was going on in that sick mind of his."

"What did he say?" Devin prompted.

"You didn't have to listen to the—" Scott paused, "Itty-it."

"I wanted to know what he had against Devin besides the color of his skin. He claimed that you faked an accident and bribed your way into controlling the construction of a building he was contracted to complete."

Devin observed the same look of disgust and incredulity on Scott's face that he knew was plastered on his. They both laughed without humor.

"He's a psychopath," Devin surmised. "Without any backbone. He didn't have the nerve to say that to my face."

"A psychopath, full of hot air," Scott added.

"Are you sure about that?" Vanessa asked.

"MyNessa," Scott used his pet name for his wife. "What you heard over the phone was the noise of a coward."

"He's right," Devin told her. Scott had already filled him in on the problem they'd had with T.J. a few years back. Devin still had trouble believing the lengths he'd gone through to keep Scott and Ness apart. "After the surprise of finding me in Scott's office, he began to make all sorts of accusations. Among other things, T.J. accused me of being responsible for ruining his chances of proving himself to his father."

"That doesn't sound like you, Bug," Vanessa told him. "What really happened?"

"Daddy! MaNessa!" Vicki yelled as she marched into the kitchen. "Megan's cheating! She's looking at everybody's cards!"

"I am not, not, not!" Megan, the accused, called from the den.

"I'll handle this crisis," Scott told Vanessa. He put his hand on her shoulder to stop her from rising. "Tell her the story, Bug. I've heard it already and don't think I'm in the mood to hear it all again."

Bug nodded in understanding. He'd prefer not to think about the situation or T.J. for the rest of his life. "Before I start, can I ask you a personal question?"

"Only if I can do the same."

"Okay," Devin agreed, "ladies first."

"When are you going to do something to get it through my sister's head that you love her?"

"What's that?"

"Bug, I like you, but I'm tired of watching you stare at Monica with those love-starved eyes of yours every Sunday. What are you going to do?"

For once Devin was stunned speechless. Vanessa always seemed so sweet, quiet and innocent. He was expecting her to ask about his intentions, not force him to do something about them. "Umm, I'm not sure," he finally got out.

"Take my advice. Stop trying to be her friend. If that's all you are now, that's all you're ever going to be. I know my sister, and I know she's holding back and why. I won't get into that, but maybe you can get it out of her. You have to do something to break out of this friendship mold she's put you in. Personally, I think you're the one for her. You have to let her know that."

"That's what I've been trying to do, but your sister's one stubborn woman."

"I know, but it's up to you now to do something about it. I've had my say. Your turn. What's the question?"

"The ear thing. What's that all about? I can't help noticing this constant exchange between you and Scott through the ear canal. If I'd have known that whispering in his ear was all I needed to do to keep him from killing T.J. I'd have tried it. A few minutes ago he was ready to explode again, and all you did was whisper in his ear and then he was fine."

A blush appeared beneath her brown skin and Vanessa answered, "That's too personal."

"That's not fair, Ness, I think you owe me something. Give me a clue."

Vanessa stared at him for a moment, seemed to come to some conclusion, and said one word, "Pleasures."

"I understand," he told her and began to fill her in with the details of his situation with T.J. by reminding her of the eyepatch he wore when she first met him. It was the last remnant of an accident caused by T.J.'s idiocy, and it happened while Devin was designing a string of condominiums contracted by the LaBranch Firm in Mississippi.

"A branch of the same architect firm of T.J.'s family," Vanessa concluded at that point.

"Yes, T.J. working in Mississippi was your luck, but my curse," he continued. "I'd already designed the condos, all the essential equipment was ordered and construction had begun. I worked with the crew because I wanted to see the job done from the drawing board to reality. I had planned on being involved in every aspect, from the foundation to the paint on the walls. Everything was on schedule, the foreman I and were of like mind. Then…"

"…along came T.J.," Vanessa guessed.

"He came, all right. Full of opinions and ridiculous ideas. When I let T.J. know exactly what I thought about him and his ideas, he tried to fire me. He couldn't."

"He couldn't?"

"No, it was impossible."

"Why?" Vanessa asked.

"Why?" Devin repeated, not wanting to brag about himself. Arrogant he was, boastful he wasn't.

"Yes, why couldn't T.J. fire you?"

"I'll tell you why," Scott answered, sliding into a chair next to his wife. "Devin is one of the most sought-after architects in the business. And I quote, 'He has a reputation for his dramatic yet tasteful original designs and replicas of architectural design, from any time period.' "

Vanessa looked at Devin, with new understanding in her eyes.

"Enough of that, Scott. What it boils down to is that I wouldn't allow T.J. to touch my design. I was finally working with my hands again and I wasn't going to let his unreasonable hatred stand in my way.

"It didn't take long for me to realize that T.J.'s animosity toward me wasn't simply from the embarrassment he'd suffered in front of the foreman and crew when he discovered that he had been trying to give orders to D. J. Preston, the foremost leader in our field instead of the simple construction worker he thought I was," Devin concluded.

"It didn't matter who you were, Dev. One look at you was all it would take for T.J. to hate you. You're black and had the nerve to have more authority than him."

"True," Devin answered matter-of-factly, "but the fact that I've accomplished more and earned money—"

"Millions more," Scott interjected.

"—more money than he ever would. That fact poured salt in the self-inflicted wound of hatred he has inside of him."

"T.J. must have been hell to work with," Vanessa said.

"Work! We never worked together. We battled. He tried to undermine every decision I made, reordered materials that were substandard, and questioned my decision to work with the construction crew."

"Sounds familiar," Scott commented, "Dirty, underhanded, and sneaky. That's T.J."

"It backfired. The crew couldn't stand him. All he did all day was walk around in his three-piece suit issuing orders that no one followed without my approval."

"That's exactly what he deserved," Vanessa said.

"I agree, but it didn't help matters."

"Your eye?"

"I'm lucky to be able to see out of both of them today."

"What happened?" Vanessa asked.

"I was at the site shaping a piece of molding for the entry hall. Next to designing, you could say wood-working is my other passion." Third in line, he thought, with Monica at the top of the list. "T.J. was in a foul mood because I had been ignoring him all day. It was the best way for me to deal with him without giving in to the urge to maim him."

"You wouldn't have," Vanessa said.

"Believe me, Ness, there were many times I wish I had. The fact that I outweighed him and could easily break him in two, plus the satisfaction of working with the crew, was reason enough to hold me back."

"I can't see T.J. tolerating taking orders from a rich, talented black man who earned more money and was respected more than he ever would be," Vanessa said.

"He couldn't, and he didn't. That day when he came storming toward me I ignored him as usual, turning my back to him. Not getting my attention, he pulled the strap of the goggles. They shot off my face and left my eyes unprotected. I couldn't move away or turn my head fast enough. Tiny splinters of wood darted straight into my eyes."

"My God, Bug!"

"Oh, I called on him. Jesus, Mary and Joseph, too. Talk about pain."

"What did T.J. do?"

"He thought it was hilarious. Besides the pain, all I could focus on was that laugh. He let me know what a stupid 'nigger' I was to get splinters in my eyes. He wasn't expecting me to retaliate. I was hurt and figured that the odds were even. I gave him a broken nose and a few cracked ribs."

"Oh, Devin."

"It all turned out fine. I had an operation on my eyes, got the splinters removed and was told over and over again how lucky I was to have my sight. One eye was worse off than the other and more sensitive to light."

"That explains the eye patch. And T.J.? How did he get away with it?"

"He didn't get away with it."

"He's not incarcerated. That's where he should be, behind bars, convicted of negligent injury. My brother's a cop, I know about these things. Or did he get off easy with community service and a fine because he knew someone?"

"I didn't press charges. It was my word against his. The goggles I wore were an old pair, that had seen better days. It was foolish, I know, but those were my lucky pair. You know the ones I always wore in college, Scott."

"I remember."

"But there were consequences. There were other ways to handle this kind of situation."

"I won't ask about them," Vanessa said studying him.

"Good, because I've said enough. The foreman finished the job and T.J. disappeared."

"Until now. Do you think he was looking for you?" Vanessa asked.

"No, he just turned to his father's firm, the only one that would have anything to do with him after being tossed out of the AIA. I happened to be there to vent his frustrations on."

"You weren't the only one," Scott added. "With how low T.J.'s stooped I'm not surprised to find that the American Institute of Architects revoked his membership. Too bad you didn't have a hand in seeing that happen, Dev."

"And of course through it all T.J. probably sees himself as an innocent victim."

As they nodded in agreement, their thoughts were interrupted by another call from the den.

"Can we have some popcorn?"

"Sure you can," Scott answered absently. He went into the pantry and just caught himself before falling flat on his face. "Why are two gallon jugs of oil in the middle of the floor?"

"I have no idea," Vanessa answered. "I haven't been in there in weeks."

Silently Devin couldn't stop himself from grinning in remembrance of the first time he kissed Brown

Eyes. He watched as Scott shrugged and put the containers on a shelf.

"What happens now?" Devin heard Vanessa ask.

"Bug and I become partners, designing and building as a team."

"Your own business, I think that's wonderful. But what about T.J?"

"What about him?" Scott asked.

"How are you going to deal with him? Unstable people are dangerous. They do crazy things. If he hurt Devin like that and laughed, there's no telling what he's capable of."

"He's a coward, Ness. I have no doubt that he enjoyed my suffering, but what happened to me was unintentional. He doesn't have the guts to do anything."

Devin watched as Scott turned to whisper in his wife's ear. Devin smiled, getting used to seeing this show of love. He found that he wasn't as jealous as before.

Megan walked into the kitchen. "Is the popcorn ready, Daddy? M-m-m," she sighed when she spotted her parents. "Daddy and MaNessa are always telling secrets. Can you help me with the popcorn, Mr. Devin?"

"Sure," Devin agreed. He handed the bowl of popcorn to Megan and once again took another look at the happy couple. Tonight he would begin to change his friendship with Monica into something more, something much more.

CHAPTER 15

It was dark outside with a light drizzle hitting the windshield as he turned down Piety Drive. Devin thought he saw Monica dash into her house. She had probably just gotten back from her movie. Devin hoped she'd missed him. Glancing at his watch, he saw that it was a little after nine, a little early for her to be back if she went to a seven o'clock show.

Devin pulled into the driveway. There was a streak of lightening, some thunder, then Monica running out the front door looking wet and wearing a long robe. She was carrying a shut-off valve key. What would she be doing with a tool used to control the main water valve?

He sat in the Durango and watched a moment. Monica obviously didn't know what she was doing. Devin got out and was standing directly behind her when she shrieked.

"Damn it! I couldn't be so stupid!"

"You're not stupid, Brown Eyes," Devin laughed, catching and holding her close.

"I'd like to think I wasn't," she answered.

"What was the 'damn it' for, then?"

"Turn off that water!" she ordered before running into the house again.

Devin turned the water to the off position with a twist of his wrist and went into Monica's house. He put the tool in an umbrella stand by the door. Everything looked normal. "Monica?"

"I'm in here!" she called.

Devin followed the sound of her voice. He stopped in front of Monica's open bedroom door. He'd never been anywhere near this part of the house. The kitchen and the den were the only two rooms he'd been allowed into.

"Devin? I'm in the bathroom. Can you give me a hand?"

"No problem," he answered, walking through her bedroom. He got a quick impression of lavender and pink, soft colors. Devin found Monica on her hands and knees mopping up water from the bathroom floor.

"Don't say a word. Grab that bucket behind you and some towels and help me, please."

Devin was proud of himself. He hadn't said a word. He didn't tell her how sexy she looked as she moved around the bathroom floor soaking up water.

And of course, he refrained from commenting on the way her robe gapped open every time she moved, allowing him a glimpse of smooth brown skin and a peek at what else lay beneath her thin robe.

Using all the towels in the house they were able to dry the floor. Monica pushed the bucket of wet towels away from her and let out a deep breath.

"Want to tell me what happened?" he asked, brushing a strand of hair out of her face. It was wet and stringy and all over her head. She was beautiful.

"I was going to take a bath."

"Are you sure it wasn't a shower?"

Monica glared at him and went on. "When I turned the cold water on, the handle broke off in my hand. I couldn't turn it off." She held the handle up to him.

"It must be stripped." He ignored the handle and took her hand instead. He held it, slowly lingering over each finger before inspecting the handle.

"I went outside to find the main shut-off valve," she said as Devin tried to fit the handle onto the faucet. "Then I couldn't find that big, long, thing-a-ma-jig."

"The shut-off valve key?"

"Right, then I couldn't turn it off. Then you showed up, thank goodness. That's when I remembered that I hadn't turned off the hot water or unplugged the tub. The house would have been flooded by the time I figured out how to shut the water off."

"Uh-huh."

Monica stood. "I've still got a tub full of water. I guess I'll take that bath now. Thanks for being such a good friend, Dev."

Friend? Devin thought. Not anymore. She was not putting him back into the friendship corner. "You plan on using that tub right now?"

"I could use a good soak in warm water," she said, pulling the wet robe away from her chest. It sprang back, clinging to her skin and perfectly molded to her breasts.

Devin couldn't help noticing. He swallowed. "That looks like a lot of water for one person."

"I'll manage," she said and crossed her hands in front of her robe.

"I could always—join you," he teased.

"No, thank you. I bathe alone."

Devin knew that would be her answer, but went on. "Where's the fun in that? Take a look a this big tub. Two can fit. I'll prove it to you," he said, taking off his shoes and standing in the tub.

"Devin, get out of my bath water. You still have all your clothes on."

"Do you want me to take them off?"

"No, I want you out."

"I don't think that's going to work. Because I want you in." Devin grabbed her around the waist lifting her over the side and into the tub with a gentle splash. There she stood facing him. He held her loosely, but firmly, his mind resigned to releasing her if she protested. The big old-fashioned claw-footed tub was wide and deep. "See," he breathed into her ear, "it's more than big enough. We'll both fit."

"That wasn't the problem." Her voice was breathy, soft.

"It wasn't? Then why are you in this tub with me, Brown Eyes?"

"I'm not actually in the tub with you, Devin," Monica protested with a sigh that didn't sound like a protest at all.

"No, not completely," he touched his lips to hers. Devin moved less than an inch away before adding, "I can fix that." Not waiting for a response, Devin's hands glided down until he cupped her behind. Devin paused. She made a sound, a noise that had nothing to do with stopping his explorations. His hands moved with a slow up-and-down motion, her head lay against his chest. His hands moved down once again then stopped. He effortlessly lifted her, wrapping her legs around his waist and then leaning back sat on the edge the oval tub.

"What are you—?" Devin swallowed her protest that with a probing, taking, giving—you-have-got-to-see-what-you-mean-to-me kiss. Before the kiss was over they had slid into the tub with a huge splash.

Monica sat on his lap. They were both wet, both breathing hard. Different emotions crossed her face, one underlying factor clear: she wanted him. He could feel it with each heavy breath she took. In the way her hands relaxed as she began to trace his hairline. And most of all from the liquid heat in her eyes. "Kiss me again, Dev."

She didn't say friend was the last sane thought Devin had as he gave her a kiss that had nothing to do with friendship. That kiss was the crack that broke the dam on the flood of emotions they had both held back for so long. There was no turning back for either of them.

Somehow in the tub as their kisses became more demanding Monica's robe was lost. He touched her everywhere. Dark brown fingers moved along her arm, trailing down her spine to the curve of her behind. Wherever he touched her Devin felt tiny electric currents shooting from her body into his own. He thought they would suffer from electrical shock if they didn't get out of the tub soon.

Devin stood holding her tight, not wanting to lose contact. Somehow he got them both out of the deep tub. They clung together in the middle of the bathroom.

What was she thinking? Devin wondered. Then, please don't let her think.

"This isn't right," Monica whispered.

No, don't say it, Devin begged inside his head. "What's not right?"

"I'm standing here naked and you have all your clothes on. I can't feel you. It's unfair," she said, looking up at him, the heat in her eyes everything he'd ever wanted.

"I can fix that," Devin said. He shed his clothes in record time.

They'd lost contact for not more than a few seconds, and then the sparks did fly. His fingers, his hands moved everywhere. There was no waiting. There was no thinking. There was just Monica and he was inside her, both of them exploding.

As they lay together in a state somewhere between electrifying pleasure and deep satisfaction, Devin heard her whisper. "And I only wanted you to be my friend?"

He smiled and closed his eyes. Devin rested his cheek against her breasts and breathed in the scent of Brown Eyes. A thought crept into his head, causing his eyes to widen. He hadn't used any protection! For the first time in his life he had been careless. Knowing he hadn't planned on making love to Monica didn't make him feel any less responsible for his thoughtlessness. But the possibility of making Brown Eyes pregnant didn't scare him. He was thrilled with the thought of having a baby with her. He just wasn't sure how she'd react. Thinking about reactions, Devin was apprehensive about what Monica's reaction was to their sudden lovemaking. She was way too quiet, for entirely too long. It was making him nervous—a feeling he didn't like at all. Might as well get it over with, Devin thought, as he lifted his head to peer at her.

She didn't stare at him with regret or anger, nor was there accusation on her face. She didn't look at him at all. Monica was sound asleep. Their first time together had tired her out more than he thought. Devin lay on his back, snuggling her warm, relaxed body against his own. He'd have to worry about her reaction in the morning. At this moment he'd simply enjoy having her in his arms. She was right where he wanted her. He fell asleep with an ease he hadn't felt in a long time.

A few hours later Devin drifted out of a deep sleep as Monica rolled over and sighed, "M-m-m, Devin."

She rubbed against him, creating a friction that aroused him. He was wide awake and ready for anything, but still apprehensive about her reaction. At this moment Devin could empathize with Scott's earlier nervousness.

She moved again. Devin held his breath. He waited. Monica crawled on top of him, her breasts rubbing against his chest—small, slow, torturous movements. She suddenly stopped and lay completely relaxed against him. Had she fallen asleep? He hoped not, because sleeping was the last thing on his mind.

Monica let out a little moan as she kissed the side of his neck. She was awake. Her lower body moved against his arousal—more than awake. This reaction, he liked. He dipped his head to give her long brown neck a kiss in return for the one she gave to him. She moaned, then sighed as he made a trail of kisses down her neck.

"I'm ready, Dev. What are you waiting for?"

What was he waiting for? For the life of him he couldn't figure it out. He would push his hesitation aside and direct his energies to accommodating her. Their first time together had been fast, wild and intense. This time Devin was determined to take it slow. The experience would be just as intense but this time slow, very slow.

For long moments he traced the curves of her body, the curve of her breasts, the indentation of her waist, moving out again to trace her hips. Slow, slow, he repeated in his head as Monica moved her hand between their, bodies making her way down. It didn't take long to reach her destination.

After a quick intake of air and a shudder that took over his entire body Devin thrust into her and grunted in frustration, "Slow is overrated."

Monica gave no response as she continued the rhythm until they were relaxed again and full of soft sighs.

That was so-o-o good, he thought, but he was so-o-o pitiful. He had no control whatsoever with Brown Eyes. And coming down from a sexual haze, he remembered what had been so important for him not to forget. He'd made love to her a second time without protection and with no finesse. He was an animal.

He paused in his self-recriminations as Monica slid to his side to rest her head on his shoulder. "Dev, that was…"

Devin waited while she ran a finger across his chest making a path around his nipples. "That was what?" he asked cautiously.

"That was wonderful!"

Wonderful! Well, he thought, if Brown Eyes didn't have a problem with his lack of finesse, he wasn't going to dwell on it. He'd just make sure that the next time was more than wonderful. He relaxed again, thinking that everything was going to be all right.

Monica opened one eye, then the other. She blinked. Something was different, very different. She was disoriented—confused, as if she hadn't gotten enough sleep. The same way she felt when Devin was keeping her awake with that loud music. Devin! Oh no! She was suddenly aware of a warm body beside her. It wasn't another dream.

The water, the faucet, the rain…The tub, the bed— Oh no, the bed! It all came back. Monica couldn't look at him. She had asked him to take his clothes off, to make love to her.

What had gotten into her? Her eyes immediately went to the nightstand. There, sitting in its usual spot, was a picture of Keith and herself on their wedding day. Pain stabbed her heart. Guilt washed over her. What had she done? Monica felt as if she'd betrayed the only man she'd ever loved. The only man she'd ever made love to. The only man she'd ever made love to, she repeated, until now.

All at once, other implications hit her. Monica didn't know how many women Devin had slept with before her. Or how many he was sleeping with right now. It could be dozens! No, hundreds, for all she knew! An even more horrifying thought shot through her head.

Frantic with worry, Monica jumped out of the bed and yanked the cover off him. "Get up, Devin!" she yelled. "Get up right now!"

He sat up disheveled, bare-chested—sexy. "What's wrong, Brown Eyes?"

"'Brown Eyes', don't you ever call me that again!" Devin pinched the bridge of his nose as he studied her. She'd taken a defiant stance at the foot of the bed.

"What should I call you? My love? My life? It all means the same to me."

"Don't tell me that, it's not true. You're only trying to butter me up to get more of what you already had last night."

He actually flinched. That surprised her. Monica knew exactly how crude she sounded. She'd done it intentionally.

"No," he answered.

"No—No! You say that one little word and I'm supposed to believe you." Before he could respond, Monica continued with her tirade. "What I do believe is that you've probably slept with thousands of woman before me. And I have no idea how many diseases are going through your body! I don't need diseases! I have three children to raise!"

"So I've slept with thousands of women?" he asked calmly, staring at her point blank.

"All right," she admitted grudgingly. "Maybe not thousands, possibly hundreds, at the very least dozens! What it boils down to is too many women who probably had God knows what diseases and passed them along to you. And now I've probably got them too!"

Monica stood in front of him completely naked, completely beautiful, and completely terrified. How could he reassure her? How could he let her know that she had nothing to worry about, that he was always careful. What a joke! Always careful. He was always careful until he met her. Would she believe that he'd always used protection in the past when he hadn't thought twice about using any last night? No, she wouldn't believe it. She was dead set against believing anything he said right now. Devin heard himself ask, "What do you want me to do Brown..." At her direct glare he continued, "...Monica. What can I do to make you feel better about this?"

"Come with me to the clinic before I pick up my children. We'll take some blood tests. I want proof that I don't have to worry about—anything."

Devin thought this over. A quick call to his doctor in Philly and he could arrange a private visit with a colleague here in New Orleans. He wasn't sure he wanted to do that. Monica would ask too many questions, wonder how he could make those kinds of arrangements so quickly. He hadn't been to a public clinic since he was a teenager, but Devin had a feeling that he should follow her lead. It was probably the only thing that would calm her fears. He loved her. He could do this for her.

But still, a small part of him protested this need for proof. Devin wished she trusted him. But she didn't. Monica still couldn't look beyond Keith. Anyone threatening his memory would be under close inspection. Maybe he should be relieved. By putting him through this, Monica was showing that he threatened Keith's memory. At least that was something.

Devin looked up as if asking for divine assistance, then back to his lovely unclothed Brown Eyes and agreed. "Okay, Monica, I'll go."

"You will?" she asked, stunned.

"Of course. I don't want you worrying for no good reason. I could tell you that you have nothing to worry about, but you wouldn't believe me. If you want proof, I'll cooperate."

"I do," she answered. Monica visibly relaxed and suddenly realized that she was standing in the middle of the room, naked. She grabbed the sheet off the bed. "Thank you, for your cooperation." She dashed off to the bathroom.

Devin looked down at his watch. It was six-thirty. How could such a wonderful night turn into such an awful morning? He knew how—single mother plus stubborn woman—that's how.

CHAPTER 16

Monica took the first two numbers from the small, free-standing hook on the counter by the closed reception window. She sat down next to Devin in an orange, plastic chair. They'd driven over in record time and got here before the clinic was open. She'd purposely chosen this clinic and time because she hadn't wanted to bump into anybody she knew. It was far enough from home to almost guarantee that. And there was no way that she was going to see her personal doctor. Just the thought of admitting that she'd had unprotected sex was too embarrassing to even think of saying out loud.

Monica handed Devin a number and stared straight ahead. She wished she could take back the last twelve hours of her life. She wanted to be her old self. She wanted Devin to be her friend again. But that had changed. She had changed. She had thrown herself at him and she knew exactly why. The idea of Devin being with another woman had terrified her. Which was why she hadn't put him back in his place when he stood in her bathtub suggesting that they share it. Devin was being Devin. There was no doubt in her mind that the invitation was real, but a solid refusal would have been all it took, even after she landed in the tub with him. But did she refuse? No, she asked him to kiss her, and then all hell broke loose. She'd crossed the friendship line and there was no going back. Now there was nothing left for them. She would not have an affair with him, and it was impossible to be just friends.

Jealousy had led her to this. Jealousy had brought all those lustful feelings to the surface with no time to bury them when Devin appeared unexpectedly. The rest just happened. Monica shuddered as she remembered the feelings Devin awakened in her. It had been pure heaven. But right now she felt like hell.

"Number one," a short round nurse in white called from her little window. "Number one," she called again. When she got no response, the nurse came from behind the window to stare at the two worried-looking people in the waiting room. They were the only people here, two numbers were missing, so one of them had to have the number she called. She pulled an orange chair behind her and placed it directly in front of the couple. Nothing. She sat down, still nothing. The pretty young woman, elbow on her knee, rested her chin in her hand and studied a blank wall. The man sat bent forward, his face in his hands. This was the look of a disturbed couple. She hoped she could help them.

"Ump." She cleared her throat, finally getting their attention. The woman jumped in her seat. She was a nervous one. The man raised his head. He wore a weary but determined expression.

"Are you two here together?"

"Ahh, yes—yes, we are," the young woman answered.

The man gave a quick nod, then drew a hand across his face.

"Okay, now that we got that out of the way, how can I help you?"

"We need some tests done," the young woman stated.

The fine man, and he was fine, didn't say a word. So it was like that, she thought. He was forced here, but she'd get them through it. "Okay, we do that here. What kind of tests?"

"Everything, the works. We want it all done," the young woman said nervously.

"Can we narrow it down some?" The nurse smiled, looking from one to the other.

The young woman looked over at her companion, back again at her, and blurted, "For V.D., AIDS, those kinds of tests!"

"I think I understand. As a couple you two are having tests done before having intercourse."

Did she have to be so blunt? "That's about right," Monica answered, thinking that was close enough to the truth. She shook her head and answered in monosyllables as the nurse asked a few more questions. Davin just sat like a bump on a log, doing nothing, saying nothing. It hurt that he was acting so cold. Just like a man. He'd got what he wanted and now that he was forced into some consequences, he was acting as if it was killing him. If he'd thought about protection, they wouldn't be stuck here now. If she'd thought at all, they wouldn't be here now.

The nurse continued to talk nonstop and handed them some pamphlets to read. Monica stared at them through unseeing eyes.

"You two are my first customers, so you don't have to wait. I'll give you a few minutes to look over those," she heard the nurse say.

Monica lasted all of thirty seconds before she called that they were ready. Getting Devin here had been fairly easy. Sitting next to him through the process was nerve-racking. She didn't want to deal with having him sitting next to her as if this was some supreme sacrifice that he had to endure. He was different. So different from last night. Monica didn't know this Devin. She didn't even know herself.

An hour later they were walking out the door. They'd come in silence. They were leaving the same way. The only sound had been the nurse's endless chatter. She repeatedly remarked on how wise it was to have these tests done before the fact. The woman meant well, but she had only depressed her more.

The nurse stopped them at the door. "Wait a second. I have something to tell you."

Devin and Monica waited at the glass door as she barreled over. "Look you two, be happy, you're doing the right thing. You both look like the walking dead. We'll be in touch with the results."

"Thank you," Monica choked out over her shoulder.

Devin stayed behind to speak to the cheerful nurse. He came out a minute later and opened the passenger door of the Durango for her. Be happy? She wished. She was happy before Devin. Her life had been fine. She was happy being his friend, most of the time anyway, when her mind stayed away from the gutter. And she was happy last night, for a short time. The feeling had been so intense, so right, but it was wrong! Could she be happy again? Maybe after she got the results of the AIDS test.

"Are you okay?" Devin asked as he got into the car, speaking to her for the first time since he'd agreed to this fiasco. He realized that he'd made the decision of his own free will, and should have given in graciously. Instead, he'd reacted childishly. Childish and irresponsible all in one day. He had to do better than that. This was the love of his life, his future he was dealing with. *Straighten up your act, Bug,* he told himself.

"I'll be fine, once I get negative results."

"I'm not so sure about that. I need to talk to you about something. Do you mind if we stop somewhere?"

"Sure, whatever you have to say can't be any worse than what we're dealing with now. Besides, I already called Ness. She said the kids could stay a little longer." Devin drove to his favorite place in New Orleans, the French Quarter. It was still early. The streets and sidewalks weren't packed with the constant flow of tourists yet. The artists and tap dancers were pulling out their easels and putting on their tap shoes. Devin parked a few blocks past Jackson Square, which stood across from Cafe Du Monde, their destination. He thought they'd eat some breakfast there, then maybe take a walk in Jackson Square. He'd try to talk to her there. Hopefully, Brown Eyes would listen to him.

As they crossed St. Peter's Street Devin took hold of her hand. She didn't protest, but her hand stayed in his listlessly. They sat outside in the large open area designed for customers to watch the happenings in the Quarter as they ate beignets and drank 'Nawlins' famous café au lait.

When their order arrived, Devin watched as she added sugar and then took a sip of the milky liquid. It seemed to revive her. He watched her take another sip. Then she actually smiled.

"I don't usually drink coffee, but I've always enjoyed café au lait," she told him.

"I can tell," Devin answered, a bit relieved to hear her speak in a more relaxed tone. If the coffee had loosened her up, he'd order a gallon. "Do you want another?"

"I think I'd like that," she told him politely, too politely for someone he'd undressed and whose skin he'd stroked and savored before losing all self control. He found himself breaking out in a sweat and forced himself to relax, to get into a frame of mind that would help him broach another delicate subject to Monica.

He watched as she looked around, as if just now aware of her surroundings. "I haven't been in the French Quarter in a long time. What made you come here?"

"I love it. The atmosphere, the people, and most of all, the architecture. The buildings call to me. They're like music frozen in time."

"That's beautiful."

"Unfortunately, those aren't my words, but they express my feeling exactly."

Monica knew a lot about him, but there was so much more he wanted to share with her. For the next hour, he did just that. He pushed aside his disappointment to share the first love of his life with the most important love of his life. That she seemed genuinely interested warmed his heart because all morning he'd felt her drifting farther and farther away. She had been his lover for one night, and it felt as if he'd lost his friend forever. As much as he dreaded the term 'friend' before, he'd do anything to hear her call him friend again. And he was at a loss as to how to mention the possibility of an unplanned pregnancy. Devin was amazed that it hadn't crossed her mind. Eventually, it would. She was too worried about other consequences right now.

Devin watched as she finished her second cup of café au lait, admiring her natural beauty. She'd somehow gathered her hair into a tight bun at the top of her head. This morning as she'd stood before him golden brown, completely naked, her hair had framed her face in wild disarray, matching her anger and frustration. She'd put on no makeup for the clinic visit, and she didn't need to. Beneath the worry in her eyes, Monica's face glowed. It gave him hope. Here before him sat beautiful music, not frozen in time as the stately buildings he loved to study and recreate. Instead, her music embodied strength, love, and warmth. He wanted it all for himself.

"I've got an idea," she said, interrupting his thoughts. "If you love the French Quarter you'll be impressed with another part of New Orleans."

"Monica, we need to talk, not travel all over the city."

"I know," she sighed sadly. "But we could do both. Algiers is only a ferry ride away. We could talk on the ferry. There probably won't be many people around."

Riding on a ferry sounded isolated enough. She was also being more receptive than she'd been all morning, so Devin agreed to go.

They walked to the foot of Canal Street where the ferry docked to transport people and cars back and forth across the Mississippi River. The downtown area of the city was beginning to bustle with the opening of businesses. This was another part of the city Monica hadn't been to in a long time. In the last twenty years the construction of indoor shopping malls all over the New Orleans area had created a preferred convenience to shoppers. The mayor, she knew, was making an effort to revitalize Canal Street. Maybe she'd make an effort to come shopping here once in a while.

Monica and Devin stood at the gated rail on the top level of the ferry. She watched as the black smoke blew from the stacks. The engines roared and the ferry moved. As the boat moved away from the dock, she turned to face Devin.

"I've been thinking about last night—and this morning."

"I'm hoping that's a good thing," he answered, the deep rumble of his voice creating a tension in her, reminding her of every detail, every bit of last night.

"I don't know if you'll think so," she said, leaning against the rail, her back facing the water. "I'd be lying if I said I didn't enjoy our time together."

"Our time together?" he mimicked. "That sounds to close to, 'That was sure a nice picnic'. We made love, Monica," he whispered. "I made love to you. Can you say that?"

"Maybe you can say that you made love to me. But, no, I can't admit to the same thing."

"You can't? It takes two. We were both there." His face full of incomprehension, he asked, "Why?"

"I can't call it making love because I can't say that I love you."

He moved in even closer, one long, muscular, deep brown arm on each side of her.

"I can say it." She knew what was coming next and didn't want to hear it. But she couldn't stop the sincerity in his eyes or the flow or words from his lips. "I love you."

"You are making this hard, Devin," she told him, unable to hold his gaze. She looked down at her sandal-clad feet—long, narrow, straight, standing firm between his own as she leaned back against the rail. She didn't need him, she didn't want to need him. Monica knew she could stand on her own two feet.

"Good," he breathed right next to her ear. "I don't want it to be easy for you to take my love and throw it right back at me."

She looked up at the frustration in his voice. "Devin, you—don't—love—me! You just want me, remember? You told me that a few days after you met me."

Devin moved away from her then. Monica sighed with relief; he'd been standing too close to her for too long. He walked across to the other side of the ferry and back again with long impatient strides. A moment later bombarding her with questions.

"How can you say that? How do you know that I don't love you? How can you be so sure?" he growled. "Where's your proof?"

As if talking to a slow child, Monica repeated, "As I said before, you only wanted me!"

"Of course I wanted you! I still want you. I love you. I want to marry you."

"Don't say that, Devin. You don't want to marry me. You can't."

"I can't? And exactly why can't I?" he asked slowly.

"Because—because…" What could she say? Monica's heart was pounding. This was too close. She was scared. This could not be happening. Not with Devin, he was her friend.

"Because what?" he asked again with an impatience she couldn't deny hearing.

"Because you're my friend!" she shouted.

"Friend," he said quietly. "Friend," he whispered with disgust. "Friend!" he shouted to the passing barges and tugboats.

"Yes, friend. And lust got in the way!" she shouted back.

Monica watched as he came toward her. She waited for his reaction, waited for understanding to sink in. Before her eyes he became calm. He turned into the controlled man that she called friend. But it was obvious from his stance, from the determination in his eyes, that nothing would ever sink in. Nothing other than what he allowed to sink in.

"Lust, okay," he told her. "I do lust after you, but it's because I love you. This constant need I have to touch you..." he paused to caress her face with the tips of his fingers, "to taste you," he gently brushed his lips across her own, "...is lust. But it's so much more, Monica. My love for you is mixed in with the need I have every moment of the day to touch you and make love to you. It's impossible to separate the two. They go hand in hand."

The sound of his calm and soothing voice when she was a bundle of nerves worked at her insides. His words were so—romantic. She was melting inside. No one had ever spoken to her that way before. Not even—Keith! Keith! She'd forgotten him again. Devin

had done it to her again. Only this time the guilt
wasn't as sharp. Maybe she had been holding on too
tight to his memory. She'd have to think about that.
She had a lot to think about.

Devin watched Monica's face as he spoke. Her eyes
held a warmth for him. Her expression was soft, not
nervous anymore. She was opening up to what he was
saying, maybe finally believing him. Her eyes lowered
and when they opened again, he saw confusion. At
least she had stopped telling him that he didn't love
her. With a thumb outlining her ears, Devin lifted her
face up to meet his eyes. "So what do you think?"

"I don't know. I need some time."

"I thought so, I can see it in your eyes."

They both jumped as the ferry's whistle blew. The
engines roared and black smoke burst from the stacks
once more. "We're heading back to the Quarter."

"I guess we missed the ferry docking. We can see
Algiers another time."

"You can give me a guided tour," he told her,
making sure she knew that there would be another
time. That they would be together. He stood next to
her with his back against the rail, not exactly content
with today's progress, but not exactly disappointed.
He quietly contemplated the best way to broach the
next problem.

"Monica, there's one more thing we need to discuss."

"There is? Devin, I have enough to think about right now. There can't possibly be any room in my head for much more."

"It's important and I think this piece of information will fit. First, I want…

"First, I want to apologize for putting you in a position that would cause you to be as worried as you were this morning."

"I have to take half the blame for that."

"I'll let you do that," he smiled. It quickly faded as he went on. "I know you believe that I've been with thousands of women. It's been nowhere near that number. I have been very selective in the past and have never had unprotected sex before—until you. Monica, last night took me by surprise, you took me by surprise. You might not believe me, but you have nothing to worry about from diseases."

"Thank you for sharing that with me, Devin."

Devin watched as she released a breath, seemingly relaxed, seemingly accepting what he said when this morning nothing would get through. "I'm not finished," he told her as she moved toward the stairs leading to the lower deck.

"There's more?"

"There may be one other thing we need to worry about. One other reason I've always used protection…"

Before he could say the words Monica shrieked, "Oh, my God! I might be pregnant!"

"I know."

"And I'm as fertile as a rabbit. The only reason I'm not the old woman in the shoe is because Keith got a vasectomy after Mark."

"It's going to be all right, Monica. We'll handle it."

"You better believe everything's going to be all right, because I'm not pregnant!" she told him as she hurriedly moved to the swinging doors. She turned to him before descending the steps, "I refuse to be pregnant!"

CHAPTER 17

Devin couldn't believe that it had been over a month since that 'wonderful' night and discouraging morning. The days had flown by. Scott and Devin had purchased fifteen acres of land on the north shore of Lake Pontchartrain in Slidell, a good 25 miles from New Orleans. On this land they would build a small subdivision. Devin had built his fortune and reputation on his ability to recreate any time, any period with such accuracy that only an experienced eye could recognize it as a replica. They planned to take a little bit of the Vieux Carre and plant it in Slidell.

Small subdivisions which provided both neighborhood and privacy were becoming popular because people were realizing that they lived in neighborhoods, but apart. People in large cities were looking for small, closed environments. The French Quarter style of architecture would interest those who loved the beauty of the Vieux Carre but didn't want to deal with all the headaches living in the Quarter brought. Scott was all fired up about the idea and they worked long hours finishing the details, hiring the crew and materials needed to start construction.

That project occupied Devin's mind most of the day. Unfortunately, when he had a moment of quiet, perhaps during a break or at lunch, his mind would wander to Monica and their in-limbo relationship. Devin would mechanically eat a po-boy or a hamburger, whatever Scott threw his way, and lose all focus on the project, and be unable to discuss even the smallest detail Scott would bring up in the fifteen minutes they gave themselves to eat.

"Bug," Scott said one day as he landed a twelve-inch foil-wrapped po-boy in front of him. "That statue of Elvis in the middle of the subdivision was a great idea!"

"Yeah, it sure was," Devin answered absently.

"And deciding to wire it with white lights—perfect idea for the sequins on his white jacket!"

"Yeah, perfect," Devin repeated, taking a huge bite out of the hot sausage po-boy. He was thinking about Monica's eyes, how they melted into his when she asked him to make love to her.

Devin continued to eat and daydream of Brown Eyes as he absently watched Scott fill out an order form from their brand-new stationary supplies. At the top was the logo for their new company, Prestway, combining their last names, Preston and Halloway. Scott stopped writing just as they heard the sounds of an eighteen-wheeler rumbling up to the site. The noise forced Devin out of his daydream in time to hear what Scott read from the order form he'd been filling out.

"Okay, we have on order one Elvis statue, a marble fountain to surround it, lights and wiring…"

"What are you talking about, Scott? Elvis statue! Are you crazy! We're recreating the French Quarter, not Graceland! What an idiotic idea! Who came up with that?"

"You did."

"Try that again."

"I'll set it straight. We've been talking about it at lunch for the last two weeks. You agreed to it. I merely suggested it."

"And why would you suggest Elvis!" Devin asked, already knowing the answer. His friend hadn't lost his old sense of humor. He'd been biding his time.

"I've been trying to break you out of the Monica haze you've been wallowing in. No use in denying it, Bug."

Scott stopped him from interrupting. "It's written all over your face. The question is, when are you going to put yourself out of this misery, future brother-in-law?"

Brother-in-law. If he could call Scott brother-in-law, Monica would be his right now. "If it were as simple as asking her to marry me, I'd be a happy man right now."

"I see," Scott answered in a clipped voice.

"Did you have to say that?" Devin asked. He imagined his mother saying just those words and the expression she'd have on her face if she knew the predicament he was in now.

"What? 'I see?' But Bug, I do see. I told you from the beginning that Keith would be an obstacle."

"The woman herself is more of an obstacle."

"But worth it, I'm sure. Everything will work out. It's true love, Dev," Scott assured him with a punch on his shoulder as they left the trailer.

Devin tried to push his problem with Monica to the back of his mind. It would still be there to torment him when he saw her later at the spa.

Devin and Scott met the foreman and the newly hired crew at the truck waiting to be unloaded. "Mr. Preston, Mr. Halloway," the foreman called, "we've got ourselves a problem here."

Problem? Devin could solve any problem, as long as it didn't involve Brown Eyes. He was ready to jump in and fix whatever was wrong. He wasn't having much luck with his personal life, but at work, he'd handle anything. It gave him some sense of accomplishment. "What is it, Harris?"

Harris was a solid man of average height with skin the color of tree bark. His booming voice and no-nonsense attitude had gained the crew's respect instantly, and most importantly, the confidence of his new bosses. Both Devin and Scott thought that they'd found the right man for the job. Devin watched as Harris scratched the bald spot at the back of his head.

"There isn't a thing in this truck here that we need."

"Then it's a shipping error. I'll handle this, Scott."

"I don't think it's as simple as all that," Harris answered.

"Why?" Scott asked, walking toward them.

"These look like your signatures on the bottom of this form and there's an envelope addressed to both of you."

"Shipments don't come with letters. Inventory Forms, yes, but a letter?" Davin said.

"What's exactly in this shipment?" Scott asked, following Devin to the open trailer door.

"Keyboards and zebra skins," Stephens, one of the crew, said seriously, a sample of the first under his arm, the latter draped across his broad shoulder.

"Fudge ripple ice cream and saddle oxfords?" Brooks, another crew member, laughed, holding what he found. "Hey man, everything in here's black and white!"

Devin questioned the truck driver.

"Look man, I just deliver it. I don't load or inspect it," was all the man had to say.

"Harris, let me take a look at that envelope." This was a real mystery. Devin tore the short white envelope open. He pulled out a white card and read out loud:

Black and white go hand and hand?
That idea I cannot stand!
In certain things those colors mix,
So this company I must jinx!

Devin handed the card to Scott. It was so juvenile it was laughable, but Devin didn't laugh. He knew this wasn't something he could brush off.

Scott looked down at the card, reading it himself. He glanced up at Devin, uttering one word. "T.J.!"

"Of course." Devin turned to Harris. "Send the driver back with this junk. We'll take care of it on our end."

"More of his immature attempts to try to get back at me," Devin growled to Scott as they headed back to the trailer office.

"It's not just you, it's both of us," Scott added, sitting at his desk.

"We have no choice but to take his threats more seriously," Devin said. "He started out with this kind of harassment before. There's no telling how far he'll go."

There was a knock on the trailer door. Scott opened it. At the door stood Stephens and Brooks, the two crew members who were in the truck. Devin motioned them inside.

"Boss," Stephens began, as they both came into the trailer, "after seeing that shipment out there in the truck and hearing you read that card, Brooks and me thought you should know something."

"Yeah," Brooks added. "We didn't think much about it before, but ever since you hired us we've seen this guy standing on the street out there, near the site. Not doing anything, just looking around. We thought he was just being nosy," Brooks said.

"And this was every day?" Scott asked.

The crew had all been hired the previous Friday. They'd only been at the site three days.

They both nodded.

"And you saw him today?" Devin asked.

"This morning when we drove in," Stephens answered. "We thought it was kinda strange, him being there and all every morning."

"Thank you, men, we appreciate you letting us know about this. It may be of some help," Scott told them, shaking each man's hand.

"Before you leave, can you describe the man?" Devin asked.

"To tell you the truth, not really. The sun was glaring on the windshield when we passed. But he was tall and white. Ain't that right, Brooks?"

"As right as right," Brooks grinned.

Devin shook his head. "Thanks again."

"Any way we can help, just let us know, boss," Stephens added.

"Yeah, we gotta get back to work to earn all the money you gotta pay us," Brooks added, slipping out of the trailer behind his friend.

"So T.J.'s spying on us, too! I wish I could get inside his head for one second—just one second to see what he's thinking," Scott said in frustration.

"You don't want to do that. You'd be up to your neck in hatred and unreasonable vengeance."

"You're right, I don't want to know what's in his head."

"There are a few things we know for sure: he's intelligent, sneaky, and has the use of technology, a dangerous combination if he wasn't such a coward."

"A dangerous combination if he suddenly discovers his backbone," Scott added.

"It couldn't have been hard for him to order that junk with our signatures."

"It would have been easy. He used to work for you, and I just quit his father's firm."

"Too easy and no proof," Devin agreed. "Nothing that would get him arrested, that is. He knows enough to watch from the street or we could get him locked up for trespassing, even if it's only for the few hours it would take for 'daddy' to bail him out."

"True, Travis, Sr., still has hopes of turning him around. How could such a twisted person come from such a nice family?"

"Black sheep?" Devin asked.

They both laughed. Devin could imagine T.J.'s reaction at being called a black anything.

"Scott, this really isn't funny, man." Devin laughed harder.

"I know," Scott agreed.

They were serious again, both under control, when Scott asked, "What are you thinking?"

"Probably the same thing you are. Get some security on the site. We can devise a code for orders and deliveries with the companies we'll be doing business with to block any more of T.J.'s interference."

"Sounds good."

Devin was satisfied that they were able to attack this problem head-on. He picked up the phone to set their precautions in motion as Scott used another line to make some contacts for security. Devin wished he could anticipate what T.J. would do next. But for now, they'd do all that they could.

CHAPTER 18

"I'm not pregnant. I'm not pregnant. I'm not pregnant," Monica chanted over and over again as she went through summer clothes that were too small for Mark to wear. So what if she was tired a lot. It was a classic New Orleans summer, hot and humid. The heat was almost unbearable at times. It was getting to her. That's why she was so sleepy all the time. And so what if her period was a little late. All this worrying had thrown it off schedule.

She put all the clothes that were too small into a plastic bag, replacing the ones that still fit into Mark's chest of drawers. Monica then got on her hands and knees. Mark was missing a swim shoe and one for church.

Lying down on her stomach, she let out a big yawn. It was only ten o'clock in the morning and she hadn't been out yet. Explain that, Monica, an inner voice demanded.

"Oh, be quiet," she muttered to herself as she spotted a swim shoe and reached to pull it out. She

yawned again. Boy, was she tired. She stopped a
second, resting her head on her folded arms. Monica
couldn't believe how comfortable it was under Mark's
bed. *I'll just lie here for a minute,* she thought as her
eyes drifted closed. She was out like a light.

"Mommie!"

Monica heard a small voice calling from far away.

"Mommie, Auntie Ness is here, can I open the
door?"

It was a child asking something. "Oh yeah. Sure.
Whatever you want, just let me sleep," Monica
thought as she grunted a reply.

The sound of running feet and more voices slowly
drew Monica out of the sleepy haze she'd fallen into.
"Where's your mom?" Monica heard Vanessa ask.

"She's sleeping under Mark's bed," her daughter
ratted.

"Are you sure about that?" Vanessa's voice carried
down the hall.

"Oh yeah, she was snoring," Monica's sweet little
girl answered.

Vanessa's laughter reached her, setting her in
motion. Monica did not want to be found by her little
sister half asleep, under the bed. She did a spider crawl
backwards and attempted to stand.

"Oww!" she yelled as her head connected with the metal support frame. How far under the bed had she gone? Monica wondered as pain shot through her head.

Vanessa walked in just in time to hear her yelp. Ness eased onto the edge of the bed, shaking her head in sympathy.

"So, you really were sleeping under the bed. What happened? Bug been keeping you awake again? What kind of music is he playing now? Rap? Reggae? Whatever it is, I bet it's loud."

"No, I haven't seen much of Devin lately," Monica answered nonchalantly as she rubbed the back of her head.

"I know. Since they started this new business Scott's been working so much I've been lucky to get a hello or a good-bye from him," Ness said sadly, laying a hand on her expanding stomach.

"I can understand why that's a problem for you, Ness. Scott's your husband. You expect to see more of him. It doesn't matter to me, Devin's just a friend. A hello and good-bye are plenty enough," Monica huffed, avoiding eye contact with her sister as she said those words.

"Who do you think you're fooling, Monica? I know for a fact that he's more than friend."

"What do you know?" Monica turned to ask, afraid that somehow Vanessa had found out about her one night with Devin. Would Devin have told Scott and Scott, Ness. She didn't think so. Nothing was resolved in her mind. With Devin so occupied right now, it was easier to avoid thinking about the situation. Monica couldn't deny that she missed him. The point was she missed him too much.

"I know enough," Ness answered, giving her a strange look.

Ness's comment brought her back to their conversation. Monica hoped Ness was only guessing. The last thing she wanted was for her little sister to lose respect for her. Monica didn't sleep around and didn't believe in sleeping around. Which was why it was so difficult to finally admit to herself that she was definitely, absolutely pregnant.

Without a doubt it was true. It made no difference that she couldn't have been any more than four weeks along. Her body gave her away. She was never late with her cycle and the changes were as clear and easy to detect as they had been with her other kids. The constant need to sleep any extra hour she could squeeze into a day and the tenderness in her breasts were two clues that couldn't be missed. She had moved from widowed mother to unwed mother.

Society might have changed from long ago when an unmarried woman was ostracized, but because of her own beliefs and morals she'd disappointed herself and her family and dishonored Keith's memory.

Monica always took pride in maintaining a good example for her younger siblings, who of course were all grown now. But what about her kids? Her nieces and nephews? How was she going to set a good example for them? *Well,* she thought, *I'm human and I made a mistake.* She let out a loud sigh.

"After hearing that sad sound, I can definitely say I know a lot," Monica heard her sister say, reminding her that Ness was in the room. "Devin has some serious feelings for you, Monica."

"I know what kind of feelings he has for me," Monica sneered.

"Don't say another word. I like Devin and I think he's sincere. Whatever you were about to say would have been something to make you feel better about rejecting him."

"What's to reject?" Monica asked, annoyed that Ness was continuing the conversation.

"You really did wake up on the wrong side of the bed today. Sleep on top next time, sis," Vanessa joked.

Monica grunted a reply; she didn't like the role reversal. It was her job to give Ness advice, not the other way around. "Do we need to talk about Devin?"

"Yes, because there's been something I've been meaning to ask you. Why do you think it was so easy for you and Devin to become friends? I've never seen you get this close to a man, outside of family, for a long time."

Monica sat next to Ness on the bed. That was a good question. Why had it been so easy? She still didn't want to discuss Devin, but she felt bad about being so grumpy.

Monica apologized. She took a long look at Ness and wondered at how well her sister still moved around with so much stomach in front of her. Soon, she'd be just as big. Hopefully, not that big. Monica didn't want to think of the possibility of having twins.

"I know you probably don't want to take advice from me because you're older and wiser . . ."

Older, yes. Wiser? Far from it, Monica thought.

When Monica didn't respond, Ness obviously took it as a cue to go on. "Since you gave me some excellent advice when I didn't want to give Scott a second thought, I owe you some. And whether you want to hear it or not, it's coming."

"Since when have you gotten so pushy?" Monica laughed, suddenly amused by their change in roles. "If I can't stop you, you might as well get it over with."

"I know how much you loved Keith, we all do."

"Now wait a minute, sis! I thought we were going to talk about Devin, not Keith!" Ness was diving right into the heart of her fears.

"Keith's part of the problem, Monica—"

"Keith's never been a problem. He was a wonderful man!" Monica interrupted.

"I know that almost as well as you, and I agree one hundred percent. But he's gone, Monica, and you have to go on."

Monica bounded off the bed and stood to close the door to the room. "I have gone on, Ness. I haven't collapsed. I haven't stopped living. I'm raising the children Keith and I had together. I haven't given up on life!" Monica insisted, not too thrilled with how well Ness knew her.

"Can you listen to me without interrupting for a minute?" Vanessa asked quietly.

"Okay," she agreed, releasing her grip on the doorknob.

"Monica, I have always admired you. You're my big sister."

"Tracy's your big sister, too."

"I know that, but you were the one who took the job seriously. Tracy was and always has been a clown. And you're interrupting me again."

"Sorry. You were saying…"

"I was saying that I couldn't imagine my life without you. And I wouldn't insult you by telling you that you've given up on life, but you have given up on love, Monica. When you lost Keith—that ended it all for you."

"I haven't given up on love," Monica denied. For the first time Ness gave her the teacher look. Monica had seen it work on her kids, Ness's girls, and every child in their family. It worked on her, too.

Ness pulled Monica down to the twin bed again. "Monica, you still love. You can't help but love. It's just that your love is directed to your kids, Mom and Dad, and all those crazy people we call family. When you lost Keith, you froze that part of your heart reserved for the love between a man and a woman."

Monica let that digest. She knew Ness was right. Her declarations and promises never to let anyone take Keith's piece were broadcast to anyone within hearing.

"Do me one little favor, Monica."

"I thought I already did that by listening to you."

"No, that was one I owed you, for Scott."

"Okay, what is it?" Monica asked, resigned.

"Let your heart thaw just a little bit for Devin. If only to find out if you really do have feelings for him. A wise person once told me that I'd be sorry if I didn't at least attempt to discover what my true feeling were for Scott. Remember? I suggest that you do the same for Devin."

They sat quietly together, lost in thought, remembering that time almost three years ago.

Monica could deny everything Ness said, but then she'd be lying. They both knew that.

"I'll give it a try, Ness. Why should I throw such excellent advice away? It came from a reliable source." Monica smiled and stretched. She grabbed each of Ness's hands to help her stand. "I suddenly feel full of energy. Maybe you ought to try sleeping under a bed once in a while."

"When I lose the stomach."

They both laughed.

"How about lunch? It'll be on us," Vanessa said as Monica began to sort through Tony's clothes again.

"I don't know. I planned on doing some summertime cleaning up and throwing out."

"Come on, we're treating. It's the least I could do since you've been taking the girls to swimming lessons every day. You've saved me from having to sit and suffer in the heat."

"Ness, it's no trouble. I work there every morning, Remember? Besides, what are sisters for?"

This summer Monica was working part-time at the Sports Spa as a tutor for kids at camp whose parents wanted to include academics as part of the day's activities. She worked from nine to eleven. Her kiddos, as well as Vicki and Megan, took swimming and gymnastics while she tutored. They'd stay afterwards, eat lunch by the pool, and swim for awhile. It gave Ness a nice morning break. She needed it. Ness looked tired most of the time.

But today was Friday, and there weren't any lessons or work.

"Mommie, can we go with Vicki and Megan on a picnic?" Jasmine came running into the boys' room to ask. Tony and Mark were right behind her.

"Ya'll are having a picnic?" Monica asked Vanessa. "That's the plan. We have tons of food. Are you coming?"

"Okay, we'll come." Monica didn't want to disappoint the kids. They seemed excited about going, and they never got tired of playing with Ness's girls.

"All right!" Tony shouted. "We get to see the site. That's where Uncle Scott and Mr. Devin are building those houses."

"All right!" Mark echoed.

"Ne-s-s-s-s!" Monica growled as she turned toward her sister.

"I'll get the kids loaded into the van."

Monica laughed at the speed that Ness moved. "Don't fall and hurt my nieces or nephews," she called, stopping Vanessa before she got to the front door. "I'm still coming."

"Good!" Nessa said, letting out a deep breath.

"And, Ness—"

"What?"

"You're a lousy matchmaker. I'm not supposed to know what you're up to."

"It's better that you do know what I'm up to. That part of the plan is honest and straightforward. I intend to use every trick I have to get you to cupid's door. It's up to you two to do the rest," Ness answered, turning to call the kids.

"That's the problem," Monica whispered the one thing she hadn't confided to Ness. "We've already done the rest."

Vanessa parked the van behind the trailer on the construction site. As the kids helped to unload the blanket and picnic basket, they talked nonstop.

"Do you think Mr. Devin and Uncle Scott will let me ride in one of those big machines out there?" Tony asked, pointing to the huge yellow monsters.

"That's a good idea, Tony. I want to ride in one, too," Mark insisted.

Monica opened the small folding picnic table as she told the boys, "You can go as far as asking to sit in one. And that's only if they have the time."

"If the boys can sit in one, can we do it too, MaNessa?" Megan asked.

"If Daddy says you can."

"He will," Vicki answered with confidence.

Monica laughed. "That girl is going to be something when she grows up."

"I know, but we've got a while before we have to deal with a grown-up Vicki," Vanessa whispered to Monica. In a louder voice she told the children, "Why don't you go knock on the trailer door and surprise them?"

Five enthusiastic kids ran to the front of the trailer. Monica could hear the sound of five impatient fists pounding on the trailer door.

There was a loud banging on the door. Devin had come into the trailer not more than ten minutes earlier. He'd been giving Josh and John instructions for a job he had them working on today. Monica's brothers had asked to work for Prestway this summer. They were somewhat familiar with construction from working with Cal and learned quickly. The twins were hard workers and put up with the good-natured ribbing they got from the other men on the crew. John got the worst end of it. Being a musician, he was always concerned about protecting his hands.

The banging got louder. "Dev, get the door," Scott called from his desk. "I've finally got the inspector on the line."

Devin put away the papers he'd been studying and went to open the door. He grinned when he found five little people outside. Three of them he was especially happy to see. If they were here, their mother had to be somewhere close by, unless Ness was babysitting. He hoped she wasn't. Devin stepped out and closed the door so Scott could finish his call.

"What do we have here? Five midgets looking for work?"

They all laughed.

"You look like a bunch of puny-looking people. Let me see your muscles."

Tony flexed his arms to show off his muscles and Mark immediately did the same. While Devin checked the boys' muscles, the girls moved into a huddle.

"You guys look strong enough, but what about these puny little girls?"

"We don't have to have muscles," Vicki informed him.

"Do you really think so?" Devin asked.

"Not at all!" Megan answered.

"But you have to lift bricks and bags of heavy cement mix!" Tony grunted, flexing his arms again. "You need muscles for that."

"Not us, we're going to be supervisors," Jasmine informed them. "We get to watch you work and tell you what to do."

Devin burst out laughing. That Jasmine was going to be something when she grew up.

Scott came out of the trailer to find Devin bent over, trying to control himself.

"What's so funny, Dev?"

"Daddy, Daddy, Daddy!" Megan yelled.

"Hello Miss Megan, and Miss Vicki, and Tony, Miss Jazz and Mark." They all came crashing into Scott, jumping and crawling all over him.

"What about me?" Devin asked. A second later they launched into him, knocking him to the ground.

Scott rescued Devin by peeling a child or two off. "What are you guys doing here? Megan and Vicki, where's your mother?"

"We brought you lunch!" Vicki told him.

"Yeah, so come eat!" Megan dragged him toward the back of the trailer.

"Lunch? Can I come too?" Devin asked.

"Sure, you can, Mr. Devin, Auntie Ness brought lots and lots of food," Mark said.

"I'll take you there." Jasmine took one hand and Mark grabbed his other. Tony walked backwards, shooting question after question at Devin about the machines, the construction, and anything about the site.

As they rounded the trailer Devin could hear Vanessa's voice.

"Vicki, Megan! Who's that stranger you have with you?"

"It's Daddy!" they giggled.

"No-o-o-o, I saw Daddy just last Sunday for five whole minutes. This doesn't look like him at all."

"I get the message, MyNessa," Scott said, reaching for his wife. He gave her a soft kiss on the lips and held her close.

"I miss you," Vanessa said after holding him tight and whispering something in his ear.

"You have missed me," Scott answered.

Devin smiled at the couple, remembering Ness's one word confession about the ear thing. Pleasures. With that thought in mind his eyes sought Monica. He found her spreading a blue blanket under a huge oak tree. She wouldn't meet his eyes.

"Come and get it! Lunch is ready," Ness called. "Children on the blanket, pregnant people and other adults at the picnic table."

Ness's comment caused Monica's head to spring up toward Devin's. His eyes questioned, *Are you?*

Monica turned away, not wanting to answer such an important question from so far away. Instead, she concentrated on settling the kids down to eat lunch. She opened a Tupperware platter of animal-shaped peanut butter sandwiches that Ness had made with the help of cookie cutters. Monica shook her head. That was just like Ness. She also found a bowl of celery and carrot sticks and some Oreo cookies for desert.

As she stood to hand plates to the kids, Monica glanced over to find Devin looking at her again, the same question in his eyes. She went back to passing out plates. Monica wasn't ignoring him. She'd promised Ness that she'd give him a chance, and Monica intended to do that. It was just that she felt a little shy around him, which was silly after what they'd shared, ridiculous after creating a baby together. But when he first came round the trailer with Jasmine and Mark holding his hand, and Tony talking a mile a minute as usual, Monica, for a second, felt as if he was home for her. Here was her family, her man. Maybe it had something to do with Scott coming 'round with his kids and then Devin right behind him with hers. It just felt right, as if this was how things were meant to be.

But then Scott was hugging Ness and Dev stood where he was, talking to the kids. If he belonged to her, she would have felt his strong arms around her. These things take time, she thought, coming to the picnic table.

As Monica sat next to him, Devin saw something he hadn't seen in a long time. She smiled at him. It wasn't her classic I-love-life-and-everything-in-it smile. It was sad, but tinged with hope. Devin's spirits lifted. He had been experiencing a little jealousy again from the warm welcome Scott received, while all he got was what amounted to a cold shoulder.

"This is so thoughtful," Scott was saying as Ness unwrapped a huge roast beef, ham and turkey po-boy made on a whole french bread loaf. "But MyNessa," he continued, "we don't have a lot of time…"

"Scott Halloway, I don't want to hear about time. I want you to sit down and have lunch with your wife or…"

Devin raised an eyebrow, and Monica cracked a smile. Scott laughed when she couldn't come up with anything. "Or else what?" he asked.

"Or else you won't be hearing sweet nothings whispered in your ear for a whole year."

Scott sat down immediately. "I can't have that. I desperately need those sweet nothings," Scott said seriously. "I'm sorry, have you felt neglected?"

"A little, but I'll forgive you if you sit down and talk to me for at least one uninterrupted hour."

"You got it," Scott promised.

Watching the comical exchange between Scott and Vanessa eased some of the tension between Monica and Devin.

"You're not hungry?" Devin asked when Monica hadn't gone beyond placing a piece of the huge po-boy in front of her.

"No, not really," Monica answered, pushing the plate away.

"Your stomach's not upset or anything, is it?" Devin asked nervously.

"No, not at all. Why do you ask?"

"I thought that maybe it might be, because…you know…well…" For such an articulate man, who had no trouble charming anyone, Devin felt like a dope.

He saw confusion, then understanding flash across Monica's face. "Oh-h-h! Oh no! My stomach's not upset, Devin."

"Then you aren't," he whispered. "Or do you know yet?" They hadn't had a real conversation since that morning after they'd made love.

"I want to talk to you about that," Monica told him.

They were interrupted by the sound of Vicki yelling, "Uncle John, Uncle John!" She ran to her favorite uncle, only addressing her Uncle Josh when she finished proposing.

The other kids came right behind Vicki, excited and surprised to see their uncles.

"Wanna eat a pig, Uncle Josh?" Mark asked, holding up a pig-shaped sandwich.

"Sure thing." he answered. He ate it right out of Mark's hand with one big chomp.

The kids thought this was hilarious and ran to get more.

Josh and John were encouraged to eat a few more animals before Monica called, "Hey, guys! Do you want to eat something more substantial than peanut butter sandwiches? We've got a huge po-boy you could polish off."

"Real food!" Josh yelled.

"It'll cost ya," Monica told them.

"What?" John asked suspiciously.

"Watch the kids for a bit while these two lovebirds spend some time together and Devin and I go for a walk."

"Piece of cake, sis," Josh said.

"Y'all take off. We'll make sure the midgets don't get into any trouble. Just don't wander off into any bushes," John warned her.

"And no funny business," Josh said around a mouthful of sandwich.

Scott stood. "If you two are keeping an eye on the kids, I'm taking my wife inside, out of the heat, to rest for a while."

Devin guided Monica further away from the noise so that they could more privacy.

"I hope I didn't take Josh and John away from their work," Monica said. She moved closer to fill in the small gap between them.

"No, it was their lunch break anyway. I'm sure they're thrilled. They won't have to go out and spend money for lunch. It's their general complaint."

"That sounds like them."

"Your brothers think Prestway should treat their employees to lunch every day."

She laughed.

It was good to hear her laugh again. Devin stopped walking. They'd gone a good distance. "Monica, you didn't suggest this walk to talk about your brothers."

"No, I didn't." Monica sat on a huge tree stump. She didn't say anything for a while.

Devin waited, in frustration. There had been a time when he could talk to Brown Eyes about almost anything. Now they could barely hold a conversation. He couldn't take this anymore.

"Monica, I hate this. Why can't we communicate? After having such a wonderful night together why can't we go on—take if from there?"

"It wasn't—"

"Yes it was," he told her, not allowing her to deny it. "And that's your word." He emphasized each syllable, "Won-der-ful! You can't deny it!"

"I won't, it was wonderful!" she whispered. "And I do want to talk to you about it. I know that you've been busy with your new business."

"I'm never too busy for you."

"Why?" she asked with tears in her eyes.

"Why? I've already told you why. Because I love you and want to marry you."

"Because I might be pregnant."

"Even if you aren't pregnant. I," he pointed to himself standing directly in front of her, "love you," he pointed to her. "Don't you get it yet?"

"Yes, I get it. It's just that I'm not ready to hear it yet."

"I'm glad that you've admitted that much. It's a start, Brown Eyes."

Monica smiled.

"Why do you look so sad?" he asked, wiping away a tear.

"You called me Brown Eyes. Thanks for not listening to me. I love hearing you call me that."

"I know. So you'll hear it often. Not only that, I'll keep telling you that I love you until you get used to it, too."

"What if I never get used to it, Dev?"

"You will," Devin said aloud, having no doubt that she already loved him. Her unwillingness to admit it to herself was wrapped up in her loyalty to Keith.

Monica let out that full-bodied laugh of hers. "Devin, you're just as arrogant as ever."

"That's only one of the many reasons you put up with me. Now and forever." He pulled her up, sat on the ground in front of the tree stump and placed her between his outstretched legs. "I need to ask you this," he said softly. "I know it's early, but could you possibly be pregnant?"

Monica sighed, "I could be."

His heart skipped a beat. "How do you know?"

"There are a few signs."

"Signs? What kinds of signs? Are you hurting anywhere? You're throwing up all the time, aren't you? I knew that's why you wouldn't eat."

"No, Dev. I don't have to deal with that—not yet anyway. That comes a little later. Sooner than I hope, too."

"But you think you are, right?"

"I'm pretty sure."

Devin's face broke out in an expression of pure happiness. He was glad she couldn't see him, because she already thought he would want her only because of the baby, an assumption that was far from the truth. "Since I'm new at this, you have to tell me more about these signs, Brown Eyes. Exactly why do you think you're pregnant."

At first Monica didn't want to talk about it. It was too personal. But this was Devin and here she sat in front of him, his strong arms surrounding her, easing her discomfort. "My period's late!" she blurted.

"That's always the first sign, right?"

"If you're regular, it's a good sign that you're pregnant."

"Are you regular?"

"Like clockwork."

All right! Devin thought, using Tony's expression.

"And my breasts."

"What about them?" Devin asked, his position giving him a perfect view of that part of her anatomy.

"They're tender, very sensitive."

"Really?" he asked, gently brushing the swell of her breast with the back of his hand.

"There won't be any of that, Devin," she told him as she sucked in a breath.

"Why not? I can't make you pregnant again."

"No, but I don't think we should. Not until I have things straight in my mind. Until I decide if I really want to get married," she told him. "I don't sleep around, Dev."

"I know," he said, kissing her forehead and wrapping his hands around her waist. "Anything else?"

"I'm always tired. I find myself falling asleep anytime, anywhere."

"Are you sleepy now, Brown Eyes?"

"Now that you mention it, I am tired."

"Rest your head on my shoulder. Take a nap."

"But the kids. Josh and John have to get back to work. You don't pay them to babysit, and I know starting a new business is expensive. I don't want you to waste your time and money on me."

"Don't worry about it. I'll wake you in a bit. Just rest, for a little while."

Waste his money, he thought. If Brown Eyes wanted to rest Josh and John could babysit all afternoon. If he was spending money on her, he would never consider it a waste.

"Okay," she yawned. "I'll just take a little nap. Ten, fifteen minutes…twenty, thirty…the most."

A baby. Devin couldn't wait to tell his mother that she was going to be a grandma. Man, he thought, she was going to be an instant grandma when they got married. Not if—when.

For the next half hour Devin held Monica in his arms as she slept. Listening to the gentle deep breaths she took followed by soft little snoring sounds and then, once in a while, a loud snort.

Lightly resting his chin on the top of her head and brushing a strand of hair from her ponytail behind her ear, Devin went over in his the mind the plans he had set in motion. Being a man of action, he'd taken care of the blood tests and getting the license the same day Monica insisted they go to the clinic. The nurse had been so helpful that day by providing him with everything they'd need. A trip downtown to City Hall had taken care of the marriage license. He'd even talked to Father Brett, the pastor at St. Ann's, the church Monica and her family attended every Sunday. He'd thought of these actions as phase one.

Phase two now could begin in earnest. He'd apply constant loving, pressure, allowing her no time to think, act or hide. He wasn't waiting for their pregnancy to be confirmed. And it was their pregnancy. They'd both created this baby he was sure Brown Eyes was carrying. His hands brushed against her flat stomach.

Next weekend seemed like a good time for a wedding. Today was Friday. They could meet with the priest Tuesday, and get married on Saturday. Perfect, he thought, wrapping his hands around her a little tighter. She stirred in her sleep and whispered his name. That confirmed it.

"Monica! Bug! Where are you two?" Vanessa's agitated voice broke into his thoughts.

"Nessa, wait! You shouldn't walk so fast. You're going to hurt yourself or the babies!" Scott shouted, waking Monica from her sound sleep. Something was wrong.

"Don't worry, I'm taking perfect care of myself and the babies. It's you I'm worried about, Scott. If you come too close I'm liable to lose control and start swinging and there's no telling where my fists are going to land!" Ness shouted as she broke into the clearing where Devin and Monica sat.

By this time Monica was on her feet, big sister armor in place. Ness moved toward her.

Scott stopped behind Devin, using him as a shield. "I'll stand here behind you, Bug. Nessa looks like she'd really like to hit me. I don't want to stand close enough for her to try it. She might lose her balance and fall. I've never seen her this mad, man." To his wife Scott pleaded, "Nessa, this isn't like you. Why don't we go back to the trailer and talk about it?"

"Not right now, not when I'm feeling like this. I can't believe you kept all that from me!"

"What's gong on?" Monica asked, disbelief in her voice. "You two are kidding, right? You are not actually—"

"Fighting! Oh, yes, we are!" Vanessa said. "I need to keep as far away from Scott as possible. If I get too close we'll both be sorry."

"You wouldn't hurt him any more than he'd hurt you," Monica said with conviction.

"MyNessa," Scott pleaded at the same time.

"What's all this about?" Devin asked, having seen enough. He realized he was probably the only completely calm, rational person here at the moment.

"Nessa just found out about the T.J. thing. She's a little upset."

"A little!" she squeaked.

"I think it's one of those pregnancy things," Scott whispered to Devin seriously.

"Oh, I understand," Devin answered in agreement.

Devin watched as Monica and Vanessa stared at each other in amazement and brought their gazes back to both men. If he went by their expression, Devin could assume that their male version of deductive reasoning was completely off the mark.

"Being pregnant doesn't make me deaf, Scott," Nessa told her husband.

"You bet it doesn't." Monica turned her nose down at them.

"But I didn't want to worry you, that's why I didn't tell you about T.J.," Scott explained.

"T.J.? The same T.J. that caused all that trouble before you two got married?" Monica asked, looking as if she'd lost a big chunk of the conversation.

"That, Brown Eyes, is a long story." Devin walked toward her, Scott still using him as a shield.

"I'm listening."

"I'll tell you later tonight. It'll be added to the long list of things we need to discuss. Right now, let's just try to save Scott from getting beaten by his wife."

"Spouse abuse, that's what it'll be, Nessa. You don't want to see our faces on the news, do you?" Scott asked.

"You don't have a clue, do you?" Vanessa asked her husband.

Scott looked to Devin for help. Devin shrugged his shoulders. He had his own problems to deal with. Scott was going to have to figure this one out for himself.

A sudden look came into Scott's eyes. "About what?" he asked.

"Let's leave these two alone," Monica suggested. "That sounds like a good idea," Devin agreed. We need to discuss the time and place for our first real date."

"You're right, it will be our first real date," Monica said sadly.

"What's wrong? What did I say?"

"It's nothing to worry about. It's okay," she told him. She'd never thought she would ever go to bed with someone she'd never even been out on a date with before. What had she become?

The walk back to the trailer was quiet. She let Devin draw his own conclusions. And he did, she realized as they neared the site of their picnic. She heard him whisper, "Pregnant hormones."

First thing she needed to do was straighten him out about myths involving pregnant women. Later was soon enough for that. Devin helped her pack and load the picnic gear while Josh and John continued to chase the kids around the wide open area near the trailer.

"The newlyweds are back!" Josh shouted. "And Scott doesn't have a scratch on him."

"They're not newlyweds, you idiot," John corrected him. "They've been married for over two years."

"Yeah, but they still act like it," Josh insisted.

"Those two over there look more like newlyweds," John told his twin, his head pointed in the direction of Monica and Devin.

"Them? They're not even touching!"

"You are blind, man. Just check out the way they look at each other."

"You, brother boy, are nuts," Josh told him. "Monica's never going to get married again. She's still stuck on Keith."

"Maybe, but I think she's getting serious about Bug. It could be that we'll get to conduct another pre-wedding inquisition."

"You're way off. You see, this is the reason I was born first. You couldn't find your way out. I had to guide you."

"Wait and see, it's just a matter of time," John told him.

"Aw, man, now you're startin' to sound like Mama."

That comment ended the conversation. Josh and John enjoyed their extended lunch, but had enough of witnessing the joys and hazards of love and went back to work.

"Thanks for the break, boss," Josh told Devin, not stopping to talk. "We'll check in with Harris."

They were gone in a flash.

"Why were they in such a hurry?" Monica asked Devin.

"Who knows what goes through their heads. About tonight, you can get a sitter," Devin stated, not giving her an option to say no.

"Sure," Monica answered. She thought she'd ask her parents to babysit.

"Six o'clock. Meet me at my place."

"So far away? I don't think I can walk that far. I might even get lost."

"Don't get smart, Brown Eyes," he smiled. "I figure we'd get the arguing out of the way. Then we could enjoy the rest of the night. How does dinner sound?"

"Arguing? You plan on us having an argument?"

"Let's just say it's probably unavoidable."

"We'll see." she eyed his handsome face, and wondered what was on this list of things to discuss that would cause Devin to predict an argument between them.

"You never answered me. How does dinner at Commander's Palace sound?"

"Fancy. I always wanted to eat there." Conscious about money, Monica asked, "Are you sure you can afford to wine and dine me like this? I'd be happy to go to a neighborhood restaurant like Eddie's in the seventh ward. It's not that far from where we live."

Devin pulled her into the trailer, leaving Scott and Vanessa with the kids. "We have a lot to talk about," he told her before lowering his head for a kiss.

He didn't completely take her breath away, but it was a good start. He did break her concentration forcing her to pay attention to nothing else but the little nibbles he was taking on her bottom lip and the soft caress he ended with. It was enough for now.

Devin lifted her face, a serious expression covering his. He kissed her again and told her; "Monica, I'm rich."

"Right," she laughed, giving him a quick peck on the lips and caressing the muscles in his arms. "You do own the biggest house on the block, but it doesn't mean you're rich. You are too much, Dev. I'll see you tonight, six sharp." She walked out of the trailer.

Devin was stunned. Brown Eyes thought he was lying. He laughed. His mother thought women were after him for his money. And the only woman he wanted and planned to marry didn't believe that he was loaded with it. His plan to conceal his wealth had worked too well.

CHAPTER 19

Two little lines crossing each other confirmed it. She was positively pregnant. The plus sign showed up as clear as day. Not that a missed period, tender body parts, and constant sleepiness weren't accurate signs. Monica just needed a concrete form of proof.

Oh well, she sighed, putting the used test back into the container it came in. It was what she'd expected. She threw the box into the garbage can, grateful that she'd asked Ness to stop at the drug store. She'd run inside while her sister stayed in the air-conditioned van with the kids.

Monica had called her mother as soon as she'd gotten home to ask her to babysit. Her mom insisted that the kids come over right away and suggested that they spend the night. She acted mighty pleased to hear that Monica was going out with Devin.

Joyce Lewis always seemed to know everything about everything without ever being told. And Monica had this confirmed when she decided to confide in her mother. As soon as they went over, the kids had run out into the yard. They had come dressed in their swimsuits to play in the sprinklers Maw-Maw Joyce had set up for them.

Mother and daughter sat in the kitchen and watched the kids enjoy the freedom and fun of being young. Love for her kids suddenly overwhelmed Monica. She knew she would love this new baby just as much.

"I have some beautiful grandbabies. You sure are doing a fine job with them, Monica."

"Thanks, Mom!"

"Thanks aren't necessary," Joyce told her. "Everybody needs a little pat on the back once in a while."

"That may be true, but you always know when to give the pat."

Joyce just smiled and nodded her head.

"Mom, I've got something to tell you," Monica said as her mother sat quietly, almost expectantly, waiting. "Mama, I…" She stopped, wondering how she was going to say this. How did the perfect daughter, the shining example, tell her mother that she was pregnant without a husband.

"What I want to say is…" Here she was a grown woman, and she couldn't say it!

"Monica," Joyce softly called her name. "It can't be that bad."

"I don't think you'll be giving me another pat when you hear what I have to say."

"That you're pregnant?" Joyce asked.

Monica's eyes widened, then watered. A smile of love and gratitude shone on her face. "You knew, you always know. How?"

"I know my children," Joyce answered. "You may be all grown up, and an adult on your own, but a mother knows."

"I just admitted it to myself today."

"It took you that long? I've known since last Sunday."

"You've known for almost a whole week and you didn't say anything. Mom, you're too much."

"Not really. I remembered how you looked when you were expecting my other grandbabies. Your face gets rounder, your skin smoother, and your eyes brighter. But this time not as bright as before."

"I guess not. I'm not married to this baby's father." Monica sadly placed her hands on her stomach.

"But you're going to be, right?"

"How did you—" Monica laughed. "I won't ask that again. I've already accepted that you know everything, but you might be wrong about that. I haven't made any decisions."

"But Devin did ask you. And you are going out with him tonight."

"Yes."

"He loves you, you know."

"Are you sure about that?"

"As sure as I am that you love him."

"Mama, I'm not even sure about that."

"Oh?"

"Now you see, I didn't want to get into all of this."

"Okay."

"What I mean is…I like Devin a lot. I enjoy being with him and talking to him, and he's great with the kids. Devin is so patient and sweet. He's also bossy and as arrogant as hell," she observed. "I admire his drive and courage to start a new business."

"It's a good thing you at least like and admire him. After all, you are going to have his baby."

"Mama!"

"Don't look at me that way, Monica Ann! I know how babies are made. And I know you're upset and beating yourself up inside because of the way this baby was conceived. And part of that is because of the way your father and I raised you. You have morals and values, but you're also human."

"I know that, Mama."

"Let me finish. I need to tell you this because you won't tell yourself. Everything will be okay. Your father and I won't think any worse of you for it. None of your brothers and sisters will, either. And your kids will only know that you love them, and that you're giving them another brother or sister, as well as a new daddy."

Joyce stood, the only way she could stand taller than her eldest daughter. "Monica Ann, what you need to worry about is not the fact that your pregnant, but how you got that way."

"Mama, that doesn't make sense."

"Of course it does. What did you do to become pregnant?"

"We...Devin and I...I mean..."

"You made love!"

"Yes," Monica admitted.

"Case closed. You love Devin. Otherwise you would have never made love to him."

"But I still love Keith! I can't love Devin!"

"But you do!"

A few hours later Monica found herself at Devin's front door. She knocked and waited. There was no answer. Nervously she rang the bell. Did she really love him? She looked down at herself. Maybe she'd overdone it. What if she were too dressy? She stared at her reflection in the huge picture window in the front of Devin's house. The sleeveless maroon dress was not exactly her style. It was too tight and too short. The only thing modest about it was the neckline, thank goodness. Monica couldn't see herself going out with her entire front exposed.

Vanessa had bought her the dress as a birthday gift last April and dared her to wear it tonight. Too bad Ness wasn't here to see it. If what she was seeing in the reflection was right, she was looking good tonight. Maybe too good. She couldn't stop staring at herself. Ness had been trying to get her to wear the dress for a year and had bought the matching choker and earrings last Christmas as enticement. The accessories were the perfect addition.

The front door opened. "Brown Eyes! I thought I heard the door." It was Devin's turn to stop and stare. "Gorgeous," he told her.

Monica made a complete circle around him, stopping at her original position to stare.

"Are you planning on coming inside or do you intend to stand outside decorating the front of my house all night long?"

"Oh no, I'm coming—it's just that…"

"I know, you haven't seen me in anything besides jeans and workout clothes."

"True, and you look good in those, but this. . . this," she said, pointing at him, "is beyond good. Maybe I shouldn't have said that."

"Not if it's true," he insisted.

Monica was smiling at him one second and then filling the air with that full laugh the next.

"See what I mean," she said, admiring his dressy attire once again. Devin wore a collarless white dress shirt, the first two buttons undone, giving her a glimpse of smooth, dark brown skin that she knew covered firm, solid muscle. She noticed the Calvin Klein label on the front pocket. He was really trying to impress her today. The fit and style of the pleated black dress pants he wore had her wondering if they were custom made. But her mind didn't stay with that thought for long because it wandered to the memory of the strong muscular legs resting between hers as they slept together that night more than a month ago.

"Brown Eyes," he called to her. "We can't stand here staring at each other all night. Come inside. I've been waiting for you."

"You have? Then why did it take you so long to get to the door?"

"Sorry about that. My mother called. She wouldn't get off the phone. She kept asking questions."

"Your mother?"

"Yes, my mother."

"I don't know, Dev. I'm beginning to wonder if you actually have a mother. It could be that she's a little excuse you use to appear sweet and keep you out of trouble."

"I've got a mother," he told her as he closed the front door. "She's sweet, pushy, demanding, and hasn't gotten over the last time I hung up on her."

"You didn't."

"I had to. She wanted to know too much. And there's only so much prying a man can take."

Monica laughed, filling the room again with that wonderful sound.

"You wouldn't laugh if it were you."

"I've got one too."

Just then a trilling noise filled the air, almost like the sound of a tiny doorbell. "What's that?" Monica asked, turning toward the source of the sound.

"My computer. I'm still on-line," Devin explained. "I was checking my e-mail when the phone rang earlier." Devin went to the computer in the corner of the living room. "It's my mother. She's IM-ed me."

"IM-ed?"

"Called me, hailed me. You know, demanded that I speak with her now. She sent an Instant Message, an IM."

"How did she know you were online?"

"A nice feature of AOL."

"I see."

Devin eyes narrowed. "Did you have to use those two words?"

"It was just a comment."

"No, it's more than that. I'll show you."

Monica read as Devin typed in an introduction and clicked the mouse.

"Tell her hello," he instructed.

"Just type it in?"

"That's right, then click the mouse."

"Devin, this is not the normal way a man introduces a woman to his mother."

"It's the modern way," he grinned. "Nowadays, with the wonders of technology, we can do almost anything."

The words 'Devin, now I see' appeared on the screen, stopping Monica from giving her opinion of his use of technology.

Monica laughed. Devin growled, "Talk to her, Monica, I won't hear the end of it if you don't."

"Okay," she agreed, sitting in the cushioned computer chair. Devin left the room, promising to return shortly.

"Monica, are you there?" appeared on the screen.

"Yes, I am, Mrs. Preston," she typed.

"I see," came back immediately.

Monica smiled as she realized why Devin protested when she used those words. They had to be his mother's favorite phrase.

"So, you're the reason my son hung up on me!" Monica read.

Talk about blunt. Monica drew a blank. The light from the screen shone on her face, the cursor impatiently waiting for an answer.

"Well, Monica, are you still there?" flashed on the screen soon after.

Not wanting to appear cowardly, Monica typed, "I'm here." At the same time she called,

"Devin, get in here!"

"Well then, answer my question, girl. Are you the reason my son hung up on me?"

What was taking Devin so long? Monica didn't want to rub the woman the wrong way. She could be her future mother-in-law. How did you talk to your mother-in- law? Monica had no idea. She'd never had one. Keith had no family other than the aunt that raised him.

She decided to be straightforward and honest. "I am," she typed and clicked the mouse.

Devin walked back into the room, his hands in his pockets. "What's wrong, Monica? Mama's hasn't got you tongue-tied already? She tends to come on pretty strong if you're not used to her." Devin stood behind her.

The word "Good" appeared on the screen. Monica couldn't help laughing at the reply.

"Sounds like you're doing fine. Do you want me to take over?" Devin asked.

"No, I have something I need to ask your mother." She smiled up at him, glad for an excuse to get rid of him until she could focus on something besides what was in his pants.

"Monica, are you still there? Is Devin standing over your shoulder?"

"Yes, he is," Monica quickly typed back.

"Tell him to go away. I want to talk to my future daughter-in-law."

Monica read the last message and calmly lifted her eyes to meet his. She was surprised to find that his mother's remark hadn't bothered her. Maybe she was

getting used to the idea of possibly marrying Devin...
"Dev, what did you tell her?"

"Not a thing. I'll go fix us a drink. What do you want?"

"Surprise me."

"You've got it, Brown Eyes." He bent to kiss her softly on the lips and whispered, "I love to see the warmth in your eyes," and walked into the kitchen.

Monica absently wondered what he meant by that as her fingers flew across the keys. "Why is that good, and what do you mean by calling me your future daughter-in-law?" she typed.

Monica continued their on-line conversation, coming to enjoy Mrs. Preston's open, blunt comments. She reminded Monica of her father. According to Devin's mother, Devin had been in love with her for some time. She praised Monica for making him work at gaining her affections.

Monica guessed that was what she had done, unintentionally, of course.

"Well I've said enough," Lisa Preston ended. "Get back to Devin before he thinks I told all his secrets. You've kept him waiting long enough, I suppose."

Having enjoyed the time she spent on-line Monica typed, "It's been nice talking to you."

"Same here," appeared on the screen. Then, when Monica was about to get up to find Devin, another message appeared. "One more thing. Don't let Devin's money bother you. I've got a feeling he thinks that will scare you off. He's never let all that money go to his head like some people do. I can tell you this: you'll have more troubles than money trying to keep that son of mine in line."

Monica waited a few minutes. When no new messages appeared she pushed away from the computer and turned to look at the room. It was a large living room with a huge white sectional leather sofa and not much else. Her eyes stared at the bare wall as she thought.

Money? Devin had said he was rich. Monica thought he was joking. His mother hadn't said anything about him being a millionaire or anything like that. She was probably trying to reassure her by letting her know that Devin had a secure job. She sounded like a practical, old-fashioned woman. Monica was sure that was what she meant.

Devin came into the room carrying a tall fruity glass of something for her in one hand and a beer for himself in the other.

"I know you're not positive that you're pregnant, but I thought it was best to play it safe. One non-alcoholic beverage for you. I call it fruit surprise."

"Thanks," she answered, absently reaching for the drink.

Devin could tell she wasn't concentrating on what he was saying. What she was doing was concentrating on him. She was staring directly into his face in deep thought. She seemed to be working out something in her mind, and held the drink he'd given her without bothering to taste it. He looked into her eyes and felt A tremendous sense of belonging as they melted and melded with his.

"Dev, you are so handsome," she sighed.

"Where did that come from?" he whispered. He'd be sure to thank his mother for whatever she had said.

"Nowhere. I realized that I'd never told you how good-looking you are."

That was the best compliment she'd ever given him. He must be doing something right.

"I think it's because you already know," she continued.

"Do I?"

"Ohh, yes, indeed." She shook her head. "It's written all over you. In the way you strut around—here, at the Sports Spa, on the site."

"So I strut," he stated, neither confirming or denying it at this point.

"Everywhere you go! And you know you look good while you're doing it."

Devin put his beer down and stooped down in front of her. He pulled the computer chair toward his open legs, her knees fitting comfortably between them. He couldn't tell whether she was amused or having problems dealing with this part of his personality.

"I admit I strut, but it's a natural thing. As natural as loving you."

"Dev," she whispered.

Her deep brown eyes had gotten a little sad, a little troubled, but they were still warm.

"Let me finish now," he told her when it looked as if she was going to interrupt. "When," he smiled, "and notice I said when, not if, when I strut it's because of the confidence I have in myself, in what I do, and who I am. And I'm warning you that I'm going to use that same confidence convincing you to become my wife, Brown Eyes."

"I'm not surprised."

"Good. And there's one more thing I need you to know. No matter how sure or confident I am, hearing the way you feel about me from these two lips will always be a welcome experience." He gently caressed first her top and then bottom lip with his thumb. "And sometime soon I anticipate hearing a few particular words from these."

"What words?" she asked.

"I do," he told her, taking the fruity drink out of her hand. He found her ring finger and held it between his thumb and forefinger.

She wasn't sure if she loved Devin, but she wanted him. He was her friend, and her lover. She was going to marry him. He had become important to her.

"I do," she answered leaning her forehead against his.

"Brown Eyes, can you say that again?"

"I do."

Devin yelled, "All right!" He picked her up and spun her around in a circle.

Monica was beyond dizzy. She felt light-headed. Light, period, as if a weight had been lifted from her body, her heart, her soul.

Devin suddenly stopped and landed on the huge sofa with Monica on his lap.

"I'm so sorry, Brown Eyes, forgive me," he was saying, kissing her lips and then each finger of her left hand.

The dizziness, the happiness, the freedom she was feeling directed her other hand to the buttons of his shirt. "Forgive you for what, Dev?"

"I'm sorry, but I forgot, for just a minute, about our baby," he told her, placing his hand on her stomach. "I didn't hurt you, did I?"

Monica stopped in the middle of finding her way inside Devin's shirt. She looked down at his hand on her flat stomach. When she'd said I do, when she said she'd marry him, she'd forgotten that she was pregnant. All she had on her mind was Devin. What did that mean? She looked up at him with surprise at her discovery and admitted, "I forgot too."

Keeping his hand pressed against her stomach, Devin pulled her closer and smiled into her hair. The emotion inside of him was so strong. He almost felt like crying. She'd forgotten about the baby when she promised to marry him. If he needed any more proof that she loved him, this was it. She was marrying him just for him. Devin had never doubted that she loved him, but this did wonders for his need to in some way be shown by Monica that it was true.

Devin quickly controlled his emotions and prepared himself for the challenge ahead—convincing Monica to agree to the arrangements he'd made over a month ago for their wedding. All without her consent, of course. He had to put it to her without making her feel as if she were boxed into a corner.

"What now?" Monica asked slowly inching her hand under his shirt.

What now? He thought, plunge right in. He'd either smooth talk his way out of this or start his married life in the doghouse.

As it turned out, he found himself landing somewhere in between as he laid out his plans in a simple, logical manner. Monica's hand slowly slipped from his chest as he explained away the reason they didn't need blood tests. She leaned still farther away from him, losing eye contact, when he informed her about their meeting with Father Brett in four days. He could no longer see if her eyes held any warmth or had turned cold as ice. Monica hopped off his lap as soon as he explained that the standard preparation for any couple getting married in a Catholic church was being modified due to their pregnancy and desire to get married as soon as possible.

Devin watched and waited. Monica had her back to him, her shoulders stiff. He needed to see her face, to know what she was thinking. He hated being in the dark about anything. If he wasn't informed, he couldn't solve the problem. He moved to stand directly in front of her.

"Would you please explain yourself, Devin?" Monica said with a chill in her voice.

Teeth clenched, he let out a huge breath. She was mad. It was not only in her stance, but her eyes and her politely worded question. He hated it when she turned into that rigid, polite person. But he knew it was all his fault.

"Okay," he agreed.

"Okay? I do hope you have more than that to say for yourself. Explain yourself, please. Why did you arrange for those blood tests?"

"Because I love you," he simply answered.

She didn't soften a bit. At least it appeared that way at first. But Devin thought she blinked.

It was quick, but it was something.

"Why did you contact Father Brett without my permission?"

"Because I love you," he told her once more. She blinked again.

"You had no right to tell him I was pregnant. I didn't even know for sure myself."

"I know. You're right."

"Don't try to…I'm right?"

"Yes you are, Brown Eyes," he admitted, trying to hold her in his arms.

Monica moved out of his reach. "There you go, confusing me again."

"I don't mean to."

"But you do it anyway. You start off being adorable and loving—"

"I'm glad you think so."

"— then I have to deal with these highhanded tactics of yours that you can't admit to being sorry for."

Devin stood staring at her, saying nothing because what she said was true. He wasn't sorry for making the plans, because at the time he felt he had no other choice. He was a man used to taking charge. The only thing he was sorry for was making her feel left out.

"I knew it, you're not sorry! And now you're feeling conciliatory. And that's supposed to make everything okay?"

"I was hoping it would help."

She'd turned her back on him again. Devin stood this for all of one minute then slowly turned her to face him again. "Okay, Brown Eyes, I can't take this. I hate when you turn away from me. Tell me how insensitive I am, how wrong, how inconsiderate. But tell me something so we can go on from there. That way I can fix it."

"Fix it? Excuse me, Devin, but you can't fix everything," she told him in a quiet voice.

"I see your point," he conceded. "I should have said we can fix it. We can fix it. Let's straighten this out together."

Monica looked at him and nodded.

"But you have to admit one thing, Brown Eyes. You drove me to arrange all those plans without you."

"I don't think so."

"I know so. Your stubbornness forced me to take drastic measures. So you'll have to forgive me. I did it all because I love you."

"Apologies and arrogance don't mix, Dev. But for you it seems to work."

Thank God, he thought to himself.

"And that reasoning of yours will work only this one time, Devin Preston. I will not put up with you excusing your inconsiderate behavior by saying you did it because you love me."

Monica allowed Devin to pull her into his arms. "Monica, I want you to know that I'm going to be the best husband and father there ever was."

"You sound pretty sure of yourself."

"Confident as always," he told her, leaning back far enough to see her face. "More than confident since you are the lady I'm going to marry, and my new sons and daughter will be Tony, Jazz, and Mark. I love every one of you."

He held her close once again and after a time announced, "Now that the battle's over and done with, what say we enjoy the rest of the evening."

"So you think it's over?"

"We talked it out. You're satisfied. I'm satisfied. Since everything came out satisfactorily what do you say about a wedding on Saturday?"

"Saturday! That's tomorrow."

"No, Brown Eyes, next Saturday," he explained. "I was thinking that we could plan the wedding together. Since I've already gotten rid of all the annoying details, blood tests, marriage license, a priest…"

Monica laughed, "You are unbelievable."

"More than that, but we can discuss it later," he answered. "Tell me, where do you want to get married?"

"Devin, we have one week to do this. The church will be fine."

"Not good enough. Tell me and it's done," he told her, oozing confidence.

Monica smiled up at him. He could tell she wasn't taking him seriously when she told him, "Outside, in

City Park, in the gardens at the Pavilion of Two Sisters."

"Day or night?"

"Night," she answered, a dreamy look in her eyes. "With the gardens lit up with tiny clear lights."

"Done!" he told her, knowing that no matter how much it cost they were getting married at City Park.

"Devin how can it be done? You can't book the Pavilion of Two Sister Gardens with a one-week notice."

"I can, and I will."

"How?"

"I'm rich! You'd be surprised at the things you can do when you have money."

CHAPTER 20

He said it again. Monica still didn't know what to think about it as he led her out the door to a waiting limousine. A uniformed driver stepped out, tipped his hat and opened the door for them.

Devin thanked the driver as he motioned for her to enter ahead of him.

Monica decided that she'd wait for the evening to unfold. Besides, she was suddenly very sleepy, a quiet reminder that she was carrying Devin's baby. She smiled at the thought, knowing that he was going to be the best father ever. Monica relaxed on the soft leather seat and leaned her head on Devin's broad shoulder. He snuggled her against him, and before she knew it she was fast asleep.

Feeling well rested, Monica slowly woke up from the best sleep she'd had in a long time. Devin's strong arms still held her close to his warm body. "Where are we?" she asked, moving to stretch and peek over his shoulder. Devin smiled at her, completely ignoring her question. "Do you know that you were wide awake one second and fast asleep the next. I guess that's one of the things pregnancy does to a woman," he said, that sweet smile still plastered on his face.

"One of many," she told him as her stomach growled. "I'm a little hungry. Weren't we supposed to go to a restaurant? It doesn't look like we're anywhere near Commander's Palace."

"We aren't."

"And it's dark outside. I must have slept longer than I thought. What time is it now?"

He twisted his wrist. Monica peered at the very expensive-looking watch, her eyebrows raised. "Nine-thirty," he said.

"It took us over two hours to get here! And where exactly is here?" she asked as a long, black iron gate slid open, allowing the limousine to drive into a gated parking lot. "We are still in New Orleans, right?" she asked since she hadn't been able to get a good look outside the window with Devin's broad shoulders blocking her view.

"Of course we are, Brown Eyes," he assured. "We're still in good ol' Nawlins. You looked so tired I told the driver to ride around for a while."

"That was so sweet."

"Not entirely. I enjoyed having you snuggle up to me the way you did," Devin told her as he solicitously helped her out of the limo. He talked in low tones to the driver,

Monica enjoyed the novelty of riding in a limousine but knew that she preferred being responsible for taking herself where she wanted to go.

Devin wrapped an arm around her waist. Monica leaned into him and asked, "Where are we going?"

"Across the street." He smiled mysteriously, holding her close as they made their way through the parking lot.

Monica stopped when they reached the sidewalk. Her stomach was doing a lot more than growling. Her face twisted as she realized what it meant. Looking up, Monica was able to forget her stomach for a minute as she took in the huge brick building with tall and wide multi-pane windows trimmed in green. Peeking over at Devin, she found the same mysterious smile and decided to stick to her plan to let the night unfold on its own.

At the door to the lobby Monica watched as Devin punched numbers in a computerized keypad and pushed the door for her to enter first. Monica took in the large, airy lobby.

Two security officers stood at a wide circular desk. A flight of stairs made of light shades of natural wood and metal ascended to the second floor. On the walls were black and white photos of the building itself, Monica realized as she looked around. The picture of a giant water tower from an unusual angle gave away their location. They were at the Cotton Mill, a complex of luxurious, upscale apartments and condominiums reconstructed from an old textile mill. If that were true, they were in the Warehouse District near the Mississippi River.

Devin nodded at the guards who waved as if they knew him. He punched the elevator button and whisked her inside as soon as the doors opened. Her stomach did the nausea dance. A flip, a turn, and then a huge roll. The elevator moved up. That did it. Her stomach easily did a triple and careened down to her feet as the elevator stopped on the mezzanine level.

Devin must have noticed the sick look on her face because he quickly moved a few steps down the hall to a wood paneled door with the letters PH and the number four on the outside.

As soon as the doors opened, Monica entered a wide spacious area that looked to be a study. She moved to the left and opened the first door she came to. A washer and dryer. The next door revealed a huge closet.

The bathroom's upstairs, Brown Eyes," Devin told her. She had spotted the stairs and was already on her way up. She passed the dining area, went through the kitchen, down a short hall, and finally made it to the bathroom.

Devin had followed her. After she finished emptying her already empty stomach, Monica found him filling the entire doorway, quietly waiting. In his hand were a glass of water, a towel and a peppermint. He put everything on the counter near the sink, traced a finger across her forehead and left. Somehow he knew that she needed to take care of herself by herself.

He was so sweet. She'd been saying that a lot tonight.

Mouth rinsed, wiped and filled with a minty flavor, Monica left the bathroom to enter a wide, spacious room. Everywhere she looked there was a view of the city through the floor-to-ceiling windows. From one angle the lights of downtown New Orleans winked at her as she viewed the Convention Center, the Bell South building, as well as the relatively new WDSU Channel Six building. Turning to her left she saw the Crescent City Connection, twin bridges that crossed the mighty Mississippi, connecting the west bank of New Orleans to the east bank. It was illuminated with lights, the bridge itself as well as the cars moving across it.

She turned to find Devin in the dining area, and a hot, freshly prepared meal on the table of a small cherry oak dining set. "I wasn't gone long enough for you to have cooked all this," Monica commented as she walked toward him.

"Long enough for me to miss you, though. Are you feeling better?"

"Much."

"Good."

"Dev, how did you do all this?" She folded her arms across her chest. "I believe you have a lot to explain. A beautiful, obviously expensive rooftop apartment, if I go by the view."

"Technically, it's a penthouse condominium."

"And the food ready and waiting?"

"I have a few connections."

"More than a few, I think. Does this place," she turned with her arms spread wide, "belong to a friend of yours?"

"No, it's mine."

Monica had turned again to admire the skyline. "So this view is yours?"

"Ours," he answered as he came to stand behind her.

His arms came around her and Monica naturally leaned into him. She let out a breath. "Out with it, Dev, exactly how rich are you?"

"Oh, I've got a few million."

"A few million? I have a feeling you're underestimating."

"Probably."

"So you have money."

"Is that a problem?" he asked, softly breathing into her ear.

"I don't know. I've never wanted to be rich. I was happy with being—secure."

"We can look at it as being more than secure."

They stood together watching the lights of the cars as they passed over the bridge. Monica spent a few quiet moments digesting the news that Devin was rich, more likely, filthy rich. He was an important part of her life. Was it so bad that he was rich too? She would just have to learn to get used to it. Just as she'd learned to accept the electrifying chemistry between them. The same chemistry that was flowing around them. Tiny sparks of electricity ran up and down her arms as he slowly caressed them.

His touch had taken her mind off her stomach. But now it began to go into another gymnastic routine. She breathed in deeply, trying to squelch the nausea. It worked this time.

"Brown Eyes?" Devin asked, turning her to face him. "If you're going to have a problem with this, tell me now so that I—I mean we," he corrected, "can fix it."

Realizing that she had made peace with the situation without informing him, Monica whispered in his ear, "I can. Excuse me, I mean we can deal with it. But if I don't get something into my stomach soon, we'll be spending the night in the bathroom."

"Not a bad idea," he told her and pulled out a chair for her. "Did you notice the bathtub? That one's big, but the one in the master bedroom is a garden tub with water jets. We'd have a lot more room to enjoy ourselves than the last time we ended up in the tub together."

"Don't even entertain that thought," she told him as she sat down and picked up a scone full of currants. "Where did all the food come from?"

"Spice, Inc. It's a restaurant/grocery store located in the building. We have private access. When you fell asleep I thought you might enjoy something quieter, so I called ahead to order a meal. I think the chef's a romantic. She whipped up a meal and sent it up in no time."

Before he got a chance to point out all the dishes, he stopped to watch as she carefully picked currants out of a scone.

"Is that all you're going to eat?"

"If I'm going to be able to eat any of this," she pointed to the full table, "then I need to get something plain and simple, like pastry, down fast. Part of the reason for my earlier stomach problem was that it was empty. If I remember correctly a completely empty stomach was worse than a full one."

"Awww, another one of those pregnancy facts."

"Are you taking notes?"

"No, this I can remember. For everything else I'm going to have to stop at a bookstore and get a few more books. There's a lot I need to know about this whole pregnancy process."

"You love to be informed, don't you."

"What other way is there to be?"

Devin watched as she slowly devoured the pastry. Earlier it had bothered him to see her so sick. He now understood why Scott had been so frantic that day Ness locked him out of the bathroom,

He absently picked up a currant from her plate and popped the chewy fruit into his mouth. Before he knew it, he had eaten all the currants on her plate. Monica looked up at the same moment he made that discovery. Without missing a beat she began feeding him currants from the half-eaten scone on her plate. When they'd demolished it, currants, pastry and all, Monica continued feeding him. She used a fork to spear grilled shrimp from a salad he tried to entice her with earlier and brought it to his lips.

Monica juggled forks and spoons as she fed him gumbo, quesadillas, and chocolate praline brownies. Devin provided her with more bits of the pastry until they were all gone. The table soon became a graveyard of half empty warming trays, bowls and platters.

"I've got an idea," he told her, standing up and pressing a light kiss on her lips. Devin ushered her down the small hall to the master bedroom. "I suggest we indulge in the worst thing we could do after eating a huge meal."

"What?" she grinned.

"Collapse until we feel like moving again."

"Dev, I'm all dressed up to go somewhere. Don't get me wrong, I love this place, it's beautiful, and the pastries were delicious. But now you tell me we're going to lie down, and do what? Sleep?"

"And talk. While you were sleeping earlier I played with the idea of going somewhere else, but since we hadn't discussed the idea together yet, and I was enjoying holding you so much, I thought it would be best for us to save New York for tomorrow. Maybe your mom can keep the kids longer or they could come with us. Whatever you want."

"New York!" Monica stopped in the doorway of the large master bedroom. "You were thinking about traveling to New York tonight? How were we going to get there?"

"Fly, of course. It would take too long to drive."

"Okay, that makes sense, but wouldn't that be a lot of trouble?" Monica asked, following him into the bedroom and watching as he sat on the bed to take off his shoes and socks.

"I planned on taking my own plane," he answered matter-of-factly.

"Plane. So you have your own plane. Next thing you're going to tell me is that you can fly it yourself."

"I can, but I didn't plan to. I couldn't hold you and fly at the same time. A pilot friend of mine flew it in and it's on standby."

"All right, Devin Prescott, I thought I knew everything I needed to know. You still have a lot more talking to do."

"I realize that." He gently guided her to the edge of the bed to remove her shoes. "But there's one thing you have to realize, Brown Eyes. You already know all the important parts. The rest are only details." He ran a finger up her leg and stood over her. "Should I take off the stockings or do you want to do that yourself?"

"I'll take care of them myself," she answered, a preoccupied look on her face. "I suppose you're right."

She leaned back onto the smooth silk comforter and watched as he got rid of the rest of his clothes. Her eyes widened, he noticed, when she realized he was completely naked, his need for her evident in every part of his body.

"Devin, I thought we were going to lie down and talk," she gulped.

"We are." He removed his watch and walked across the room to place it on top of a beautifully-carved chest of drawers, giving her a view he hoped would throw her.

"But you don't have a stitch on."

"I want to be comfortable. And I want to feel your skin touching mine." He came back to the bed and offered her his hands.

Monica reached out to him. Devin slowly pulled her up to him. He stretched his arms around and lowered the zipper of her dress. Giving a gentle pull, Devin watched as it fell to her hips. Another tug and it landed softly on the floor.

"You sure you don't have anything else planned?"

"Not at all," he insisted, releasing the clasp on her bra and quickly peeling it away. He pulled her back into his arms. "Ahh, doesn't that feel good? Skin to skin contact."

"Yes," was all she said. Then after awhile, "Dev, promise me all we'll do is talk. It might seem kind of strange to you, but I don't think we should make love again, at least until we get married."

A spasm went through his body as she said those words. It gripped him so hard Monica couldn't help feeling it.

"Am I asking too much? Because if you can't handle this I think we should leave now…"

He pulled back and looked into her face. "I can handle it." Devin watched as she peeled away her pantyhose, enjoying the sight of her long, brown legs. She didn't realize it, but Brown Eyes had just told him she loved him—again. She said make love, not have sex, not a lustful tumble, but make love. He was going to show a tremendous amount of restraint tonight if it killed him. He slid between the cool sheets and lifted the covers for her to join him. Devin held back a comment and even the grin that threatened to appear on his face as Monica joined him, her maroon silk underwear still hugging her round hips. "I know you'll be a gentleman," Monica was saying, "and not mention my unmentionables."

."Not mentionable."

"These sheets feel so good."

"Mmm," Devin answered, wrapping his arms around her.

"You feel good."

"I won't argue with that. I'm also full of good ideas, this being one of them."

Devin held her, satisfied with all the changes that had occurred today. When he woke up this morning he'd had no idea that all his efforts would be rewarded with having Monica in his arms tonight. Fitting her perfectly against him, Devin began, "Tell me what you want to know."

."All right, let's start with New York," she said, not wasting any time. "Why New York?"

Before he answered Devin reached for her left hand, gently caressing her ring finger. "Monica, we haven't talked about this, but I know that Keith's been a major obstacle between us. I've been jealous. Wait," he said when she took a breath to interrupt him. "I don't want you to feel as if I'm trying to take his place. I want my own place in your heart, Brown Eyes. Your heart is so big— you love everyone. I want you to save a little room for me because my heart is already full of love for you."

"Dev," she whispered, "I think you've already bull-dozed your way there. It's just…"

"I know. Don't say anything. This was something I wanted you to know. That's all."

"Okay, I understand," she whispered after a tense silence. "I want you to know that as far as Keith's concerned, I'm trying. He was my first love, and I can't simply throw the feelings I had for him out the window."

"I know, Brown Eyes."

"I care so much for you, Devin. More than I've cared about any man in a long time. I hope that's enough."

"For now. We'll work on it," he answered, contin-uing to massage her ring finger. "Monica, there's one more thing?"

"Yes."

"Where are your wedding and engagement rings? Feeling the way you do about Keith, I always found it strange that you didn't wear them."

"I lost them about a year ago. For the longest time I felt naked without them. But I can honestly say if I found them today I wouldn't be tempted to wear them. The ring you place on my finger I'll be more than proud to wear, Dev."

"How do I love you, let me count the ways," he whispered, more to himself than Monica. There were so many ways she'd said I love you tonight. He pulled her tighter against him, if that were possible.

"Speaking of rings…"

"Does that bring us back to—"

"New York," Devin finished for her. "Yes, New York," he continued. "When I began my career and stumbled into becoming the number one architect for the rich and famous—"

"I'm sure there was more talent than stumbling."

"True, which is how I found myself making more money than I could ever imagine. I've always had a dream of going to New York, walking into Tiffany's with my fiancée beside me and being able to tell her to choose any ring she wanted. I knew that whoever that woman might be, she would become the love of my life and would deserve the best. And you do, Brown Eyes."

She made no reply, only leaning back into him even more. "Afterwards, I thought that we could go shopping at Saks or Bloomingdale's for a wedding dress."

"I'd like that," she quietly agreed.

"Good, then it's settled," he quickly surmised while she was in an agreeable mood. It wasn't often that Monica agreed so readily.

Devin spent the rest of the night filling in some details he'd mentioned earlier about his life. Monica was surprised to find that he was the famous D.J. Preston, whose work was in demand across the nation. She vaguely remembered seeing his pictures splashed across the covers of *Newsweek* and in *People Magazine* as one of the nation's most eligible bachelors. That's why he looked somewhat familiar when she first saw him in the French Quarter.

They continued to talk for hours about important issues as well as trivial things, such as how to squeeze toothpaste. As the night wore on she experienced a wide range of emotions. She wasn't sure if that was due to her pregnancy or simply Devin. She felt everything from worry about his safety from T.J. to contentment to silliness to absolute seriousness. The current of electricity flowing between them was a steady but controlled hum throughout the night. With heavy eyes she savored the feeling of knowing that she'd made the right decision for herself and for her kids, to marry this sweet, sweet man.

Devin lay wide awake. His control was a fragile, thin thread of spun glass as he listened to Monica's even breathing. Maintaining physical contact for the last three hours had to be the biggest challenge of his life. And all for the love of one woman. Designing a Tudor castle on a small island off the coast of Maine or a seventeenth-century plantation house in upstate New York was a breeze compared to the last three hours. He let out a slow breath and sucked it back in again as Monica moved, rolling directly on top of him, fitting herself perfectly to his body. Talk about *déjà vu*, this was how they got pregnant to begin with. Monica moved her hips, slowly, torturously, to the right and then to the left. He was wrong. This was more of a challenge than the last three hours. Devin gently but quickly eased out from under her. Monica murmured a small sound of protest before curling up with a soft pillow. In no time she was breathing deeply, a slight frown replacing the look of contentment on her face. Good, she was as miserable as he was.

In the top dresser drawer Devin found a pair of boxers. He'd had some of his clothing delivered with the furniture a few days earlier. On one of his visits to the Quarter he'd ventured through the Warehouse District, stopped to have a tour, and bought the last condominium before it disappeared. He didn't plan on living here. The plan at the back of his mind was

to use this penthouse beauty as a retreat just for them.
A secret place for him to sneak off to with Monica
once in a while.

It was luxurious and prestigious, and something
one might expect someone with his income to buy.
But for Devin this was no status symbol. He'd broken
away from needing or wanting those, and had grown
tired of people who did. This was a retreat—their
retreat, which is why, he realized, he brought her here
instead of Commander's Palace. Devin had wanted
Monica all to himself. And tonight he'd had an over
abundance.

Moonlight from the floor-to-ceiling windows
guided him to the overstuffed chair where he'd left his
briefcase. He pulled out a thick, hard covered book
and positioned the chair closer to the window taking
in the beautiful landscape below him. The huge water
tower stood right outside and towered above the beautiful courtyard filled with a variety of plants, tables
and chairs. Devin also remembered that there was a
pool out there somewhere. They'd have to take a swim
sometime soon. He would have to buy Brown Eyes
one of those pregnant bathing suits. He couldn't help
glancing her way. He walked to the bed and covered
Monica with the satin sheet, hiding a delicious view of
her breasts.

Now to get down to the business of being informed. Devin went back to the window and sat in the plush chair switching on a small lamp. He opened the book. "Chapter 1: The First Trimester."

Devin sat for the next few hours reading and rereading details of the first trimester of a pregnancy. He'd never realized the importance of the first three months of a baby's development. So much happened in that short amount of time. Had Monica seen a doctor yet? If not, they'd set an appointment tomorrow for next week.

And all the symptoms. He'd looked back at the list, his long finger tracing the page as he read. The nausea and vomiting he'd witnessed already. Swollen, tender breasts she'd mentioned earlier. Walking across the room to the bed, Devin moved the sheet down to take a peek. Were her breasts any larger? Yes, he thought so. Even though he only had that one opportunity to hold and caress them, he remembered the texture, the weight in his hands, their size. They were definitely bigger. He put the sheet down, hiding the brown nipple that stood erect, tempting him.

He closed the book and walked across the room to check his watch: four A.M.

He'd get in a few hours sleep, then see if he could charm an order of scones, maybe some without fruit, from the bakery chef. The store didn't open till later, but maybe he'd luck out. Some juice and milk would be good for Monica, too. He'd take care of it.

Devin settled in next to Monica relaxed enough to enjoy the feel of her in his arms again, skin to skin, but with a little added insurance. This time they both were wearing underwear.

CHAPTER 21

Monica opened her eyes and slowly stretched. The unaccustomed feel of cool satin sheets reminded her that she wasn't in the middle of her own bed. She raised up on her elbows, searching the room for Devin. Not finding him and not one to lounge around in bed, Monica quickly scooted to the edge. She stopped when her stomach protested her quick movements. There was a sound at the bedroom door. She was under the covers in a flash, causing her stomach to lurch again.

"Breakfast, Brown Eyes," she heard Devin say, still hiding under the covers.

Feeling silly, Monica sat up, securing the sheets around her. There stood one fine man with one fine breakfast. He carried a wooden tray with three fat scones, a cup of hot tea, and glasses of juice and milk.

"Oh Dev, you're so—"

"Sweet, I know. Eat up. Settle your stomach and get dressed. We've got some traveling to do." Devin gave her a quick kiss on the cheek and sat on the end of the bed. Monica watched as he picked up the cord-less phone.

"Who are you calling?" Monica lifted the mug to take a sip of the hot tea.

"Your parents. I'm going to tell them we're getting married."

"Mr. Take Charge is making all the arrangements again?" she asked, eyebrows raised.

Devin stopped dialing and hung up the phone. He placed a hand on each side of her face. "Do you mind if I tell your parents the good news?"

"Since you asked so nicely," she nodded.

Reaching for the phone again he stopped to ask, "What about the kids? Do you want them to come with us?"

"No, this trip should be ours, but we'll need to stop by my parents so that we can talk to them together. It'll be a big change in their lives."

"Sounds good."

Monica picked up a scone as Devin began to dial once again. She felt an enormous bubble of happiness floating inside of her. She smiled at the scone, no currants. She smiled at an image of what her parents' reaction would be; her father's scowl because he was once again left in the dark, her mother's face full of satisfaction because she knew it would happen. She smiled just for the sake of smiling.

"Good morning, Mr. Lewis," Devin said into the phone.

"Dev? Bug?" Monica could hear resounding loud and clear from the receiver. "How many times have I told you? It's Cal, or if you have to be formal, I can deal with Mr. Cal. What are you doing calling my house so early in the morning!" he blustered.

"I called with some good news," Devin told him, capturing Monica's hand to take a taste of her breakfast.

"What? You went and got yourself a new boat or something?"

Monica shook her head at her dad's shouted reply. This was one reason she rarely talked to him on the phone. Calvin Lewis could bust an eardrum.

"No, I'm getting myself a wife," Devin told her father, this time leaning over to press a kiss on her forehead.

"Oh congratulations, Bug, but you could have waited for a more decent time of day to call."

"I would have, but we'll be leaving soon for a trip to New York."

"Okay, good luck. Have a safe trip," Monica heard him bellow and the distinct click of the phone.

Monica laughed as Devin stared at the phone. "Your father's a character."

"True, but you can't help but love him. You have to give him information quick and straight, Dev. Especially if it's early in the morning."

Devin handed her the phone. She dialed. The phone rang once.

"Hello."

"Good morning, Dad."

"Hey, sweetheart, did you have a good time last night?"

"Yes I did. I'm calling to see if you can keep the kids for the rest of the weekend. I'm going to New York to get a ring and a dress."

"New York!" he shouted louder than before.

Monica moved the phone a few inches from her ear, laughing with Devin. "I'm getting married, Daddy."

"To who? No, don't answer that. Bug, right?" he asked, his voice losing the deep timber it carried a second ago.

"Yes."

"When did that happen?"

"Right under your nose," Monica could hear her mother respond.

"Why don't you children tell me anything? Why didn't your mother tell me anything? So you're going to New York," he continued nonstop.

"Just for today. Can you and Mom keep the kids?"

"We'd be more than happy to." Her mother came on the line.

"Devin and I want to tell the them the news. We'll be there in about an hour. Love you both. See you soon." She handed the phone to Devin. "Done."

Devin took the phone and removed the tray. He crawled across the bed to lie down beside her. "It won't be completely done until you're Mrs. Devin Preston," he told her, inching the sheet down to her waist.

"What are you doing?"

"An inspection."

"What kind of inspection?"

"A thorough breast inspection."

"Why?"

"I've been reading about this strange phenomenon that occurs when a woman is pregnant. A woman's breasts become swollen and extremely sensitive," Devin answered. Having exposed them to his view, he grazed a thumb against her nipples as he spoke.

Monica let out a moan. "It's true."

"So I've discovered by the look in your eyes and the sounds coming from deep in your throat. But I need a more tactile approach to this study."

Devin gently held her breasts in the palms of his hands massaging, feeling, and finally kissing each raised nipple.

He suddenly pulled away. "It's all true," he breathed, "and lucky for me."

"Dev," she said, wanting him to discover more.

"Next Saturday, Brown Eyes, I promise. Just keep those eyes hot for me."

"That shouldn't be a problem. These eyes have been burning for you for a long time," she said. She slipped out of bed and headed to the bathroom.

"Everything you need is in there," Devin said. "There are towels, some of that Tropical Blossom soap you like, a toothbrush and toothpaste that has been squeezed from the bottom." He walked up behind her and whispered, "And even some unmentionables."

Monica laughed at his silliness, closing the door on him. It helped to break some of the electrifying tension in the air, which was what he intended, she was certain. The things you could do when you had money, Monica mused as she took in the amount of supplies in the bathroom. She didn't remember seeing any of these things here last night. Devin must have contacted a twenty-four-hour 'we got what you need' store. It was sure to be expensive.

She took a quick shower, dried off and dressed in a light Nike windsuit hanging on a hook near the door. It was white and trimmed in aqua and navy. She pulled on the shorts, leaving the pants and light-weight jacket to bring along with them. There was also a white and aqua striped t-shirt. A pair of matching tennis shoes completed the outfit. Next she found a curling iron that did wonders for her hair.

Monica walked out of the bathroom to find Devin wearing a similar outfit. "I thought these might be comfortable for the plane ride," he was saying. "You can bring a change of clothes or we can buy another outfit while we're there—"

"That's okay, you've bought and will be buying quite enough already. I think I can make do with this today," she said, taking in the way the navy t-shirt filled out his broad shoulders. "I want you to under-stand that I don't expect you to shower me with pres-ents. I don't want you believing that you need to buy things left and right for me or the kids. I do work. I have a good job, and I make money."

Work. Job. He could see another battle ahead. Not that he minded her working, but with the baby coming and three kids to take care of already...one thing at a time, he thought. "I hear what you're saying, Brown Eyes, but I want you to understand that I share my wealth with my family. I have with my mother and brother, and I want to be able to share it with my new family."

"As long as you don't spoil us."

"Deal," he readily agreed. There was bound to be a wide difference in his view of spoiling and Monica's.

Joyce and Calvin Lewis were on the front porch as they pulled in front of the house. They sat side-by-side on a wide wooden swing sipping mugs of coffee.

"The kids are still sleeping," Joyce explained. "They did a movie marathon last night. But don't you two look cute together. Cal, don't they look cute together? They were made for each other."

"Never would have guessed it, Joycie, but you're right as always. Come on up, have a cup of coffee, and let me be the first to say congratulations. I knew you were a good luck charm. I never thought in a million years that Monica would ever get married again."

"Cal!"

"Daddy!"

Devin watched as his future father-in-law looked from his wife to his daughter. "The man's not dumb. I'm sure he knews about Keith."

Joyce shook her head, "Cal, Cal, Cal."

"I meant it as a compliment." Calvin stood to shake Devin's hand. "I'll be proud to have you as a son-in-law."

"Thank you Mr.—Cal," Dev finished, remembering the older man's request from this morning, "but there area a few things I think that you should know about me."

"You've been keeping secrets, son?" Calvin asked.

"Not anything notorious, but something you should know."

"Spill it."

Remembering Monica's advice and never one to hold back, Devin spilled it in a straight forward manner. "I'm a millionaire."

Joyce nodded, Cal grunted, Monica grinned.

Surprised at their lack of response, he elaborated, "You might have seen me on the cover of a magazine or in the newspapers. In the architectural world I'm known as D.J. Preston."

"Good name," Calvin commented, "solid, firm. It fits you."

"I'm glad you think so, Mr. Lewis."

"Cal. I told you before, son. Cal."

"Somehow, Dev, I think my parents already know."

"You were always so smart," Joyce told her daughter. "We found this last night at the grocery store."

Her mother handed Devin a magazine. On the cover was a gorgeous picture of Devin. His well-shaped body was covered by a fashionable double-breasted suit. Slashed across the cover was the question, "Why is our architectural icon in HIDING?"

Devin stared at the cover. "So I'm in hiding," he mused. "I guess in a way, I am. That's a picture of the me I have no desire to be anymore."

He handed the magazine to Monica, who'd been peering over his shoulder. Monica was worth all the fame and potential riches he'd left behind.

"Monica and I discussed this last night. That part of my life is over. I'm no longer interested in being so swamped with demands that I'm unable to help create what I've designed. That's the reason I started the new business with Scott. I won't take your daughter and grandchildren away. In fact, I look forward to being a permanent fixture in this family."

"You already are, Bug," Calvin told him.

"Most definitely," Joyce agreed.

"Speaking of grandchildren," Monica continued, "you're going to be having another one soon."

"You mean two more. Ness is due sometime soon, right, Joycie."

Her mother nodded, a spark of knowledge in her eye.

"Dad, you better make that one more."

"Ness is having triplets!"

"No," Monica let out a breath, "I'm going to have a baby."

"You? What!" he bellowed, then slowly added. "Oh, now I see."

Devin cringed inside. Since when did everyone start using those two words. "I don't think you do, sir," Devin explained. "I've wanted to marry your daughter for some time now. I knew she was special from the moment I set eyes on her. Our pregnancy is just an added bonus."

"Okay, I think I see things better now," Cal grunted. "Joycie, you can explain the rest to me later."

"I intend to," Joyce answered.

"Mommie, Mr. Devin!" Jasmine shouted as she came through the front door. "You look like twins." Hugging her mom, she added. "I like what you're wearing. Can I have one, too?"

"Sure you can, Jazz," Devin promised. "Where are your brothers?"

"Inside watching T.V. Maw-maw Joyce!" she screeched as if she suddenly remembered something. "You should see the giant bowls of cereal Tony and Mark are eating!"

"Well, they'd better eat every bite," Joyce commented. "I told them one bowl," she explained. "I guess they figured out a way to make sure they got a lot."

Everyone walked into the house to find the boys in front of two huge mixing bowls overflowing with cereal.

"Don't you think that's a bit much?" Monica asked them.

"Maw-maw Joyce said one bowl and this is one bowl," Tony explained.

"Don't get smart with me, young man," Devin heard Monica say. He didn't know how she kept a straight face and talked in such a firm voice, when all he wanted to do was laugh. This parenting business was going to be tough.

"Tony said it was okay," Mark wailed. Devin watched as Monica delivered "the look." She was good. He'd have to perfect his own look if he was going to be a good father. Monica did not have to utter another word. The look prompted the desired reaction.

"I'm sorry, Maw-maw Joyce," Tony said, hopping off the chair to get a normal-sized bowl.

"I'm sorry, too," Mark echoed.

Standing next to Joyce, Devin was able to keep a stern look on his face as the boys apologized.

"I love being the grandmother," Joyce whispered to him. "When the parents are here I get to sit back and watch."

As Monica supervised the transfer of cereal into normal-size bowls, Joyce whispered again, "She loves you, you know."

"I know.

"She doesn't realize it."

"I know that, too."

"You'll help her see it," Joyce told him, patting his shoulder.

Having finished his normal-sized bowl of cereal, Tony came over for his triple shake and asked, "Why are you and Mom dressed alike?"

"Yeah, why?" Mark asked, coming over for his turn. "We don't have to leave already, do we?" Tony asked Monica.

"No, you don't," Monica told him, "and this outfit is a gift from Mr. Devin. I guess he liked it so much he got one for himself." She turned to Devin, a secret grin on her face. "We also have some good news to tell you."

"You kids go talk in the den," Joyce advised. "We old folks are going back out to the porch to enjoy a second cup of coffee."

Devin was pleased to find both his hands claimed, one by Mark, the other by Jasmine. Tony moved closer to Monica, putting an arm around her waist, hugging her as they moved into the den.

Devin was concerned with the cautious glances Tony was throwing his way. He obviously sensed something different in the relationship between Devin and his mother.

Tony knew something important was going to happen. Monica could feel it in the tight grip he had around her waist. She hoped he was only nervous because he didn't know what to expect. Monica began to explained, "Mr. Devin and I have been good friends and neighbors for a long while, and we've gotten to know each other very well. We've found that we like each other a lot."

"Like boyfriend and girlfriend?" Jasmine asked.

"Yes, like boyfriend and girlfriend," Devin agreed, winking at Monica. She was glad Devin didn't have to be prompted to participate in the discussion. It was important that they do this together. Monica smiled as Devin reached for Jasmine and placed her on his lap. "Exactly what do you know about boyfriends and girlfriends? You don't have a boyfriend, now do you, Miss Jazz?"

"No, I'm too little. Mommie says I have to wait until I'm sixteen, and that's a lo-o-ong time from now."

"Yes, it is," Monica agreed, pleased with how easily Devin lapsed into teasing her daughter, their daughter soon. Monica was certain that they would accept the news of the marriage with excitement. They all loved Devin.

"Mom?" Tony asked. He scooted closer to her and anxiously peered at Devin on the other side of her. "What did you want to say?"

Monica looked down at her oldest son. He was more than a little anxious. She hadn't anticipated this. The best thing to do was just to say it. "What I want to tell you is that just like some boyfriends and girlfriends get married, Mr. Devin and I are going to get married."

"Then we'll be more than neighbors and friends. We'll be a family," Devin added. His concern for Tony's reaction reached Monica.

"Yippee!" Jasmine yelled, throwing her hands up in the air.

"All right!" Mark shouted, grabbing one of Monica's and then Devin's hand in each of his chubby ones. He jumped up and down, moving their arms to whatever beat was bouncing in his head.

Tony didn't move an inch. His only comment was a whispered, "Oh."

Monica could feel the tension in his body. Of all her children she'd thought Tony would be the happiest. He talked about Devin nonstop and was always asking him question after question. Monica raised her head to Devin's. The same puzzlement was mirrored in his eyes.

"Hey, Tony, what's wrong?" Mark asked, catching his big brother's mood and immediately becoming subdued.

"Oh, nothing," Tony answered, keeping his head down.

"I think it's something," Monica told him.

"I agree," Devin added. He moved to sit on the other side of him.

"Tell us what you're thinking," Monica asked.

"I don't know."

"Okay then, why don't we go through a list of what the problem could possibly be?" Devin suggested.

Jasmine and Mark sat down to hear what problems Mr. Devin was going to list. The expression on their faces suggested that they didn't have a problem.

"Tony probably ate too much cereal," Monica heard Jasmine whisper to Mark, who nodded in agreement.

Monica sat up straight, once again wrapping her arms around her son as Devin began his list of problems.

"Problem number one: I make the worst pancakes in the world. They're so bad even the pigeons won't eat them."

"That's not true," Tony answered, a smile in his voice.

"Then it must be problem number two: I don't know how to have fun. All I do all day is growl and work and tell everybody to stay out of my way."

"Ah-ah," Tony looked up a Devin, "you're one of the funniest grown-ups I know, besides my mom and Auntie Ness and Uncle Scott…"

"A…and everyone of your aunts and uncles, I'll bet," Devin finished for him.

"I guess so." He smiled again, obviously relaxing some more. "You're nice. You helped us build the tree house and let me sit in the big machines at the site and all. I like you, Mr. Devin."

"Then why do you look so sad?" Monica asked.

"It's just—why are you getting married? Who's making you get married?"

"Nobody's making me get married, Tone." Monica was surprised at the question. "Mr. Devin and I want to get married. We care a lot for each other."

"But you said you would never get married again, so somebody must be making you do it."

Tony, her oldest, always in tune to her moods, must have heard her say that dozens of times over the past three years. Monica was sure the conviction in her voice when she repeated it over and over again had come across to him and he'd taken it to heart. Tony believed it as strongly as she had.

"Tony, I think you helped me learn a new lesson."

"I did?"

"Yes, you should never say never. I cared for your dad so much. That's why I thought I would never get married again. But guess what? Now I care for someone else."

"Mr. Devin?"

"Yes, Mr. Devin. Since you like him so much, I think you should let him know that it's okay to marry us, all of us."

"That means he'll be my new dad, right?

"Right."

"And I don't have to forget my real dad?"

"Of course not," Devin answered with a gentle grip on Tony's shoulders. "Those memories are special. There's always room for more."

Monica felt those words directed at Tony were meant to reassure her as well as her son.

Tony leaned closer to Devin and confessed, "I've wanted you to be my new daddy for weeks and weeks, but not if someone was making Mommie marry you."

"Then that settles it," Devin said, rubbing his hands together.

"All right!" Jasmine and Mark shouted, once again celebrating the coming wedding.

CHAPTER 22

Time had passed quickly. It almost seemed impossible that a week had gone by since they'd flown to New York. The shopping expedition in New York's Upper East Side was one of the best times he'd had spending his money. Monica refused to allow him to spend money on anything beyond the ring and the gown. He insisted on keeping his promise to Jasmine, buying her a windsuit with matching shoes as well as and one for each of the boys.

Walking into Tiffany's with his fiancée had been a moment in time worth waiting for. At first they had only been able to get mere glimpses of the famous Tiffany diamond that had been mined in Africa in the late 1800s. The stone's sparkle had been spectacular even through the crowd surrounding the display case. The ninety facets had sparkled brightly, holding people's attention as others vied for a chance for a closer look. Finally making their way up to the display, Devin had stood behind her; together they'd quietly admired this beauty of nature.

When they moved into the store Monica had told him that she would have to be paid to wear a such a huge diamond. Most women would pay to be able to wear the famous Tiffany diamond that Audrey Hepburn wore during a publicity shot for the movie *Breakfast at Tiffany's.* But not Monica, not his Brown Eyes, she'd claimed that the diamond would fall off, roll out of the store and down a manhole to be gobbled up by some alligator living in the sewers.

Devin laughed in remembrance, just as he'd laughed then. He removed the jacket to his tux and unbuttoned his shirt. He sat, then stretched out across the bed, thoughts of his wife easing more laughter from him. Monica was the only woman he knew who wouldn't jump at the chance to wear the famous Tiffany diamond. She was his diamond. Brown Eyes was sparkling with humor and brilliance. Her personality was filled with so many different facets he'd live a lifetime discovering or being challenged by them all.

Devin stretched and laid his hands behind his head. His eyes strayed toward the closed bathroom door where Monica had disappeared not long ago, still in her wedding dress. She was beautiful. Devin closed his eyes, seeing his dream of marrying Monica come true all over again.

They were married in the Pavilion of Two Sisters in City Park, just as she wanted, surrounded by family and friends. The night was warm and clear. The ceremony and reception weren't extravagant, but kept quiet and personal. Devin didn't want to be discovered by the media. He'd gladly announce his marriage sometime in the future, but for now, he wanted privacy.

Father Brett said the mass and united them as a couple. Devin had proudly lifted the wedding ring from the traditional blue box, a hallmark of Tiffany's. He'd handed the box to his brother Joseph not more than five minutes before the ceremony, afraid it would get lost. As usual, Joseph had commented with some wisecrack that Devin ignored.

Devin had handed the powder blue box back to his brother, the best man. His eyes had quickly scanned the front row behind him. He smiled and nodded to his mother. She mouthed the words "I see" with tears in her eyes. Devin had then repeated the words as the priest directed. "With this ring, I thee wed." The engagement ring, a classic Tiffany setting with a round, brilliant cut had sparkled in welcome as he slid the matching platinum wedding band onto Monica's ring finger, signifying their new bond. Not friends, not lovers, but man and wife representing them all.

It was suddenly quiet. The running water stopped.

"Devin," he heard her call. Monica's voice held a hint of seduction. He was up in an instant. This was their wedding night and they were spending it in the Cotton Mill Penthouse, where Monica wanted to stay. Devin wanted to travel, to take her anywhere she wanted to go, but she chose the penthouse. He was more than happy to oblige.

Devin opened the door to find Brown Eyes standing in the middle of the bathroom, perfectly, and he meant perfectly, naked.

"I ran this water for you," she whispered. "I thought you might enjoy a nice warm bath."

Her eyes connected with his as she spoke. They were hot, they were melting as she stepped into the tub. "Well, what do you know, Dev. I'm standing in the middle of your tub this time."

"I can see that," he grinned, enjoying the sultry facet he was discovering.

"Do you want me to get out?" she asked. She raised both eyebrows and lifted one leg out of the tub. The water dripping down her calf to her toes was an unbelievably erotic sight.

"No," he answered, watching the last droplet fall from her toes, at the same time pulling his shirt off. "No way," he affirmed as his pants and underwear came off in one motion. "Absolutely not," he answered, stepping into the tub.

Monica laughed at the speed with which he undressed. The laughter abruptly ended as Devin smoothly maneuvered them into a sitting position. She sat before him, their bodies intimately touching everywhere.

"I'm going to have to time you," Monica breathed into his ear.

"For what," he asked, moving his hips slowly, provocatively against her.

"I want to see," she gasped as he moved again, "exactly how fast you undress. I bet you beat a world's record."

"It's all about incentive, but we'll talk about that later," Devin told her, his lips traveling down her neck creating a meandering, route to her full, perfect breasts. "I've been dreaming about this." He stopped before his lips touched the dark brown tips.

"You have?" she whispered in that same sultry voice.

"Yes, I have Mrs. Preston." He pressed a kiss against the brown tip before him.

"I like that." She let out in a long breath.

"The name or the kiss?" he asked.

"Both."

"Good."

"Dev, show me what you've been dreaming."

"I am. I have been. Be patient, Brown Eyes."

Monica felt both patient and impatient as he made slow, electrifying love to her. In the tub, out of the tub, and eventually on the silk-covered bed. She couldn't remember ever feeling so fulfilled. Not even with Keith. She'd overcome her feelings of betrayal, realizing it was impossible to betray a man who had died three years ago.

Now as she lay in her new husband's arms, a different feeling began to emerge. It was guilt, not the same guilt she'd experienced before. This was one without shame, which somehow made her feel even guiltier. It stemmed from the fact that not only did she enjoy Devin's lovemaking, she absolutely drowned in the electric energy he created for her. Devin's touch, his love, were all that any woman could ask for, which was why she felt guilty.

Stop it, Monica! she demanded. She didn't understand the hows or whys, and she wasn't going to dwell on it, not right now. With an effort she squelched those feelings of guilt, locked them in some unknown part of her mind until she was ready to deal with it. The last thing she wanted to do was ruin her honeymoon weekend.

Monica and Devin woke up the next morning to the sound of growling stomachs. They fed each other crackers until Monica declared it safe to get up without having to rush to the bathroom. Leaving the bed, they both donned matching red silks robes as they went into the kitchen to fuel their bodies.

Devin laid a huge terry cloth blanket on the hardwood floor of the living room as Monica buttered toast and collected breakfast from the fridge. "Fruit, yogurt and whole wheat toast will have to fill us up. I'm afraid I'm not in the mood for cooking."

"Not to worry. I don't want you to take the time to cook. I'll fix a lunch that's out of this world after we've rested up a bit."

"I think we're starting a bad precedent here," Monica stated, eating a spoonful of yogurt and plopping a grape into her mouth.

"Are we?"

"All we do when we stay here is eat and lie around."

"And…" he added expectantly.

"And what?" she asked, a slight challenge in her voice.

At this Davin stood. He dropped his empty yogurt container, the spoon clanging as it hit the floor. Monica took a quick peek as he towered over her, then pretended not to care. She quickly ate a few more spoons of yogurt, knowing from his expressions that it would be a long time before lunch. The last thing she wanted was an empty stomach making her nauseous.

"Brown Eyes, I know you are not seriously asking me that."

Monica stretched her feet. She picked up a bunch of grapes and tried to eat as many as she could without being obvious.

"Another facet, I've discovered," Monica heard him whisper.

"What's that supposed to mean?" She stopped chewing long enough to ask.

"Not a thing. I'll give you one more chance to finish the sentence. A-n-n-d…"

"And I don't know," she answered, tossing the rest of the grapes into the bowl and carefully standing. That's as far as she got. Devin lifted her into his arms and carried her straight to the bedroom, just like she wanted him to.

Two hours later, Devin sleepily pulled her toward him, snuggling her spoon-fashion into his arms. "And what?" he asked again.

Satisfied with the end of the game, Monica answered without missing a beat, "And making love to me until I'm completely drained and all I want to do is sleep in your arms until we..."

"Make love again?" Devin asked.

"Eat again," she answered, filling the room with her deep laughter when he grunted.

"I'm too worn out to respond to that right now, Brown Eyes. Sleep, you're going to need it."

They didn't move until a delivery man from Commander's Palace rang at the door to the lobby. Devin went to collect the food.

That night when Monica made love to Devin she felt a desperate need to savor each spark that ignited between them. Each touch was important and had to be remembered. In some corner of her mind Monica knew that once they left the penthouse she'd have to fight harder to keep her memories of Keith at bay.

The penthouse was exclusively theirs, hers and Devin's. It was here that she felt free to show her love to Devin. Without a doubt, she loved him, though she was having trouble telling him that. But she did. How else could he have broken through the barriers she'd created?

Much later Monica lay awake, on her side, gazing at her sweet husband. She traced his eyebrows and moved up to trace the beginnings of a receding hairline. She smiled in remembrance of the day she first saw him. D'Juan had been with her. Was that significant or coincidental? At the reception D'Juan had insisted that she was Monica's personal cupid, destined to lead her to the loves of her life. Would Monica have noticed Devin that day without her friend's help. Yes, she admitted, if not that day, eventually.

Monica traced his lips, as smooth as the words that come out of them when he was trying to maneuver his way into or out of a situation, his arrogant, pushy ways bittersweet because there was always a good, honest reason behind them.

Monica laid her head against his warm chest. The tight curls of hair tickling her ear. "I love you, Devin," she whispered almost to herself. "I'll tell you soon, I promise." Having said what was in her heart she instantly drifted off.

Devin's eyes opened, then closed. In his head he performed a dance that would have rivaled anything anyone from Chuck Berry to Michael Jackson could have choreographed.

CHAPTER 23

"No bay leaf or thyme. No file, not even any salt and pepper," Monica muttered as she went through the pantry in Devin's kitchen. She was making gumbo for their first dinner together as a family. Monica knew how much Devin enjoyed gumbo on his regular Sunday visits to her parents' house. She was going to make every effort she could to ease into the role as Devin's wife.

"Jasmine, Mark, Tony!" she called out into the yard. Monica grabbed a bag of groceries full of ingredients for a delicious seafood gumbo. The kids had helped her bring the groceries inside. She had bought only the main ingredients because she always had a good supply of seasoning in stock. Devin had none. If she was going to make gumbo she might as well do it next door where the other ingredients were. Her gumbo pot was there and she didn't particularly like the idea of using Devin's electric stove.

They had decided to live temporarily in Devin's house, which made more sense because it was bigger.

Monica was planning on renting her half of the house. The house she and Keith spent so much time remodeling. She was moving on. Monica was even going as far as leaving it completely furnished, the children's furniture and all.

Before the wedding the children had each chosen new bedroom furniture. The bedroom sets should have been delivered and set up the Friday before they got married, but were now four days late. Something obviously happened to the shipment.

The kids helped her bring the groceries next door, running outside to finish whatever game they were playing. Before Monica could get inside her neighbor called out, "How ya doing there, girl?"

"Hello there, Mr. Reaux."

"What are you doing here? I thought you were moving next door since you married that nice boy."

"I am. I just needed some things from inside."

"I won't keep you. I'm going to miss ya, though."

"I'm going to miss you too, Mr. Reaux."

"Call if you need me, hear?"

His front door slammed. Monica was going to miss his daily greetings.

She put the groceries in the kitchen and dug through a cardboard box until she found her gumbo pot. She searched through another box until she found the seasonings. Everything was packed and ready to move next door.

As Monica walked around her kitchen beginning to prepare the meal she felt a knot in her stomach begin to unravel. She suddenly realized that more than cooking on a familiar stove and her seasonings had brought her here. Monica began chopping onions and making a dark roux for the gumbo from a mixture of flour and oil. The tension in her shoulders began to ease. Just like the knot in her stomach, she hadn't noticed it was there. Thinking back, Monica realized that it had begun the moment she walked into Devin's house as Mrs. Preston with her three kids and the luggage from their honeymoon weekend.

"Brown Eyes," Devin had said, "do whatever you want, make any changes you want. We'll be living here for a while, at least until *our house* is built."

That was another decision they'd made. Devin was going to design a house for them, with everyone's ideas included, of course. He'd left to visit his work site at her insistence. She needed some space. The idea of building a new life with Devin and the possibility of enjoying it too much were the things that had her running next door.

Gumbo simmering, rice cooked and french bread warming in the oven, Monica called the kids inside to wash up. It was after six and Devin had said he'd be home by five with some help to move the boxes. The phone rang. Wondering what was keeping him, Monica absently picked up the receiver.

"Monica, what are you doing there?" Ness's voice rang in her ear.

"What do you mean, what am I doing here? Where else am I supposed to be?" Monica answered, thinking she'd forgotten an appointment or something.

"You're supposed to be in your new house. Where you now live with your brand new husband."

"That's right," she answered, embarrassed that she'd forgotten.

"Now I understand why Bug couldn't get in touch with you."

"Devin was trying to call? I was wondering what could have happened to him. He was supposed to be back an hour ago."

"Scott, too. I got a call from my husband and my new brother-in-law. They're both stuck in traffic."

"Oh."

"There's been an accident on the Twin Span."

"Is anyone hurt?" Monica asked, moving to grab her keys and purse, her heart in her throat.

"No, Monica. I didn't mean to scare you. Both the guys are fine. The accident had something to do with an eighteen-wheeler. Traffic's at a standstill."

"Why didn't Devin call?" Monica asked her sister, her heart inching back to where it belonged.

"He's been trying all afternoon."

"You did say that," she sighed.

"I guess he didn't figure that you would move back to your old house after only three days of marriage," Ness joked, unintentionally hitting a nerve.

"Don't be ridiculous, Ness. I was only cooking dinner. All my things are still over here. I guess he didn't think to try calling my house."

"No, but I did." Vanessa paused a minute and asked, "Monica, are you sure you're only there to cook?"

"What other reason would I have?"

"I don't know. Just go call your husband and let him know you're okay," Ness said, a hint of exasperation in her voice. "He sounded worried."

"I will, see you tomorrow."

If she were going to call Devin, Monica had to go next door to get his car phone number from the door of the fridge. He'd written it on one of Prestway's business cards for her this morning.

She took the french bread out of the oven and reminded the kids to wash up before going next door to get the number.

The phone rang as soon as she walked into the house.

"Brown Eyes! Thank God! I thought something had happened to you. I've been calling everywhere. Where have you been?"

"Next door," she cautiously answered, feeling guilt over running to her old house for comfort.

"Next door? All afternoon? Why?"

"I'm cooking gumbo, I needed my gumbo pot and…" she trailed off.

"I understand," he told her softly. "I should have stayed home with my new family. The traffic's moving at a snail's pace. There's no telling when I'll be home."

"I'm sorry I convinced you to go."

"I'm sorry I listened. I miss you."

"Me too," she answered, wanting to be with him as much as she wanted him away earlier.

"That's good to know," he whispered into the phone. Then more loudly. "Don't try to move any of those boxes yourself. Brooks and Stephens will have to take care of them tomorrow."

"I won't," Monica promised.

"So you made gumbo."

"Just for you."

"Does it taste good?"

"I don't know, I haven't eaten any yet." Using the cordless phone she walked to the back of the house and peeped out the window. She could see into the kitchen and den next door. The kids were watching TV.

"How about you?"

"Me?" she asked, caught off guard.

"Do you still taste good?"

"I don't know, Dev," she laughed. "I'm not in the habit of tasting myself."

"I'll find out for myself as soon as I get out of this traffic. I love you, Brown Eyes," he said. A click immediately followed. He'd disconnected before Monica realized it. He wasn't expecting a response; Devin knew he wasn't going to get one. It hurt to do that to him.

"Me too," she whispered. Talking to Devin had reassured her. She would go next door, bring dinner over, and eat with the kids in their new house.

Monica walked back into her old house to find the table completely set with the bowls she'd left on the counter, napkins and spoon. The children were calmly eating french bread.

"Surprise!" they yelled.

"I'm starvin', let's eat!" Mark suggested, french bread crumbs falling from his chin.

So much for moving next door for dinner. After dinner Tony, Jasmine and Mark helped to clean the kitchen. Monica still had every intention of going back to Devin's house, but making love to Devin for most of the night before, keeping busy all day and her pregnancy had her eyes drooping. She'd lie down in her room for just a minute and then they'd all go back to Devin's house before he got back home. She dragged herself into the bedroom and was fast asleep in no time.

Devin pulled into the driveway beside Monica's truck, a puzzled look on his face. The house was in total darkness. Eight o'clock was a little early for everyone to be in bed. A glance to his right gave him all the explanation he needed. The house next door was blazing. He'd thought Monica would be back at their house by now. He didn't want to spend their first night together as a family in Keith's house. It wasn't that he wanted to deny that Keith had been

Monica's husband and the kids' natural father. The problem was that he needed the opportunity to develop a place for himself in their lives, and it couldn't begin there.

Devin felt like an outsider as he knocked on the door. Mark's round, curly-topped face peered at him through the window.

"Mr. Devin's home!" He opened the door.

"All right, you finally made it!" Tony yelled, coming to greet him.

"Mr. Devin, you're late!" Jasmine told him, her hands on her little hips.

Mark paused, his hands mid-air, a thoughtful expression on his face as he stopped in the middle of the triple shake.

"Something wrong?" Devin asked.

"No, I was just thinking."

"How about thinking out loud. I might be able to help," Devin encouraged.

"Shouldn't we call you Mr. Dad or something? You are our new dad, right?"

"Not Mr. Dad, just plain Dad, or Daddy," Jasmine told Mark.

"But only if you say it's okay," Tony insisted.

Three hopeful faces staring up at him made a lie of his feelings of being an outsider. "All right is what

I say!" Devin answered, using the boys' favorite expression and sealing the agreement with the traditional triple shake with each happy child.

"Where's your mom?" Devin asked as he lifted Jazz, who without any reserve whatsoever, had stretched her hands out to him. As reward, he received the sweetest of hugs.

"Well, Daddy," she whispered. "This is gonna sound weird, but Mommie's sleeping again. The Rugrats aren't even off yet," she added with a shake of her head, as if she couldn't believe it.

"Why don't I wake her up with a kiss."

"We'll help you," Mark yelled, running toward Monica's old bedroom.

"Wait, Mark," Jasmine warned, jumping out of Devin's arms attempting to stop him. "Let Daddy kiss her first."

"I think it's too late," Devin said, passing a hand across Tony's closely-cut hair.

"I know, Mark is loud." Tony stopped long enough to tell Devin, "I'm glad you're my new dad. I missed having one. I'm sure glad Mom changed her mind about getting married."

Devin's heart swelled with the reception he received from his new sons and daughter. Maybe Monica had a good reason for being over here still.

That thought and the fullness in his heart immediately deflated with the first word that came from Monica's lips.

"Daddy's home! Daddy's home! Daddy's home!" Monica heard sung in her ear over and over again. Was that Tony? No, it sounded like Mark. Tony used to sing that song every evening when his dad came home. Monica rolled over. She'd been exhausted, she was still exhausted. The room was dark. Trying to clear the cobwebs out of her head she pushed up on her elbows and found two of her children at the foot of the bed.

"Mom, Daddy's home," one of the them said, pointing to the doorway.

Monica tried to focus her eyes on the two silhouettes near the door. Confused and groggy she asked, "Keith?"

The room suddenly filled with light. Immediately realizing what she'd done, Monica froze in shock at the huge mistake she'd made.

She couldn't bring herself to look up at Devin, instead focusing on the kids who were now all standing at the foot of the bed staring at her. Only Mark felt the need to correct her mistake.

"It's our new daddy, Mommie. The old Mr. Devin."

If she weren't so shocked, Monica would have laughed at how cute he sounded. Instead all she could say was, "I know, sweetie."

Forcing herself to look up, Monica's eyes sought Devin's for understanding. He wouldn't look at her.

"Kids, why don't you go finish watching the Rugrats. Your mom and I need to talk," Monica heard him suggest in a light tone. He closed the door behind the children. His face wore a ragged expression. He let out a huge breath. "It's me, Devin. You might wish that it was Keith standing in this doorway, but it's not."

He took a step toward her. Monica could see the hurt in his eyes, the pain she'd caused.

"Devin, I'm—"

"No, whatever you do, don't say you're sorry." He was across the room in no time, sitting on the bed beside her. "Just know that I'm Devin Preston, and that I am your husband."

"I know that."

"Really? Than why is my new wife, my new family, in the house of your first husband?"

"I don't know," she admitted. "I was scared. There were so many changes happening so fast, and there were so many reasons for me to come over that before I knew it, we were here all day."

"I see," he answered.

"I don't think you do. After a while, I realized that I had been making excuses to be here."

"And?"

"And I planned on going back to your house—"

"Our house."

"That's what I meant."

"Then say it, Brown Eyes! Our house."

Those words shouldn't be hard to say, but somehow they stuck in her throat. When she'd said 'our house' in the past it had always been in reference to this house. The house she and Keith had worked so hard to repair. The house they had lived in as a family. Monica looked into Devin's face, her new beginning. The words 'our house' could mean something special for them too, an opportunity to make new memories.

"I planned on going to our house," she emphasized, hoping she hadn't waited too long to say it. "But the kids were hungry and had already set the table, and then I fell asleep. I was so tired after last night," she said, hoping a reminder of their honeymoon would change his mood. She didn't like to see him with so much sadness in his eyes.

"I see," he answered, focusing his gaze on her, the sadness quickly being replaced by what looked like arrogant determination.

Monica relaxed. This was more like the Devin she knew. "Dev, you've said that twice," she teased.

"What?"

"I see."

His eyes widened. "I am not turning into my mother."

"I don't think you'll have that problem," she said reaching over to caress the muscles in his arms. "Ever."

Devin stood up. He was obviously still upset by her slip earlier. She'd explained her reasons for being here, but could she blame the man for still being upset? Reversing roles, Monica imagined what her reaction might have been. A huge knot of jealousy immediately twisted inside her stomach. Devin didn't deserve this.

Suddenly the framed wedding portrait of herself and Keith gently landed on her lap. Monica always kept it on her nightstand. What was going on in his head? she wondered.

"I've only been in this room one other time, and that night I didn't notice this picture. Do you keep it there all the time?"

"Yes."

"Did you plan on taking it to our house to sit in our bedroom?"

"No, I was going to give it to Jazz."

"Sounds like a good idea," He rubbed his hand down his face.

Monica waited. She knew there was more to come. "He was a good looking man," Devin grunted, "as far as a man can admit."

"So are you."

"He's got curly hair like Mark's," he continued, as if he hadn't heard her, "and skin the same complexion as your mother."

"Yes."

"We're almost complete opposites."

"Is that significant?"

"It could be. That's something, at least. I'm relieved that Keith is so different from me, but in light of tonight, I'm confused. How could you mistake me for him?"

"I told you already, I was sleepy and confused, and the kids were calling you Daddy—"

Monica stopped. "The kids were calling you Daddy."

"It was their idea." He sat on the edge of the bed again. "They already have a place for me in their lives. I need you to find one too."

"Oh, Dev."

"It's true. You've let me into a tiny crack of your heart, but I want more."

"You deserve more. I told you before we got married…I'm trying."

"Together we're going to try even harder. We're going to fix this. Tonight we're going to sleep in this bed with that picture of you and Keith staring at us all night long, and you're going to tell me everything you need or want to reveal about him. Keith needs to be out in the open."

"But why?" she asked, bewildered. It seemed beyond strange for him to want to know about Keith. He'd already admitted to being jealous of him.

"Monica, have you ever had a deep-down, soul-searching talk about Keith since he died?"

"Well—"

"Before you answer," he moved in closer to her, his deep voice demanding her full attention, "I don't mean the many times you've sworn never to get married again or repeated a funny story about him. I want to know if you have ever talked, really talked about your life with him, how he made you feel. How you felt before and after he died."

"No, not really," she quietly admitted, not sure she ever wanted to.

"Then we will. Together."

"But this isn't normal!"

"What's not normal, Brown Eyes," he told her, pulling her into his arms, "is this obsession you have for Keith. I don't want to banish him from your heart. I only want you to share what you had with him so you can find a place for me...for us."

With that he stood and kissed her forehead. When he got to the door Monica asked, "Where are you going?"

"To get the kids started on their baths so we can have some uninterrupted time together. Is there a certain way you do this?"

"They take turns in the bathroom. I think it's Jasmine's turn to go first," she answered. "And we were reading *The Stories Julian Tells.*"

Devin smiled at that. "Do you read with them every night?"

"Yes."

"I'd like to join you if you don't mind."

"No, not at all. The kids would like that."

"Why don't we show a united front, walk out there together, to show the kids that everything's okay. Then maybe we could have a bowl of that delicious gumbo I've been smelling."

"I'd like that." Monica reached for his outstretched hand. At the door she stopped to glance back at the framed portrait and then again at Devin. She had a feeling that tonight they would erase that last layer of resistance.

Devin knew that discussing Keith with him was going to be awkward for Monica, but he would ease her into it, help her relax. He suggested they take a shower together. Devin and Monica took turns washing each other, and despite the heat between them, they did not make love. Devin, with one last intense look, left the bathroom, grabbing a towel on the way out.

Making love was not on tonight's agenda. If they got Keith out in the open and then made love here before moving next door, Devin would be more certain of their future together. He slowly dried the droplets of water from his body as he envisioned that future. They'd share many evenings similar to this one: getting the kids ready for bed, reading a book together, giving and receiving goodnight hugs and kisses. Then they'd end the night in each other's arms.

Monica came out of the bathroom smelling like tropical blossoms and wearing a t-shirt nightgown. Although Monica wore it, Devin knew, in an attempt to douse a little of the sexual tension between them, it wasn't working. It wasn't going to work. He already knew what was under the gown, and had no problem bringing up a visual imagine.

Devin slipped between the sheets and invited her inside.

Monica protested, "Dev, you don't have any clothes on."

"I know, they're all next door."

"You didn't complain yesterday."

"That was different. This door doesn't have a lock. What if one of the kids comes in?"

"They do know how to knock if the door is closed, right?"

"Yes, Keith always…"

"Don't stop, Brown Eyes," he encouraged, pulling her closer to him. "Keith…" he waited, and when she didn't continue, said "see, I said his name without turning into a green-eyed monster. Keith does not threaten me. It's the memories that you keep locked up inside your heart with no room for anything else that threaten me. Let them go, Brown Eyes," he pleaded. "It's me, your friend, your husband, you can tell me anything."

Monica discovered that she could. She lay back against Devin's strong, hard chest and with encouragement and gentle probing shared memories of her first husband. At times he laughed at something she'd say or became intense as he listened. He held her tight when she surprised herself with a string of 'damn its' after reliving the day Keith died. He caressed her arms and pushed her hair back to rain kisses on her forehead as she cried for herself three years ago.

She had cried then, at the hospital where she identified his body, at the funeral, and even in this bed, but not like this. Those were silent, careful tears. Tonight in Devin's arms, she let out the agonizing moans of a woman whose hurt had run so deep that this was the only path to relieving the pain. Through it all, Devin held her and repeated over and over again, "I'm here, Brown Eyes. It's me, Devin, your husband."

Monica fell into a deep sleep. Soft hiccups accompanied the deep breaths she took as she slept. Devin felt a tremendous sense of relief and thought he could feel the same in Monica. He had never seen her so relaxed. There had always been a tension in her body, even during their honeymoon weekend, even when she slept. It was gone, as well as the tiny doubts in the back of his mind as to whether he had done the right thing.

Always a man of action, Devin had followed his instincts. He'd been afraid to learn more about Keith. After all, dead or alive, the man was his competition. Now Devin was relieved to find that he was just a man. A man who took the responsibilities of caring for his wife and kids seriously, but a man just the same.

There was a surprising feeling of gratitude as well. Devin was grateful that Keith had loved and cared for Monica, grateful that he was a good father to his children. Devin made a promise to himself to make certain that Keith's children remembered him and he would not deny the fact that some part of Monica would always love Keith. As long as Monica opened her heart to him, he could not begrudge her those feelings.

With that last thought Devin pulled Monica tighter in his embrace, falling asleep with her warm body cradled against him.

Devin opened his eyes, wide awake in an instant. Monica moaned in her sleep, turning her head one way then the other. Her hand brushed against his bare chest, grazing a flat nipple. She made another soft moan, slowly inching her body until she was on top of him, covering him completely.

Devin's eyes widened. This was a nice predicament. Of course it was *déjà vu* all over again, but he liked it. His body was hard and ready. Monica was soft and warm where his fingers touched. Her whole body moved against his. The t-shirt nightgown was all the way up to her waist. Had he pushed it up that far? When she slowly sat up, peeled the cotton night gown off and threw it to the other side of the room, he knew it wasn't his doing.

Monica stared at him with those warm, warm eyes communicating her intent. She'd made love to him before, but tonight she was going to *make love* to him.

Monica leaned forward and traced each thick eyebrow with her thumbs. "You are beautiful, Devin, from the outside in, and inside out."

"Thanks," he whispered, lying as still as before, wanting her to do as she pleased. His entire being, his heart and soul, was tense in anticipation. Her body was like water in motion, warm water in motion. She moved all over him, touching, exploring.

This time Monica wasn't simply a participant; she was the catalyst, and he wanted her to explore. Devin was barely hanging in there. He knew he wouldn't last long once Monica decided to free him from his misery. She guided him inside her and three seconds later they both came apart. She'd made love to him. Really made love to him, in Keith's bedroom. Devin was overwhelmed.

He rolled her beneath him, and hugged her to him repeating over and over again, "I love you, Brown Eyes, I love you."

"I do, too," she answered before they both fell asleep.

CHAPTER 24

The phone rang, waking Devin a whole lot earlier than he intended. As a matter of fact, he'd planned on skipping work altogether for the rest of the week. There was nothing happening that Scott couldn't handle. "What?" he asked when he finally found the phone on the opposite nightstand.

"What are you doing there?" Scott asked by way of greeting. "I tried calling your house but didn't get an answer. Nessa said to call you at Monica's. Did she change her mind about moving?"

"Not exactly," Devin grunted, still not completely awake.

"Okay, I'll let you go with that for now, brother-in-law. Sorry I had to call so early, Mr. Newlywed, but I just opened a very interesting letter addressed to the Prestway Corporation. I picked it up on the way out yesterday with the other mail but didn't get a chance to look at it until now. Since I have a pregnant wife keeping me awake at night because she can't sleep, what else should I do but paperwork?"

"You could rub my back," Devin heard Ness request over the phone.

"See what you have to look forward to, Bug?"

Devin chuckled, "About the letter?" He knew it had to contain some serious information for Scott to call at five in the morning.

"We may have ourselves a potential problem."

"Wait a minute," Devin said, getting out of the bed. Scott sounded worried. They hadn't heard anything more from T.J. since they'd begun building. Devin had hoped he'd given up on harassing them.

Jumping into his shirt and pants from yesterday, Devin took the cordless phone out into the hall, even though he doubted he would wake Monica. She was sleeping like a completely satisfied woman.

"So, what's in the letter?" Devin asked.

"The North Shore Civic Organization is coming for a visit."

"Why?"

"They have concerns about the types of buildings we're constructing in their community."

"What kind of concerns?"

"They aren't specific, but they are prepared to protest and I quote, our 'lewd and morally corrupt influence.' "

"Constructing homes in a residential neighborhood is lewd and morally corrupt? That makes no sense."

"I agree, but you know whose hands have to be elbow-deep in this?"

"T.J.'s."

"Who else could it possibly be, Bug?"

"No one else." They were within zoning laws, everything was moving along smoothly. The last thing Devin felt like doing was butting heads with a civic organization. "I wonder what kind of crap T.J. told these people to get them all riled up?"

"We're going to find out today," Scott answered. "This letter says that they'll be at the site at ten o'clock. They are willing to discuss the situation."

"I planned on taking the rest of the week off."

"I figured as much. You shouldn't have come in at all," Scott told him. "The two of you are okay, right?"

"We're getting there."

"Nessa was worried."

"Tell her not to. I'm taking care of her big sister."

"I guess I'll see you at work then?"

"I'll be there by seven. I want to keep a lookout for T.J. If he set this up, I'm sure he'll be around somewhere to witness the action."

He wrote a note to Monica, leaving it on her pillow as he kissed her goodbye. He peeked in on the kids and found them all to be fast asleep. Devin stopped at the front door, at the last minute deciding to leave each of the kids a note, then went next door to change.

Devin closed the pregnancy book he'd been reading for the last fifteen minutes. All morning he'd been making rounds at the site, hoping to spot T.J. If he was around, he'd hidden himself well. Devin was disgusted. He hadn't wanted to leave Monica today. He was hoping to wake up to the words 'I do, too,' changing to 'I love you.' "

Devin glanced at his watch. It was after ten. He wanted this to be over with so he could get back home to his wife and kids. If those civic-minded people didn't show up in the next ten minutes he was leaving.

Devin stood and stretched, trying to relieve the tension in his neck and shoulders. He walked out of the trailer, his eyes scanning the grounds for Scott. He was taking a turn searching the site.

"Excuse me."

Inside, Devin jumped. He really was tense. He'd been concentrating so hard on the wide field before him he hadn't heard the three men approach.

"Can I help you?" Devin asked, showing an outward calm he didn't feel. He was certain these three men were representatives of the North Shore Civic Organization. Looking toward the site entrance, Devin spotted a line of cars, vans, trucks and Suburbans parked along the road. People began pouring out of the vehicles, pulling signs out behind them: 'No French Quarter Here', 'No Bourbon Street Drunks', were the only two signs Devin could read. His eyebrows rose. These people meant business. The question was, what exactly was their business?

The speaker, a man dressed all in black like a minister, noticed the direction of Devin's gaze and turned to see what had caught his attention. The minister's face turned as red as the roots of his hair. He reminded Devin of a real life Howdy Doody. Was the man embarrassed or angry? Maybe both.

"Give us a moment," the minister said. The three men moved a few feet away and began a heated discussion. Devin couldn't help overhearing.

"Luke," the minister said forcefully, "there was no need for demonstrators today."

"I don't agree, Rev," the steely-eyed man in the three piece suit answered. "We've got signs and volunteers, Prestway needs to know what they're up against. We won't stand for weirdoes and drunks moving into our neighborhood."

Three-piece suit glared at Devin. This guy was the one he was going to have trouble with, Devin knew. The Reverend sounded reasonable, and the other man, dressed in dark pants and a polo shirt with the logo of a local bank, stared at him with a perplexed look on his face.

Devin stood his ground, continuing to listen to and study his adversaries. When a group of overzealous people got together there was a potential for danger. For now the milling crowd was quiet. People were lounging on the ground, even using their signs as ground cover.

Polo-shirt-guy was dividing his attention between the argument and Devin. Mr. Three-piece kept a suspicious eye on Devin, as if he were a major threat to him.

Devin had had enough. He was wasting precious time listening to this foolishness. It was time for it to end.

T.J. swallowed the rest of his micro-brewed beer. He grinned as he watched the action begin. It had taken him weeks to think up this plan. Preston was chummy with so many people T.J. had found his little interferences blocked from every direction. His poem and the shipment had been his only successes so far. What was it about that nigger that made so many people like him?

T.J.'s plan had taken him as far as following the foreman. What was his name...Harris? T.J. had followed that pathetic man Harris to a local bar hoping to bribe him into causing a few minor disasters. But damn it all, he showed the same kind of loyalty as those fools in Mississippi. Harris had gone on and on about Prestway. T.J. couldn't stomach it and had left the man talking to his beer.

T.J. leaned back against the tree trunk, fuming. Scott, his one-time friend and associate, was now partners with that black man. T.J. wasn't surprised. It had all started the minute Scott got involved with that Vanessa woman, the wrong color woman. T.J. had tried to save him, but Scott turned on him. So now, both Scott and Preston were going to get what they deserved. He was too smart for them. T.J. had seen them searching for him. The stupid fools never thought to look up. The sturdy branches of the huge oak and the Spanish moss created a perfect hiding place. He'd been sitting here since six A.M.

T.J. studied the scene. The protestors were standing and waving their signs. This was looking good. Then Preston walked up to the three men huddled together. Before he could blink an eye, the crowd settled down. Everyone was shaking hands. Then he spotted Scott walking up to the group. Preston was the only black spot in the midst of respectable people, and he looked as if he had the audacity to make introductions.

T.J. watched the group of men walk toward the crowd of protestors. In a flash they were loading the signs and then themselves into the parked vehicles and were gone. Scott, Preston and the three men went into the trailer. Enraged and forgetting where he was, T.J. leaned forward, nearly falling out the tree.

What had happened? He had to do something, but first he needed a drink. T.J. frantically climbed down the tree, not caring if he was spotted as he jumped the last few feet to the ground. He zig-zagged drunkenly to his car which he had hidden more than five blocks away. "What happened? What went wrong?" He kept repeating.

Devin used his silver tongue to clear the hostility in the air. The fact that Mr.-Polo-Shirt-Guy had recognized him as the designer for his aunt's castle, one of his first replicas, brought Devin's name and reputation out in the open. Hence, the three men's willingness to discuss the issue and realize that they were on the same team.

The North Shore Civic Organization was, of course, misinformed by an anonymous source.

"You received an anonymous tip in the mail?" Scott asked. "You mean, on the basis of one letter you came ready with signs and protestors?"

"We already know who's responsible for this," Devin stated.

"The North Shore Civic Organization did exactly what he hoped it would do," Scott added.

"What are you saying? That we've been tricked?" Dave, the polo-shirt-guy, asked.

"That's exactly what we're saying," Devin answered. "But we have a copy of the blueprints. They show designs for bars and striptease clubs . . ."

Luke, the three-piece suit guy, sounded unsure of his evidence.

"If you have them with you, we can settle this right now," Scott announced, walking to his desk and pulling out the blueprints for the subdivision.

"I don't like the idea of being used," the Reverend said, placing a long, cylinder-shaped container on Scott's desk.

"We don't care for being the brunt of lies and false accusations," Devin said.

Thirty minutes later the three men left the trailer, a new bond developing between the North Shore Civic Organization and the Prestway Corporation.

CHAPTER 25

Monica stretched, slowly waking from a deep sleep. She felt really good this morning. There was such an intense feeling of relief she decided to lie back and get lost in it. Monica hadn't felt this good—this free—since Keith died.

Keeping her eyes closed, Monica stretched again and reached for the firm, athletic body that should be sleeping next to her. Instead her fingers came in contract with a piece of paper on the pillow next to hers. The pillow that used to be Keith's. Now Devin's imprint was on it, and she didn't feel any twinge of guilt. Today she was a guilt-free woman.

Disappointed at not being able to share this with Devin, Monica opened the folded piece of paper.

There's a minor emergency at work, otherwise I'd have never left you.

I love you always,

Devin

Not more than a second after she read the note Mark flew into the bedroom, his body springing ahead of the hand he used to open the door. His other arm was waving back and forth. A piece of paper was crushed by the tight grip he had on it.

"Mommie, look what I have! It's a letter! It's from my new daddy! Look it says Dad, D-a-d. That spells dad."

Relieved that she was completely covered Monica told her excited son, "That's something I'd like to see, but," she remind him, "you need to go into the hall, close the door and knock again."

"I forgot," he giggled, and ran back into the hall. "Knock, knock, knock," he called as he banged on the door.

"Who can that be knocking on my door?" Monica asked. She got out of the bed to put on her robe and then dived back under the covers.

"It's me, Mommie, Mark," he yelled.

"Then come on in!"

Mark walked in all smiles. "You are a silly Mommie."

"I know. Now let's take a look at that note."

Devin was so sweet. He'd left a note for each of the kids. Tony and Jasmine came in while Monica read Mark's note. After sharing what Devin wrote to each of them, Monica suggested, "Let's get out of this bed and get ready for swim lessons."

Monica dressed and walked out of the bedroom, stopping now and then, her eyes fixed on a certain part of each room, reliving a memory. They were precious to her and weren't going to leave her because she was moving. Taking in the boxes spread all around the house, Monica made a decision. She was going to have everything moved this morning, before Devin got home. She was going to show him how ready she was to start a new life with him.

Monica picked up the phone to recruit the help of her neighbors from across the street. A few weeks ago her neighbor had been complaining about how lazy her sons were getting this summer. At the ages of thirteen and fourteen they were too old for camp and too young for work. Monica would put them to work today.

Finishing her arrangements on the phone, Monica went to check on the kids. Tony and Mark were creating a mess as they dug through a box of clothes searching for their swimsuits. Monica quickly found them on the top of the mound and told them to get dressed. She went to help Jasmine with a similar problem.

Breakfast, she thought, as her stomach started to act up for the first time today. Yesterday she'd bought yogurt and fruit with the gumbo fixings and stored them in the fridge. She set out the yogurt, grapes, and orange slices for the kids at each of the stools. She was finishing off a cracker when the doorbell rang.

"Good morning, Miss Monica, you have a job for us?" Dwayne, the older child, asked.

"And how much does it pay?" Lance, the younger of the two, asked.

"Man, you are so rude!" Dwayne told his brother with a look of disgust. "Whatever you can pay us will be fine, Miss Monica. We should do it as a wedding present."

"No, I don't mind paying you, and how much depends on how fast you can move these boxes."

"Is that all? We can handle that," Lance assured her.

"Good," she answered, directing her gaze to Lance, the more outrageous of the two. "But before you do anything I suggest that you tie your shoes."

They all looked down at his shoes. The double set of laces was loose and hanging.

"That's the style, Miss Monica."

"Not when you're working for me. I don't want to have to take a trip to the hospital."

"I get your point."

Shoes tied, Monica directed them to start moving the boxes in the living room. She carried the lighter ones. She imagined the look on Devin's face if he caught her carrying any of these boxes, then blocked it out of her mind. These boxes were light.

By the time she'd made a few trips the kids were finished with breakfast. Monica assigned them the job of unloading the boxes full of pots, pans and cooking supplies.

Her tenant peeked his head past the security bars for the first time to ask, "Do you need any help, girl?"

"No thanks, Mr. Reaux. I'm working these two young men here."

"Call me if you need me."

"I will," she smiled up at him.

Lance and Dwayne had finished moving the boxes in less than an hour. All she had to do was move the pot of gumbo from the fridge. She paid them, adding a bonus since she was satisfied with how well they'd handled the boxes.

Pleased with this morning's work, Monica placed a miniature grandfather clock on a small table in her new living room. Noticing the time, she called Ness to let her know they'd be going to swim lessons this morning.

Ness picked up the phone after the first ring. "It's about time you made it to the right house."

"I'm going to pretend that I don't know what you're talking about," Monica told her, remembering that Ness had caller ID. "Just don't tell Devin or Scott anything if you happen to hear from them."

"You sound excited."

"I am. Ness, I want to thank you."

"For what?"

"That little push you gave me a few weeks ago."

"Did you think I was going to miss out on such a golden opportunity to play big sister for a change?"

"It was a strange experience, but I needed it," Monica laughed into the phone. "Just don't think you're going to get away with it again."

Ness laughed too. "O-h-h-h-h."

"You okay?"

"Just one of those aches and pains you get near the end."

"You're probably closer to the end than you think. You know twins come early," Monica reminded her.

"That's what I'm hoping for," Ness grunted. "The doctor said the babies have really grown in the last two weeks, and if they came early she was sure they'd be fine."

"Ah, but you can hold out, Ness. What's another week or two?"

"Just wait until you're eight months pregnant. I want to be there to witness you waddling around carrying triplets."

"Triplets, not that again. You're going too far."

"Maybe, maybe not."

"I had my other kids one at a time."

"That doesn't mean a thing. Things change."

And she was right, things did change. Sometimes you don't want them to, but sometimes it's for the better. Monica planned on enjoying these new changes in her life.

Monica picked up Megan and Vicki and they spent the morning at the Sports Spa as usual. Ness had sounded so tired that Monica took them out to lunch and was conned into a trip to City Park to feed the ducks. She'd given in to the outing but warned that it would be short.

Monica had a canister of popcorn left over from Christmas. Now was as good a time as any to get rid of the stale popcorn. The ducks could enjoy Christmas in July.

Tony and Mark climbed one of City Park's huge oaks and attempted to throw popcorn from there to the lagoon. But as soon as the girls began to throw popcorn to the ducks they came racing to the shore, surrounding the kids and quacking.

There was one particular duck who made sure he got his share and then some by stealing kernels of popcorn from the smaller ducks. Vicki and Jasmine refused to feed the rude duck and shooed him away so that Megan could feed the other smaller ducks.

Monica laughed. Those girls were really going to be something when they grew up. They had a strong sense of what was fair and unfair, and they definitely knew how to go about making things right. They worked as a team. Jasmine and Vicki were the aggressive ones with Megan going about it more quietly. The boys, however, could care less.

Monica turned to share this with Devin, then remembered that he wasn't with them. It felt as if he should be. She'd felt so close to him all morning that she had forgotten that he wasn't actually with them.

Preoccupied with her thoughts Monica hadn't noticed the change in weather. Dark clouds hung low in the sky, blocking the sun giving an appearance of dusk.

When rain began to fall, Monica called the boys out of the tree and they all dashed to the nearest shelter. She stood behind the children as they stretched their arms out into the rain.

"You've got a mixed bunch there, huh?" a deep gravelly voice asked behind them.

Monica turned toward the voice, a little of her enjoyment fading with the interruption. She didn't have to deal with the ignorance some people displayed as often as Scott and Ness, but she found that when she did her reactions were always very guarded.

"Excuse me?" she asked, using her coldest tone.

A tall, dark-skinned man who had to be more than eighty years old narrowed his eyes and repeated, "You heard me girl, I said you've got a mixed bunch there."

Just as Monica was going to politely tell him off, he cleared his throat and bellowed, "That's good."

Surprised, Monica's eyes widened.

The man sighed and glared at her as if she were dense. "You must know some of those kids over there are white and some of them are black."

Of course she knew that, but more often than not she would forget that fact and simply see them as children. "Yes, I noticed."

He stood beside her watching the children as they played. They were sticking various body parts out into the rain, laughing away and having the time of their lives.

"That's how it should be. If we play together as little children, we know that deep down we're all the same."

Touched by his words, Monica looked up at the man, the gray in his hair evidence of his wisdom and age. He stood straight and tall, an obvious contradiction. "I agree," Monica told him.

"Good," he said. "You keep doing what ya doing, and thinkin' what ya thinkin', and ya gonna have a good life."

"I will," Monica told him, not knowing how else she should respond.

The old man began to walk away. He stopped a second later and without turning said, "That's what he said. That's exactly what Keith said."

Hearing the name of her first husband, Monica moved to stand in front the old man. "Excuse me sir, but what did you say?"

"I said," he told her with a look of exasperation on his face, "that ya gonna have a good life."

And he walked, disappearing into the mist and a cluster of oak trees.

Not knowing what to make of him, Monica decided it was time to make a run for the truck. The kids were wet anyway, a little more water wasn't going to hurt them. The rain had been a welcomed relief.

Getting everyone settled and buckled in, Monica opened the glove compartment to find napkins so they could dry their hands and faces.

They drove through the park, the canopy of oaks above them, the grey Spanish moss hanging down like tiny curtains.

"This is spooky, spooky, spooky," Megan said, voicing what all the kids were feeling.

"Not really," Monica whispered, a sense of disquiet affecting her as well. "It's just the rain and the trees, and look up ahead," she told them, "I can see a patch of light up in the sky where the trees end."

The children stretched their necks. Mark sneezed. Monica automatically reached into the glove compartment again for a napkin. Something sparkling caught her eyes just as they came out of the trees and into a ray of light.

The rain stopped. Monica pulled to the side. She reached inside the small compartment and couldn't believe what she'd found. Her wedding ring. She held it up and stared at it. Monica was stunned. She had searched everywhere for this ring. She'd gone into that glove compartment so many times she couldn't count them, and not once had she seen it. Not even when she was pulled over for speeding a few months ago and had to pull everything out to find her insurance papers and registration.

"What is it, Mommie?" Jasmine asked.

"My wedding ring."

"But you're wearing your wedding ring. I saw Uncle Devin put it on you," Vicki told her.

"But this is my wedding ring from Tony's, Mark's and Jasmine's first daddy."

"Are you going to wear it?" Tony asked.

"No, I'm going to save it with my memories."

Monica put the simple gold band back into the glove compartment for safekeeping and drove toward home puzzling over the strange afternoon.

Losing the ring a year ago had begun her first real separation from Keith. Gradually, without her realizing it, her heart had healed and softened enough to let Devin into her life first as her friend, then as her husband.

Monica didn't believe in ghosts or psychics or any of that mystical kind of foolishness. But she believed in God. Monica knew in her heart that Keith was in heaven with God and somehow was able to send his blessings by guiding her to the ring, but only after she married the right man.

CHAPTER 26

Monica pulled into the driveway of her new house. She couldn't wait to see Devin and tell him that she loved him. 'I do, too' wasn't good enough. She would change and drive over to the site.

Monica left the kids with Ness, who was suddenly full of energy and in a cleaning frenzy. She had insisted that Monica leave the kids with her for a few hours.

Monica committed herself to a limit of two, three hours tops. Ness, she knew, was going through the nesting stage, where she felt the urge to clean like crazy. That meant that those babies would be coming sometime soon.

Before she could close the door Monica heard a squeal of tires and turned to find the Durango coasting into the driveway.

Her truck was parked in the correct driveway. His wife was standing in the doorway of the right house, squeezed into those skintight biking shorts she liked to wear when she exercised. This was good. Devin was standing in front of her in two seconds. A beautiful smile lit up her face and her eyes were as warm as sunshine. This was better than good.

"I have to tell you something," she whispered, backing through the door, pulling him inside,

"I'm listening," Devin shut the door.

"You were right."

"I usually am."

"Some of the time, Mr. Arrogant," she agreed, "and this is one of those times. You know me so well, Dev, what I need and what I want. I am so happy that you took a chance on me, that I took a chance on you. You opened my heart again."

"I had to. You already had mine," he told her.

"And you have mine. What I find amazing is what I didn't tell you last night."

"Tell me what?" Devin asked, tracing her full lips with his thumb, knowing that she was going to say the words he'd been dying to hear for so long. He was ready to hear them, to taste them from her lips.

"I love you, Devin Preston."

He kissed her then, savoring the feel, the taste of her just after she poured her feelings out to him. It was so sweet. "Would you like to show me how much? I hated to leave you this morning."

"I know," she said as she led him to the bedroom. "I knew it had to be something important to take you away."

"Just a civic uprising with protestors and picket signs," he answered, stopping to place a kiss on her neck.

"Oh, no!"

"Oh, yes, but I'll tell you all about it later." He closed, then locked, the door as he thought of the possibility of the kids disturbing them. Wait a minute, he thought, frowning, the house was way too quiet. "Where are the kids?"

"With Ness."

"Why?" he asked, already sure he would like the answer.

"I was coming to tell you that I love you."

"Tell me again. Better yet, do some of that showing you were talking about earlier."

"Right," Monica answered, going for the button of his pants.

And did she show him? The time Monica would have wasted driving to the site was better spent expressing the love that had always been hidden inside of her, love for him.

They lay close together, swallowed by the king-sized bed, sometimes talking, sometimes quiet and content to be in each other's arms. Devin shared the morning's happenings and Monica revealed the strange conversation she'd had with an old man, and the discovery of her wedding ring.

"It was so strange, Dev. At one time I was desperate to find it. Now all I feel is relief. Not because I needed to find the ring, but because it was a precious memory of my past." Monica held her left hand before him. "This particular ring is my future, and it already has a special memory attached to it."

Devin didn't know what to say to this. All he wanted was an 'I love you', but he'd gotten much more. What else could he say but, "I see."

Monica filled the room with her laughter before rolling on top of him to show him once again how much she loved him.

An hour later Devin left to get the kids. Since she'd neglected to eat anything since lunch, Monica's stomach rebelled on her. A mid-afternoon snack was usually enough avoid this problem, but she had been too busy to think about it.

Monica sipped her decaffeinated tea and nibbled on a cheese covered cracker. Devin had fixed her a tray before leaving, insisting that she didn't have to come along. "Dads do this kind of thing all the time," he told her.

Twenty minutes later, after finishing her snack and showering, a stampede of tennis shoe-clad feet and shouts of, "Ma! Hey Ma!" and "Mommie!" echoed up the stairs and ended as each of her children ran to their own room. Waving arms and legs were all that she saw as they flew by the bedroom door.

"You did go to pick up the kids and not a bunch of wild animals," Monica asked as Devin came up the stairs at a much slower pace.

"Those were our children, Brown Eyes." He wrapped both arms around her waist and laid his hands on her stomach. "When we have a few more, this place might turn into a circus."

"A few more?" she laid her head back against his chest and peered up at him.

"Maybe. We can discuss it after our new arrival, and talking about new arrivals, what's up with Ness? She couldn't keep still the whole five minutes I was there. Is this something I'm going to have to worry about in seven months?"

"I don't know. What was she doing?"

"She was cleaning our pantry."

"Our pantry, huh?"

"Yeah," he grinned. "The one you lured me into so you could hit on me."

Monica swatted a hand at him and headed down the stairs. "I don't remember it being that way."

"Whatever way it was, that's where it all started." Devin stopped on the stairs, a calculating look in his eyes. "If Scott and Ness ever sell that house we're buying it."

"For the pantry?"

"I'd buy the pantry if I could, but we might have a problem with that."

"You're right, as always, of course," she said, playing right along with him. Devin followed her into the kitchen. She took the leftover rice out of the fridge and was lifting the big pot of gumbo when Devin yelled, "What are you doing?"

"Getting dinner ready. Gumbo's better the second time around. All the flavors blend together overnight."

He was already in front of her taking the pot out of her hands before she could realize what was happening. Not really surprised, Monica stood with her hands on her hips, waiting to hear it all.

"I don't want you lifting something that heavy." Devin looked around the kitchen, and then he went into the living room and came back again. "How did all these boxes get over here? You didn't do this by yourself! Did you, Monica?" Devin had a worried frown on his face. "Stephens and Brooks were coming to move everything."

"No, Dev, I hired two boys from across the street. I wanted to surprise you."

"You did—you have. This has been an amazing day." Devin hugged her tight against him, then pulled back an instant later. "Brown Eyes, I know you didn't stand by and watch those boys do all the work."

"I might have carried a small box or two."

"You shouldn't be lifting anything! According to the doctor, it's not good for you or the baby."

"Baby? Somebody else is having a baby?" Tony asked, coming into the kitchen.

"Well, Auntie Ness is having two babies. Who else?" Jasmine asked.

"Yeah, who else?" Mark repeated.

Monica and Devin turned toward the three questioning faces waiting in the middle of the kitchen for answers. "We might as well tell them now," Monica whispered.

"Are you sure?" Devin asked.

"They're going to know sooner or later, and it's better if it comes from us."

Apparently, having waited long enough, Jasmine asked, "Who's having a baby?"

"We are," Monica and Devin answered.

"We are?" Mark asked.

"All five of us!" Devin confirmed.

"All right!" they all shouted.

Devin stayed home the next two days helping to get the house settled. The kids' furniture had finally arrived. It had been delayed due to a shipping error. Devin wondered if T.J. had had anything to do with it. He didn't like the possibility that T.J. could be interfering in his personal life too.

Dev, Monica and the kids were busy, but an easy transition had taken place. The children, who'd accepted Devin from the first moment they'd met him, loved having him around all the time. He continued to read with them at night and helped to supervise clean up and bath time.

Monica was so well organized with the kids all he had to say was, "Bath time!" They knew there was no arguing. The kids would trudge up the stairs with Jasmine informing them whose turn it was to go first.

At the Sports Spa, Devin had convinced Monica to slow down her power walk. During their initial visit, the doctor had approved light exercise. Brown Eyes complied with Devin's suggestion, but the expression on her face and the patronizing smile told him that she was only humoring him. He'd have to check out that chapter on exercise and pregnancy again.

The kids had thrown out a barrage of questions about babies, how they grow, and where they come from. Monica handled them with quick, short answers that satisfied their curiosity. Thrilled about the baby, they called every aunt, uncle and cousin to tell them the news.

Late Thursday evening Devin tucked the covers around Monica and quietly left the bedroom. She had gone to lie down after dinner and was out like a light. It was only eight o'clock, but Monica would probably sleep the rest of the night. If Devin hadn't read that this was normal, he would be worried. He checked on the kids and promised them that they could watch two more shows but then it was bedtime.

Devin went into the back room. It was designed as a study but he'd turned it into a weight room. It had been too long since he'd done any weight lifting . He started with dumbbells working on his arms. Devin had finished two sets of biceps curls and was getting in position for skull-crushers when the doorbell rang.

There was the sound of running feet and then Tony informing him, "It's Uncle Scott, Daddy. Vicki and Megan are here too. Can I open the door?"

"Sure, tell Uncle Scott to come back here."

Tony stood at the door, hesitated, then asked, "Dad, can you show me how to lift weights one day?"

Devin stood still, affected by the ease with which Tony called him Dad. "We'll have to buy some weights for someone just your size. Then I'll teach you."

"All right!" he said, running for the door.

"I can't stop her!" Scott complained as soon as he spotted his friend.

"Stop who?"

"Ness. If we hadn't left the house, she would have dusted, polished, and waxed us all. She's suddenly full of energy. I wish she'd find another way to use it."

"You could always whisper a suggestion in her ear," Devin advised.

That advice wiped the aggravated look off Scott's face. Devin thought he was going to bolt out the door, leaving right then, without his daughters, and without telling Devin the reason for his visit.

"T.J.'s been hanging around again," Scott told Devin. "I saw him myself. One of the security guards spotted him first and we went to give him a little warning."

"How'd that work out?"

"We didn't get close to him. He drove off when he saw us coming. But I was close enough to realize that we're dealing with a crazy man."

"We already knew."

"But, it's worse, Bug. His eyes were wild, he looked like he hadn't shaved in days, and we could smell the alcohol fumes from his car before we were close enough for him to hear us. That's when he drove off."

"Was that all?"

"We called the Slidell Police and reported him as a drunk driver, gave his license plate and all. Maybe he got locked up for the night."

"If we were lucky. He didn't do any thing else? Leave any more notes?"

"No, he just yelled a few obscenities out the window. You know, stuff like 'nigger lover.'"

Devin shook his head. He lay face down on the bench, ready to attack his gluteals and hamstrings by doing a few sets of leg curls. He would rather get his hands on T.J. Since that wasn't possible, this exercise might help relieve the knot that was twisting inside his stomach.

"Bug, we know the man's a racist. He hates our partnership, he's obsessed with it. He's going to try something."

"I know. I hate this wait-and-see game. I thought about putting a restraining order on him, but we have no proof that he's done anything. He's covered himself."

"What do you suggest we do, partner?"

Devin sat up and wiped his face with a towel. "We tell our wives and family to be careful. Scott, I'm praying that this obsession won't spill over to them."

"You and me both, brother-in-law."

"What I want to do is track him down myself and give him my own personal warning. Better yet, have him followed."

"People do it all the time on TV. I don't see what it can hurt. We might get what we need on him that way. Do you have anyone in mind?"

"I do."

"Good. How about the wives? Do you think it's safe for them to bring the kids over for lunch tomorrow?" Scott asked. "Ness is already talking about fixing lunch and even bringing a cake. She figures this will be her last Friday lunch before the twins are born."

"I don't see why not," Devin answered. "We'll keep everyone close to the trailer."

"Talking this out with you makes me feel…"

"Less restrained. I know. There's not much we can do."

"I'm off."

"You don't have to rush. How about a beer or something?"

"No way. Ness is wasting all that energy on cleaning. I've got other ideas."

"Scott, remember, she's eight months pregnant."

"There are many ways and pleasures, my friend." He left and actually remembered to take his daughters with him.

Ness might have an abundance of energy, but Monica had a complete lack of it. He had kept her up pretty late two nights in a row. Tonight he decided to make do with the pleasure of holding her in his arms all night long.

Devin woke up at five-thirty the next morning. He made a tray of crackers with melted cheese. Monica liked these almost as much as the scones she'd eaten at the penthouse. He'd have to remember to stop at Spice, Inc., to get some more.

"Brown Eyes," he called. "Wake up." Devin didn't want to leave today without warning her about T.J.

Monica sat up. Spotting the tray, she reached for a cracker an appreciative smile on her face. The smile was lost to a worried frown as Devin filled her in on the latest news about T.J.

"I'd feel better if that man was behind bars."

"He hasn't broken any laws."

"He's interfered in our lives. Look at what he almost did to Scott and Ness," Monica yawned.

"You're still tired."

"I'm pretty worn out. I still haven't caught up from those last two wonderful nights, and I didn't have my nap yesterday."

Monica had started taking naps so she wouldn't feel so drained by the end of the day.

"I going to miss my naps when school starts. I hope it doesn't leave me feeling like this every morning."

"You know, you really don't have to," Devin suggested. This was as good an opening as any. He'd been wondering about how he was going to approach this subject.

"What do you suggest? That I nap during lunch? That's barely thirty minutes. It won't work, Dev," Monica said taking a sip of her tea.

Devin picked up his own mug. He'd taken to having crackers and tea with her every morning, not that he'd admit it to anyone. "Why go to work at all?"

Monica's eyes narrowed, then widened and cooled a few degrees in no time. But they hadn't turned ice cold. Maybe it wasn't going to be as bad as he'd thought.

"Excuse me, please explain that statement," she demanded in a polite tone.

It was going to be bad. Monica was being polite, way too polite. "Brown Eyes, I was only thinking about your health and the baby's."

"The baby and I will be fine," she informed him. "I've always worked when I was pregnant."

"You've always had to work. It's not necessary during this pregnancy."

"You don't have to work either, Dev. Why don't you stay home? You've got millions of dollars in the bank, enough to last a couple of lifetimes."

"I realize I don't have to work, but I love my job, and can't stay home all day doing nothing!"

"Well, I love my job, too!" she told him, not backing down a bit.

This was getting frustrating. This conversation was not going the way it was supposed to. Monica should be telling him how sweet he was for worrying about her health. Sweet? The expression on her face shouted sour.

"Monica, I understand all that," he told her, struggling for patience. He did understand a women's role in the work force, but he thought if it was unnecessary for a woman to work; it was better all around for her to stay home with the kids. "It makes more sense for you to stay home. You're the one carrying the baby!"

"Well, isn't that a convenient reason?" she said, moving the tray from her lap and grabbing her robe, the same robe she'd worn that night when she couldn't turn the water off. Devin couldn't help responding to that memory, his body hardening, his face softening with a smile.

"What's so funny Devin. Why are you smiling?" she asked indignantly. "I guess you think that you can make a suggestion about something as important as my career and expect me to agree just like that." Monica snapped her fingers.

"No, that's not what I'm thinking."

"You aren't grinning from ear to ear because you think you're going to get your way?"

"No, this robe, it brings back a particular memory,"

"Oh," she answered, her eyes becoming warm with the memory.

"Come here," he said reaching a hand out to her. Monica was standing on the other end of the bed, the width of it separating them.

"You're trying to change the subject. I'm not quitting my job."

"We'll talk about that later. Maybe we can think up a compromise," he suggested, coming toward her because she hadn't moved an inch.

"A compromise?"

"Yes."

"I'm not forgetting about this," Monica let him know before she melted against him, the argument completely forgotten, for the time being anyway.

CHAPTER 27

"Does that sound like a good compromise?" Monica asked, turning to her sister. Ness was sitting at the kitchen table coating chicken legs with flour. Monica had come over to help fry chicken for their lunch with the guys. Ness insisted that this was her last Friday as a pregnant person. By this time next week she expected to be holding two healthy babies in her arms.

"Hm-m, what did you say?"

"I said, I just thought up a compromise for the argument Devin and I had," Monica repeated.

"Sorry, I wasn't really listening," Ness admitted sheepishly. "But from the little I heard it didn't sound like much of an argument."

"It was. Devin's really good at turning things around so that it doesn't seem like an argument, but officially, it was."

"I know what you mean. Scott has his own way of getting around things. He thinks I don't know what he's up to."

"I know exactly what Devin's up to. He's used to getting his own way, and he'll use every trick in the book. Being complacent and offering a compromise are just ways to confuse me."

"Maybe, maybe not. Would it be so bad to stay home, Monica? Bug does have a point. You don't have to work for the money."

"That thought's been running through my head all morning. It think that's part of the problem. I like making my own money. I like being independent. But then I think about the chance to be home with my baby for a change. I never liked putting my babies in child care centers."

"I'm looking forward to staying home with these two." Ness patted her stomach.

"It makes even more sense for you to stay home, Ness, you've got two."

"Don't forget, you're carrying triplets."

"Ness, I've heard enough of that."

"Hey, if it's happened, it's already happened. Nothing I say can change it."

"You're just hoping that in seven months I feel as miserable as you do now."

"I'm feeling good right now, but I still want you to drive."

"No problem."

"Now, tell me again about this compromise," Vanessa said, all ears as they fried the rest of the chicken.

T.J. hadn't been to work all week. He couldn't take being near those people anymore. Especially after his father had hired that Hispanic man and put him in the office next to him. It was unbearable. T.J. would never understand why his father hired all these different kinds of people. It infected the office and forced people to think that this was normal, that it was okay to mix things up like that. But it wasn't. It was not normal.

There was nothing he could do about his father. T.J. would be breaking all ties with him anyway. Unable to take the pretense anymore, he was breaking all ties with everything and everybody he'd ever known.

T.J. had heard about a place in a remote part of the South. There were people there who thought as he did. He'd leave today and join them. His bags were already packed, his bank account cleaned out. He would need the money. They'd take him for sure if he offered a big donation.

This world was going to hell. He hadn't accomplished his mission to bring Prestway down and he couldn't stay around to finish the job. The thought sent a sickening twist in his stomach and caused his head to pound. But there was something he could fix, something that he could make right before he left. T.J. had plans to save those two little girls of Scott's. The thought was like consolation to his soul. He'd take them away and raise them the right way.

That's why he'd been here since before dawn. Waiting. They came here, the wives and children, every Friday, acting like the perfect family. They were anything but perfect. Most of these people were the wrong color. But he'd take care of that. It had been easy to get in to find a hiding place. Preston didn't know how lazy their night watchman was. This was the third time T.J. had gotten past him.

He'd take care of it, T.J. promised himself again. He sat hidden in the bushes, carefully rationing a six pack of his special beer, waiting and watching the trailer.

Mid-morning Scott and Devin had a meeting with the entire construction crew. They wanted the men to be made aware of the possible threat T.J.

represented. The six-man crew was more than anxious to cooperate by following the extra precautions. They even volunteered to help track T.J. Devin and Scott declined the offer and instead handed a stack of flyers with T.J.'s picture to Harris to post near and around the site. Harris took one look at the picture and exploded. "Well I'll be damned!"

Everyone turned toward him.

"How about telling us what you're damned about, Harris?" Devin asked.

"I remember this man. I saw him at a bar one night. He was real friendly. You know the kind of guys who are real nice, but you can't help but think that they're after something. I was thinking that he was gay."

"What was he after?" Scott asked.

Harris seemed a little uneasy with everyone staring at him. "Hell if I know!" He cleared his throat. "What I mean is, I never found out. We were talking one second and he was gone the next."

Devin mulled over what Harris said. "Can you remember the last thing you were discussing?"

"Yeah, I remember. We were talking about Prestway."

"What about Prestway?" Josh asked, bursting from the group of men, John right behind him. The twins' interruption made the older man even more uptight.

"Don't get all crazy on me, kid, I know this is your family and all," Harris told Josh, his voice turning hoarse. "I was only telling the man that this was the best job I ever had."

The twins visibly relaxed.

Scott laughed and Devin joined him but there was no humor in the sound. "I can guarantee that sent him running," Devin informed them. "Thanks for the help, Harris. Men, go back to work, but keep your eyes open."

Harris, Josh and John hung back as the rest of the crew walked across the field toward the construction site.

"I suppose this T.J. man was trying to use me to get back at you," Harris muttered, a look of disgust on his face.

"Without a doubt," Scott answered.

"He obviously wasn't very successful," Devin assured the foreman. "He sensed your loyalty. That's why he disappeared. We appreciate it."

Harris nodded. "Five minutes," he told Josh and John. "Just because you're related to the owners don't mean I expect you to be slacking off."

"We'll be there," John promised for both of them. Scott and Devin invited the twins into the trailer. "T.J. is nuts!" Josh said without preamble. "Scott, you know that!"

"What are you doing to protect our sisters?" John wanted to know. "We already know what he did to Devin. God knows what else he's capable of."

"And what do you know?" Devin asked, trying to be patient with his two in-laws. They were only concerned about their sisters. He didn't expect anything less.

Josh told him.

"And you got this information from who?"

"Thomas, his cousin, worked in Mississippi with you, before the accident."

"I see," Devin said, then cringed inside. He was bound to pick up something from his mother besides her strong will and determination. He'd better get used to those two words slipping out of his mouth once in a while.

"What I want to know," Josh asked, "is if this crazy man is going to go beyond harassing you here at Prestway. Are my sisters, nieces and nephews in danger too?"

"We hope not," Scott answered, glancing Devin's way. Both knew the answer was completely inadequate. "We've been discussing the same possibility. Don't worry, we're taking care of everything."

"I guess that will have to do for now. We trust you, but only because we know how you feel about Ness and Monica," John told his brothers-in-law.

"Is there something we could do to help?" Josh wanted to know. The frustration he was feeling was obvious by the expression on his face.

"For one thing, you can hang around here at lunch time," Devin suggested.

"Monica and Ness are bringing lunch today! Are you crazy?" Josh shouted.

"They'll be safe enough," Scott said. "Ness was determined to come…"

"…and there was no stopping her," John finished. "All right then, we'll be back at twelve."

"Make that eleven-thirty," Devin told them, thinking to have them visible before the girls arrived.

"John, man," Devin and Scott heard Josh say, "when I get married I'm gonna make sure my wife uses common sense."

"I know, Josh, I know," his brother agreed.

Devin shook his head at their ignorance. They knew nothing about women and marriage. Turning to go back into the trailer, his foot kicked an envelope, sending it across the floor to land right at Scott's feet.

Scott bent to pick it up. "Looks like some mail we miss—"

"What is it, Scott?"

"This stationery looks familiar."

"Labranche and Son. It has to be from T.J.!"

"He's gotten bold, using his own stationery. I don't think it's a thank-you note," Scott said.

"It's more than likely that he's gotten reckless." Devin took the envelope from Scott. That possibility was what scared Devin. "If he's getting reckless, then he feels as if he's got nothing to lose. If that's the case, we can count on something happening soon." Devin read the note and handed it to Scott.

The white sheet of paper was almost empty with the exception of two words and a signature. It said, "I'm coming. T. J."

"He signed his name." Scott threw the note at Devin and went for the phone. "I'm calling Ness."

"Tell them to stay put." Devin put the note, their only evidence, into his pocket. Devin grabbed the other phone to call the police. This should be enough to get a restraining order on T.J.

"There's no answer!" Scott slammed the receiver down.

"Call my house, Monica's old number and try your house again. They might be outside with the kids."

"I hope you're right," Scott muttered. After a few minutes he hung up. "I got my answering machine and nothing but constant ringing at the other houses."

"Call Miss Joyce," Devin suggested.

A few minutes later Scott groaned, dropping the phone onto the cradle. "They have to be already on their way!"

Devin finished his call and hung up.

Scott was pacing up and down the trailer muttering to himself about hard-headed, pregnant wives.

Devin understood his feelings exactly. They were the same ones coursing through him. T.J. was coming, but what would he do? He was determined not to panic.

"Calm down, Scott. We've done everything we could. We know they're on their way. Let's go out to meet them."

"Yeah, that's a good idea, then we can send them right back."

Scott followed Devin outside. They stood outside the trailer, shielding their eyes against the glare of the sun and scanning the road for the van.

"Bug, if he does anything, if he comes near my family…"

"I know, I feel the same way."

T.J. swallowed the last drop of beer. He carefully put the bottle back into the carton and scratched. He'd been stuck in these bushes hours now. Bugs had crawled up his arms and found their way up his pants legs. Now he was itching. T.J. hoped he wasn't unlucky enough to have landed in poison ivy. He decided not to think about it. The most important thing here was the mission.

T.J. carefully shifted into a more comfortable position. A maniacal grin appeared on his face as he spotted Preston and Scott coming out of the trailer. They had obviously found his note. He could tell. He wasn't more than fifty feet away. The fools stood glaring at the road. Scott was moving back and forth, pacing up and down. T.J. was loving this. He had to fight the laughter that attempted to erupt from his gut. Worst yet, he thought he'd wet his pants from the effects of all the beer he consumed. T.J. couldn't give in to the urge to do either right now. The nature of his mission kept him glued to his place of concealment. It was a good thing too, he thought, when ten minutes later his golden opportunity drove up in a maroon mini-van.

Monica was relieved to finally reach the site. She felt as if she'd ridden across the country instead of Lake Pontchartrain. Ten minutes after they'd left her mom's house, the kids had started arguing about who could throw a tennis ball the farthest.

To make things worse, halfway across the bridge Ness had gotten really uncomfortable. Reclining the seat had helped her a little. All in all, it had not been a good drive.

Monica found it unusual for Devin and Scott to be outside waiting for them. Before she could dwell on that thought, several things seemed to happen at once. The guys were at the van in a flash. Before she could turn the engine off, Ness had swung open the door. Only Scott's quick reflexes saved him from being seriously injured. The kids had poured out of the back door and run for their dads, trying to get their attention, something they were finding hard to do.

Devin opened Monica's door. "You have to go back home, Brown Eyes."

At that exact moment Scott was talking to Vanessa. "Nessa, what are you doing? You need to get back into the van. I want you to go home right now."

Monica, her body turned sideways with feet dangling a few feet from the ground and Vanessa, her legs stretched forward ready to slip out of the van, both stopped to stare at their husbands. At the same time they asked, "Why?"

As Scott and Devin explained the situation to them, out of the corner of her eye Monica watched the kids throw the ball around. They were probably warming up for the challenge. They'd be disappointed she knew, but their safety was more important.

"The police are coming?"

"Yes, they are, Brown Eyes. I don't want you to worry. We've got everything under control."

"With a madman running loose! How can you have anything under control?"

"As long as I know you're safe, we can handle T.J."

"Okay," she said, reaching up to trace his eyebrows. "It's just that I don't want to lose you too, Dev."

"You won't, Brown Eyes. T.J. has gone too far. He's dug his own grave. Drive home and call me when you get there."

"Nessa, what are you doing?" Scott was saying. "Did you hear anything I said? Come back to the van."

"Don't be so nervous. I need to get some of the kinks out. That drive left me feeling like one big ache," Nessa told him as she walked the length of the van and back, Scott attached to her side.

"We better get the kids loaded up," Monica told Devin, trying not to show how worried she actually was. "I love you, remember that."

"I'll never forget it, because I'm going to hear it again at the end of the day. Every day."

"That wasn't even halfway, Mark!" the couple heard Jasmine yell. Monica and Devin turned to see Mark run and scoop up the ball. When he acted as if he was going to investigate some unknown creature in a group of bushes, Monica called out, "Mark, come back. Kids we have to leave!"

"Aw, man. Why, Ma?" Tony moaned. "Mark's only one who got to throw."

"Next time, Tony," Devin told him sternly. "I need you to go home and listen to your mother."

"Okay, Dad," he quickly answered, probably sensing the tension in the air.

Monica could feel it too. Something was about to happen.

Tony and Mark were already in the van when Vanessa let out a soft moan, "Monica, no!"

"Nessa, what is it? What's wrong?" Monica shouted.

"My water broke," she whispered, loud enough for the other couple to hear.

Vanessa and Scott looked down. Monica and Devin looked down. Scott's work boots and Ness's tennis shoes were soaked.

"Nessa's water broke," Scott yelled. "We're having our babies!"

"What? Auntie Ness is having the babies?" Jasmine yelled, running around the van with her cousins.

"MaNessa's having the babies!" Vicki sang over and over again.

Megan joined in with, "Babies, babies, babies!"

Not to be outdone the boys jumped out of the van yelling their favorite phrase, "All right!"

Monica helped Ness into the passenger seat and guided Scott to the driver's side of the van.

"Take your wife to the hospital," she commanded.

"But she's supposed to have the babies at Oschner."

"I don't think that's going to happen. North Shore isn't far away."

"I don't want to have my babies there. My doctor won't be there," Vanessa said, a slight panic in her voice.

"But your husband will. You don't have much of a choice, Ness. You're going to be fine."

Devin stood behind Monica. "Don't worry about anything. Do you know where you're going?"

Scott nodded his head. "I've passed it often enough."

"We'll take care of the girls!" Monica shouted as they drove down the road leading to the highway.

Devin wrapped his arm around her as they watched the van disappear. "Don't worry about Ness. She'll be fine."

"I'm not worried about Ness. Scott's with her. What has me tied up in knots is imagining the things T.J could possibly do to you."

Before Devin could answer, the calm that had descended with the departure of Scott and Ness was suddenly broken with a high-pitched scream.

His chance was finally here. T.J. could feel it in his bones. Even when that little black boy threw the ball and stood looking at him without knowing, T.J. knew he'd have his moment. The shouting, the running around when Scott left to take that wife of his to the hospital to have those mixed-up children was a perfect distraction. The security guard was nowhere to be seen. Scott was gone, Preston was occupied, and one of the cute little blond-haired girls he was honor bound to save had just thrown a tennis ball into his lap.

"I did it! I did it! I threw the ball right into the bushes!" she yelled, running to retrieve it.

As the little girl came around the bushes, T. J. stepped forward.

The little girl stopped immediately. She took a few steps back. "Did you lose this?" T.J. asked, holding the ball in his hand, attempting to sound non-threatening. There was a wary look of caution in her eyes. She'd been taught well about strangers.

"Don't be scared. I know your dad. We used to work together. His name is Scott Halloway."

T.J. could see she wasn't fooled. She began to back away. "You can have the ball, mister."

He had no choice but to grab her then. He tried to cover her mouth but her little body moved in so many directions it was impossible to reach. The little hellcat started to kick and let out a scream that vibrated in his eardrums.

The other two girls came around the bush, the hellcat's sister demanding, "Let go of my sister, you bad man!"

"You leave my cousin alone!" the black girl yelled.

"Cousin!" T.J. yelled, knocking her to the ground with a quick shove. His sense of indignation gave him the strength and will to complete his mission. If they got hurt in the process it would be worth it. He was saving these girls from an unnatural lifestyle. In the long run they'd thank him for it.

In a matter of seconds he managed to maneuver them into a secure hold, their heads hanging, feet and arms moving the entire time. T.J. didn't stop to do anything about it, there was no time. With a burst of energy he raced across the field. His car wasn't far. All he had to do was cross the highway. He was almost across the field. The strain of carrying the screaming, squirming and now scratching girls was slowing him down. He could hear noises behind him. Preston and somebody else were in pursuit. But he was almost to the highway, almost home free...Until a small foot connected with his groin.

The pain hit him fast and hard. It spread from the point of impact to every part of his body. His legs refused to move. He collapsed to the ground, dropping both girls as he fell. He had to save them. Through the haze of pain that thought gave him strength to keep a firm hold on an arm of one girl and the leg of the other. Why didn't they understand that he was their savior?

It had all happened so fast. The scream, the chase, and now Devin had T.J. exactly where he wanted him. Devin grabbed T.J.'s wrists and squeezed, forcing him to release the girls. He dragged T.J. away from the gravel shoulder and flipped him on his back as if he were a squirming cockroach.

"Get up!" Devin demanded. "Get your crazy, kidnapping, sick—" Devin stopped, not wanting to say more in front of Vicki and Megan, their sobs having penetrated his anger.

"Maybe you had better wait for the police," John suggested as Vicki clung to him with a death grip. Megan was hanging on to Josh just as tightly.

Devin looked up long enough to see that the twins were comforting the girls. "How did you get here so fast?"

"We heard the screams," Josh said.

"Are they hurt?" Dev asked, his eyes boring into T.J.'s.

"No, just scared, I think," one of them answered.

"Good," Dev finally answered. "Take the girls back to Monica. Make sure Jazz is okay. I saw this sorry excuse for a man push my daughter."

The twins left, not questioning Devin further. If T.J. had had the a nerve to lay a hand on any one of their nieces, then whatever Devin decided to do was okay with them.

Devin leaned down toward the man who hated him. From the first, the hatred had been there. Now it had gone too far. The man had dared to mess with his family. Devin yanked T.J. up, dragged him a few feet and propped him against a tree. The fact that he was so much bigger than T.J. had always kept Devin from beating him to a pulp. That didn't matter in the least now. Stuck in Devin's head was the image of T.J pushing his daughter to the ground, a child less than half his size. The rage inside him grew.

"Know that you are about to be beaten by a black man who is richer and more successful than you, not only in business but in life." Devin's fist rammed into T.J.'s stomach once, twice, three times, once for each of the girls. Then Devin stood back.

T.J. slid down the tree. Somehow hatred gave him the strength to mutter, "White is the only right."

Devin stared down at him. T.J. belonged behind bars. Was overdue to be behind bars. Sick of looking at him, Devin moved away. He leaned against a tree, not knowing how long he stood there attempting to rein in the hatred he felt toward this man. He looked up at he sound of sirens.

Devin explained to the police officers the attempted kidnapping and all their earlier problems. Anxious to see T.J. in handcuffs, Devin led them to the tree he had been slumped against. Devin was shocked to find him gone. T.J. had disappeared.

EPILOGUE

Monica lay back on the hard cushioned table in the doctor's office. She let out a long sigh. "Do you think everything's okay? I mean that the baby's okay."

"From what the doctor says, Brown Eyes, baby might not be the word."

Monica gave him a look that said, "I don't want to hear that."

"Well then, we could be wrong about the date. Maybe that's why you're growing so fast. You could be further along than four months."

"That's impossible!"

"I know that too."

The doctor chose that moment to walk into the exam room and begin the ultrasound.

The next day Monica was in the living room braiding Jasmine's hair when Devin called out to her.

"We're in here," Monica answered.

She finished Jasmine's hair just as Devin walked into the room.

"Can you go outside with me Daddy?" she asked.

"Yes in a minute, Jazz. I want to talk to your mom. Why don't you see what the boys are up to?"

"Okay," she answered. Jasmine was still her feisty old self but happier playing indoors unless there were adults outside. Vicki and Megan, Monica knew, were having the same type of reaction. Talking about what had happened, and a little bit of professional therapy was helping them get through it. The emotional scars were more serious than the minor scratches they'd received.

"She'll be okay, Brown Eyes," Devin assured her, wrapping his arms around her stomach.

"I know she will. I just wish it had never happened. I wish they'd caught him."

"You are not the only one, but worrying about T.J. will get us nothing but worry. There's an arrest warrant out on him as well as a restraining order," he reminded her. What Devin didn't add was that he had his own man out there hunting T.J. down. He would have to hide deep and long to get away for long. However long and however much money it was going to take, Devin was going to find T.J.

Feeling a tiny movement under his hand brought to mind the reason he'd sought her out. "It's been twenty-four hours. Has the shock worn off?"

"Almost."

"Now, aren't you glad that I convinced you to quit working."

"It was a compromise."

"But you quit, and now you can follow the doctor's orders to relax, take things slow for the babies' sake."

"I can admit that it's a good thing I'm not working for the school board at the moment, but for the record, I did not quit. It was a compromise. I still work twice a week for half a day, at home, in my own little office."

"But you quit, just for me," he insisted.

"Mr. Preston," Monica told him in exasperation, "I've had enough of your arrogant, know-it-all ways." She left the room to gather the kids for the Labor Day celebration.

All the way to her parents' house Devin wore a smug expression. The kids jumped out of the Durango as soon as they parked.

Devin hopped out and ran over to the passenger side to help Monica. She was already carrying a load. He was relieved that she had agreed on a compromise.

Just before walking into the house, Devin couldn't resist teasing her once more. "Just admit it. You quit for me."

"If it will shut you up, I'll admit anything. I quit, just for you."

His smile grew broader, his chest puffed out.

"I did it because I love you," she added.

"Ah-h, Brown Eyes," Devin let out in a huge breath. Right there in the open doorway, he held her as close as her stomach allowed and kissed her tenderly on her soft brown lips.

"That's what got you two in the trouble you're in now," Scott snickered, carrying one curly, light brown-haired baby boy in his arms. "And trouble has yet to begin. I'm talking from experience here," he yawned.

"Long night?" Devin asked.

"Long nights," Scott corrected.

"Be happy you're only having one," Ness commented, walking into the room with the other baby, a carbon copy of the first.

Monica and Devin laughed so long and hard at this that the entire family came into the front room to see what was so funny.

"Since everyone's here why don't we tell them," Monica suggested.

"Tell us what, for heaven's sake?" Calvin bellowed.

"We're having triplets," Devin announced proudly.

"I was right? What are the chances of that?" Ness laughed just before the family exploded with good wishes.

Monica took it all in. The good-natured teasing, the hugs and kisses. Then she reached out to Devin, the most important man in her life. The one who took a chance and softened her heart so that she could love again.

2009 Reprint Mass Market Titles

January

I'm Gonna Make You Love Me
Gwyneth Bolton
ISBN-13: 978-1-58571-291-5
ISBN-10: 1-58571-291-4
$6.99

Shades of Desire
Monica White
ISBN-13: 978-1-58571-292-2
ISBN-10: 1-58571-292-2
$6.99

February

A Love of Her Own
Cheris Hodges
ISBN-13: 978-1-58571-293-9
ISBN-10: 1-58571-293-0
$6.99

Color of Trouble
Dyanne Davis
ISBN-13: 978-1-58571-294-6
ISBN-10: 1-58571-9
$6.99

March

Twist of Fate
Beverly Clark
ISBN-13: 978-1-58571-295-3
ISBN-10: 1-58571-295-7
$6.99

Chances
Pamela Leigh Starr
ISBN-13: 978-1-58571-296-0
ISBN-10: 1-58571-296-5
$6.99

April

Sinful Intentions
Crystal Rhodes
ISBN-13: 978-1-585712-297-7
ISBN-10: 1-58571-297-3
$6.99

Rock Star
Roslyn Hardy Holcomb
ISBN-13: 978-1-58571-298-4
$6.99

May

Paths of Fire
T.T. Henderson
ISBN-13: 978-1-58571-343-1
ISBN-10: 1-58571-343-0
$6.99

Caught Up in the Rapture
Lisa Riley
ISBN-13: 978-1-58571-344-8
ISBN-10: 1-58571-344-9
$6.99

June

Reckless Surrender
Rochelle Alers
ISBN-13: 978-1-58571-345-5
ISBN-10: 1-58571-345-7
$6.99

No Ordinary Love
Angela Weaver
ISBN-13: 978-1-58571-346-2
ISBN-10: 1-58571-346-5
$6.99

2009 Reprint Mass Market Titles (continued)

<u>July</u>

Intentional Mistakes
Michele Sudler
ISBN-13: 978-1-58571-347-9
ISBN-10: 1-58571-347-3
$6.99

It's In His Kiss
Reon Carter
ISBN-13: 978-1-58571-348-6
ISBN-10: 1-58571-348-1
$6.99

<u>August</u>

Unfinished Love Affair
Barbara Keaton
ISBN-13: 978-1-58571-349-3
ISBN-10: 1-58571-349-X
$6.99

A Perfect Place to Pray
I.L Goodwin
ISBN-13: 978-1-58571-299-1
ISBN-10: 1-58571-299-X
$6.99

<u>September</u>

Love in High Gear
Charlotte Roy
ISBN-13: 978-1-58571-355-4
ISBN-10: 1-58571-355-4
$6.99

Ebony Eyes
Kei Swanson
ISBN-13: 978-1-58571-356-1
ISBN-10: 1-58571-356-2
$6.99

<u>October</u>

Midnight Clear, Part I
Leslie Esdale/Carmen Green
ISBN-13: 978-1-58571-357-8
ISBN-10: 1-58571-357-0
$6.99

Midnight Clear, Part II
Gwynne Forster/Monica
 Jackson
ISBN-13: 978-1-58571-358-5
ISBN-10: 1-58571-358-9
$6.99

<u>November</u>

Midnight Peril
Vicki Andrews
ISBN-13: 978-1-58571-359-2
ISBN-10: 1-58571-359-7
$6.99

One Day At A Time
Bella McFarland
ISBN-13: 978-1-58571-360-8
ISBN-10: 1-58571-360-0
$6.99

<u>December</u>

Just An Affair
Eugenia O'Neal
ISBN-13: 978-1-58571-361-5
ISBN-10: 1-58571-361-9
$6.99

Shades of Brown
Denise Becker
ISBN-13: 978-1-58571-362-2
ISBN-10: 1-58571-362-7
$6.99

2009 New Mass Market Titles

January

Singing A Song…
Crystal Rhodes
ISBN-13: 978-1-58571-283-0
$6.99

Look Both Ways
Joan Early
ISBN-13: 978-1-58571-284-7
$6.99

February

Six O'Clock
Katrina Spencer
ISBN-13: 978-1-58571-285-4
$6.99

Red Sky
Renee Alexis
ISBN-13: 978-1-58571-286-1
$6.99

March

Anything But Love
Celya Bowers
ISBN-13: 978-1-58571-287-8
$6.99

Tempting Faith
Crystal Hubbard
ISBN-13: 978-1-58571-288-5
$6.99

April

If I Were Your Woman
La Connie Taylor-Jones
ISBN-13: 978-1-58571-289-2
$6.99

Best Of Luck Elsewhere
Trisha Haddad
ISBN-13: 978-1-58571-290-8
$6.99

May

All I'll Ever Need
Mildred Riley
ISBN-13: 978-1-58571-335-6
$6.99

A Place Like Home
Alicia Wiggins
ISBN-13: 978-1-58571-336-3
$6.99

June

Best Foot Forward
Michele Sudler
ISBN-13: 978-1-58571-337-0
$6.99

It's In the Rhythm
Sammie Ward
ISBN-13: 978-1-58571-338-7
$6.99

2009 New Mass Market Titles (continued)

July

Checks and Balances
Elaine Sims
ISBN-13: 978-1-58571-339-4
$6.99

Save Me
Africa Fine
ISBN-13: 978-1-58571-340-0
$6.99

August

When Lightening Strikes
Michele Cameron
ISBN-13: 978-1-58571-369-1
$6.99

Blindsided
Tammy Williams
ISBN-13: 978-1-58571-342-4
$6.99

September

2 Good
Celya Bowers
ISBN-13: 978-1-58571-350-9
$6.99

Waiting for Mr. Darcy
Chamein Canton
ISBN-13: 978-1-58571-351-6
$6.99

October

Fireflies
Joan Early
ISBN-13: 978-1-58571-352-3
$6.99

Frost On My Window
Angela Weaver
ISBN-13: 978-1-58571-353-0
$6.99

November

Waiting in the Shadows
Michele Sudler
ISBN-13: 978-1-58571-364-6
$6.99

Fixin' Tyrone
Keith Walker
ISBN-13: 978-1-58571-365-3
$6.99

December

Dream Keeper
Gail McFarland
ISBN-13: 978-1-58571-366-0
$6.99

Another Memory
Pamela Ridley
ISBN-13: 978-1-58571-367-7
$6.99

Other Genesis Press, Inc. Titles

A Dangerous Deception	J.M. Jeffries	$8.95
A Dangerous Love	J.M. Jeffries	$8.95
A Dangerous Obsession	J.M. Jeffries	$8.95
A Drummer's Beat to Mend	Kei Swanson	$9.95
A Happy Life	Charlotte Harris	$9.95
A Heart's Awakening	Veronica Parker	$9.95
A Lark on the Wing	Phyliss Hamilton	$9.95
A Love of Her Own	Cheris F. Hodges	$9.95
A Love to Cherish	Beverly Clark	$8.95
A Risk of Rain	Dar Tomlinson	$8.95
A Taste of Temptation	Reneé Alexis	$9.95
A Twist of Fate	Beverly Clark	$8.95
A Voice Behind Thunder	Carrie Elizabeth Greene	$6.99
A Will to Love	Angie Daniels	$9.95
Acquisitions	Kimberley White	$8.95
Across	Carol Payne	$12.95
After the Vows	Leslie Esdaile	$10.95
(Summer Anthology)	T.T. Henderson	
	Jacqueline Thomas	
Again My Love	Kayla Perrin	$10.95
Against the Wind	Gwynne Forster	$8.95
All I Ask	Barbara Keaton	$8.95
Always You	Crystal Hubbard	$6.99
Ambrosia	T.T. Henderson	$8.95
An Unfinished Love Affair	Barbara Keaton	$8.95
And Then Came You	Dorothy Elizabeth Love	$8.95
Angel's Paradise	Janice Angelique	$9.95
At Last	Lisa G. Riley	$8.95
Best of Friends	Natalie Dunbar	$8.95
Beyond the Rapture	Beverly Clark	$9.95
Blame It On Paradise	Crystal Hubbard	$6.99
Blaze	Barbara Keaton	$9.95
Bliss, Inc.	Chamein Canton	$6.99
Blood Lust	J. M. Jeffries	$9.95
Blood Seduction	J.M. Jeffries	$9.95
Bodyguard	Andrea Jackson	$9.95
Boss of Me	Diana Nyad	$8.95
Bound by Love	Beverly Clark	$8.95
Breeze	Robin Hampton Allen	$10.95

Other Genesis Press, Inc. Titles (continued)

Other Genesis Press, Inc. Titles (continued)

Other Genesis Press, Inc. Titles (continued)

Other Genesis Press, Inc. Titles (continued)

No Commitment Required	Seressia Glass	$8.95
No Regrets	Mildred E. Riley	$8.95
Not His Type	Chamein Canton	$6.99
Nowhere to Run	Gay G. Gunn	$10.95
O Bed! O Breakfast!	Rob Kuehnle	$14.95
Object of His Desire	A. C. Arthur	$8.95
Office Policy	A. C. Arthur	$9.95
Once in a Blue Moon	Dorianne Cole	$9.95
One Day at a Time	Bella McFarland	$8.95
One of These Days	Michele Sudler	$9.95
Outside Chance	Louisa Dixon	$24.95
Passion	T.T. Henderson	$10.95
Passion's Blood	Cherif Fortin	$22.95
Passion's Furies	AlTonya Washington	$6.99
Passion's Journey	Wanda Y. Thomas	$8.95
Past Promises	Jahmel West	$8.95
Path of Fire	T.T. Henderson	$8.95
Path of Thorns	Annetta P. Lee	$9.95
Peace Be Still	Colette Haywood	$12.95
Picture Perfect	Reon Carter	$8.95
Playing for Keeps	Stephanie Salinas	$8.95
Pride & Joi	Gay G. Gunn	$8.95
Promises Made	Bernice Layton	$6.99
Promises to Keep	Alicia Wiggins	$8.95
Quiet Storm	Donna Hill	$10.95
Reckless Surrender	Rochelle Alers	$6.95
Red Polka Dot in a World of Plaid	Varian Johnson	$12.95
Reluctant Captive	Joyce Jackson	$8.95
Rendezvous with Fate	Jeanne Sumerix	$8.95
Revelations	Cheris F. Hodges	$8.95
Rivers of the Soul	Leslie Esdaile	$8.95
Rocky Mountain Romance	Kathleen Suzanne	$8.95
Rooms of the Heart	Donna Hill	$8.95
Rough on Rats and Tough on Cats	Chris Parker	$12.95
Secret Library Vol. 1	Nina Sheridan	$18.95
Secret Library Vol. 2	Cassandra Colt	$8.95
Secret Thunder	Annetta P. Lee	$9.95

Other Genesis Press, Inc. Titles (continued)

Other Genesis Press, Inc. Titles (continued)

Dull, Drab, Love Life?

Passion Going Nowhere?

Tired Of Being Alone?

Does Every Direction You Look For Love

Lead You Astray?

Genesis Press presents
The launching of our new website!

RecaptureTheRomance.Com

Ignite
The Flame!

Order Form

Mail to: Genesis Press, Inc.
P.O. Box 101
Columbus, MS 39703

Name _____

Address _____

City/State _____ Zip _____

Telephone _____

Ship to (if different from above)

Name _____

Address _____

City/State _____ Zip _____

Telephone _____

Credit Card Information

Credit Card # _____ ☐ Visa ☐ Mastercard

Expiration Date (mm/yy) _____ ☐ AmEx ☐ Discover

Qty.	Author	Title	Price	Total

Use this order

form, or call

1-888-INDIGO-1

Total for books	_____
Shipping and handling: $5 first two books, $1 each additional book	_____
Total S & H	_____
Total amount enclosed	_____

Mississippi residents add 7% sales tax